CRITICAL
BUT
STABLE

ALSO BY ANGELA MAKHOLWA

The 30th Candle

Red Ink

Black Widow Society

The Blessed Girl

CRITICAL BUT STABLE

ANGELA MAKHOLWA

LAKE UNION
PUBLISHING

Text copyright © 2021, 2022 by Angela Makholwa
All rights reserved.

Published by Lake Union Publishing, Seattle

First published as *Critical, But Stable* by Pan Macmillan in South Africa in 2019. This edition contains editorial revisions.

www.apub.com

Amazon, the Amazon logo, and Lake Union Publishing are trademarks of Amazon.com, Inc., or its affiliates.

ISBN-13: 9781662504471
ISBN-10: 1662504470

Cover design by @blacksheep-uk.com

Printed in the United States of America

CRITICAL
BUT
STABLE

The Body

He stares at her quiet, peaceful face.

So much love in that face. Such passion.

This woman embodies everything he ever envisioned love to be. She is caring, intelligent, sensual, sensuous. A beautiful person inside and out.

Looking at her now . . . That body . . . underneath those covers, that body's the same.

How strange to be thinking about its eroticism at this moment.

This is the thing about his body. It always betrays him. Even now. The shame of it.

Yet here she is. Voluptuous, smooth, perfect, naked in his bed.

The thought stirs something in him. Unbelievable. That his body can be responding so rudely in the circumstances.

He collapses to the floor, weeping.

Can it really be over?

He thinks of all the good times they've shared. The laughs, the kisses, rubbing her feet . . . The passion!

The remains of their meal is still there, their empty wine glasses on the table.

As his heart constricts with loss, the tears roll down his face. He is a heap of grief.

Suddenly, a new emotion takes over.

It is fear.

What is he going to do with this beautiful body now, lying so still – and so finite – in his bed?

He will have to call someone.

An ambulance? No, too late for that.

The police? No! No police, not for a man like him.

Her husband? And say what exactly?

Oh shit, oh shit! What has he done?

The Manamelas

'Nomathando! Sweetheart! Come, we're running late. Noma!'

After twenty-five years of marriage, he still could not believe how long it took his wife to prepare for occasions. And this wasn't even an occasion. They were just going out for a quiet early dinner, trying out a new restaurant up the road that had been featured in some glossy magazine or other. It didn't matter to Noma. It could be something as banal as a visit to an old friend, a family *braai* or a PTA meeting, yet she'd still go to great lengths to ensure she was the most beautiful woman in the room.

As he regarded his reflection in the antique gilt mirror in their ostentatious foyer, he tried to calculate how many hours he had spent waiting for his wife. How long on average?

After taking a shower, it took her probably one to two hours to prepare for an occasion. Never less than that. Not ever.

If he calculated the number of events and occasions they attended every year, he reckoned her preparation time clocked up to about one hundred hours per annum.

He found himself taking out his smartphone and clicking on the calculator app.

He sat down on the occasional chair beneath the arched staircase that led to one of the three floors in their behemoth of a house.

He typed in 1.5 hours x 100 x 25 years.

He had been waiting on this woman for approximately 3750 hours.

If you divided those hours by twenty-four, this amounted to 156.25 days of waiting for the same woman over a twenty-five-year lifespan.

More than five months of waiting for someone to finish applying her make-up, switching between two to three outfits until she found the perfect one to suit the occasion. Then more waiting for her to match the bag, the shoes, the jewellery . . . endless waiting.

He shook his head.

Were they all worth it? All those hours of waiting?

He heard her velvety voice dripping down the staircase.

'Honey, look! What do you think?' she said, twirling to show off her designer dress, matching shoes and bag.

He looked up the stairs to catch a view of the latest result in the five-month (and counting) exercise in vanity. He considered her face, now lined with a few crow's feet and laughter lines in spite of her regular visits to the skin clinic and the expensive creams that lined her bathroom cabinet and vanity closet. He took in her glowing skin, long legs, curvy body and tiny waist.

He was quiet for longer than was comfortable. Especially for his wife.

'Well?'

'Honey . . . I've never seen you looking more exquisite, but . . .'

'But what?'

'Won't you be cold in that thin material?'

'It's not for now, silly – it's for our trip to Zimbali. It's always hot down there, even in winter.'

'But Zimbali's not until next weekend.' His stomach rumbled.

'I know that. I'm going to change for dinner in a minute. I just wanted you to approve my choice of outfit for the social club

4

event.' She posed and pouted. 'Am I going to be the most gorgeous creature in the room?'

Like a well-rehearsed thespian, he responded, 'You're always the most gorgeous creature – in the room, in Zimbali, in the world!'

He knew his lines.

His wife blew him a kiss.

'I'll just be a minute,' she said.

The Jiyas

Moshidi stared at her office PC for the umpteenth time. A flat screen. Black, stern and menacing. The screensaver that bore a photo of her and her family did nothing to calm her unease.

If she clicked on her mailbox, she knew that the email would still be waiting. The one she had not been able to bring herself to open yesterday when she'd left her desk.

It was still there. Lurking darkly in the pile of unopened mails.

FINAL DEMAND – that was the subject line. Was it better in the era of snail mail, when the message took weeks, sometimes months, to land on one's desk, thanks to the inefficiencies of the postal system?

She sighed and shook her shoulders as if to ward off the tension and stress that had been accumulating over more than a year.

How did they get into this mess?

It was her. She knew it. Though Solomzi was not much better than she was.

They were both so competitive. So . . . shiny. She knew what her sister Lerato would say about their dilemma.

'Show-offs. Why are you two so superficial? You already have it all. Why can't you just be happy?'

For the life of her, Moshidi could not imagine being any other way.

The biggest mistake was joining the social club. The Khula Society was the final nail in the coffin for them. They'd always had a huge appetite for the grandiose, her and Soli.

She sighed and leaned back in her executive swivel chair, opting to dream about 'The Way They Were' instead of facing the nightmare that loomed large, so inescapable. So suffocating.

She remembered how Solomzi stole her from her accountant boyfriend by showering her with an endless array of luxurious gifts and extravagant excursions.

Shame. What was his name again? Ludwe. Such a gentleman he'd been. And so . . . level-headed. Maybe if she'd stuck with him, she wouldn't be facing this mountain of debt now.

A true-to-type accountant, he always watched his rands and cents. He'd taken her to a McDonald's on their first date. A McDonald's!

Solomzi was the polar opposite of Ludwe. He was extravagant, tall, bow-legged, with an intelligent face that belied his mischievous nature. He was so sexy then. Still sexy even now.

This year marked their ten-year anniversary.

Sometimes she wondered how they'd made it.

The seven-year itch had gnawed away at different areas of their marriage like a swamp rat. Nibbling here, nibbling there until every aspect of their union felt discombobulated. They went through marriage counselling and miraculously found their footing again, but it hadn't been easy.

She sighed, thinking about all the hurdles they had surmounted, and now this new demon was creeping in to disturb the equilibrium that they had somehow managed to find.

To ward off her frustration, she decided to do what she did best – daydream.

She'd met Solomzi at a farewell party for her colleague and friend Thandi, who'd just been headhunted by a multinational financial services firm.

Thandi had invited a few close friends to her penthouse apartment in Hyde Park to celebrate the new job over wine and canapés. Moshidi had just been promoted to senior HR manager at the bank where they worked and was thrilled to accept her official introduction into Thandi's high-flying circle of friends.

They were all in their late twenties but were already known as the 'The Glam Set'. All their parties were catered and were either held at tastefully furnished apartments located at the 'right' addresses or at a rented upscale venue if the host was still saving up for the right address.

Most of them had Instagram accounts that looked like professional photoshoots from magazines. Her sister looked down on her choice of friends, but she didn't care. She had always been ambitious.

She'd been having a funny conversation with Tshego from marketing when a tall, good-looking man with a deep Xhosa accent came up to introduce himself.

She had registered his presence a few minutes before when he'd made an energetic entrance into the room, hugging two of the men whom Thandi had introduced as her university friends.

For some reason, she had felt his energy from the moment he walked in. It was an odd sensation. She had last felt that kind of magnetic pull to someone when she was much younger – when love was spontaneous and did not require the ticking of a long list of boxes.

When Solomzi proffered his large, muscular hand by way of introduction, her head felt heavy, as if by lifting it and locking eyes with this stranger, her fate would be sealed. There would be no turning back.

A rush of panic overcame her. What if he was drawn to Tshego and not her?

'Hi, I'm Solomzi, but everyone calls me Soli,' the tall stranger said.

Tshego took his hand and responded, 'I'm Tshego and this is my friend Moshidi.'

Embarrassed by her adolescent coyness, Moshidi managed to raise her head, shaking his hand formally.

'Sorry. I just, um . . . I'm Moshidi.'

Solomzi grinned, a huge, full-toothed grin. 'Pleasure to meet you, ladies. I'm an old friend of Thandi's. Yeah . . . we go way back. Varsity days. How do you two know her? She's such an alpha female. I'm always terrified of her friends. Confident, beautiful women—' He sounded like he was going to go on forever, till Tshego mercifully interrupted him.

'*Shoo*. You talk a mile a minute. And I thought I was Thandi's chattiest friend.'

Moshidi and Solomzi laughed nervously while Tshego stayed completely at ease.

'Well . . . anyway, I'm going to go grab a drink while you two, eh . . . I dunno. So awkward.'

The minute she left, they looked at each other and grinned like idiots.

'This is weird,' said Moshidi.

'Yes . . . um, can I offer you a drink? You look like a champagne girl.'

'Ah well. I'm holding a champagne glass.'

'You're a quick one, aren't you? I like it. I'll be right back. Don't move an inch.'

And that was it.

She hadn't left his side since.

Over the next ten years, they would go on to cohabit for a year, get engaged in the traditional fashion with Solomzi visiting her family in Rustenburg with his uncles to negotiate her *lobola* – the traditional bride price or dowry that the groom's family pays to the bride's family as a means of securing her hand in marriage.

The feminist in Moshidi had had strong opinions in her youth against the *lobola* practice, but as she grew older she had gained an appreciation for this custom, especially after she had gone through her sister Lerato's own *lobola* negotiations.

Unlike the commercial transaction she had perceived it to be, *lobola* negotiations involved a process aimed at bringing the families of the bride and groom together. Indeed, in Xhosa culture, it is said that 'One never stops paying *lobola*' because relations between the two families are expected to continue for the entire lifetime of the marriage and even beyond the death of one of the spouses.

As per tradition, it is mostly the uncles on both sides of the family who are involved in the negotiations, and the aplomb with which her Uncle Lemogang took on leading the process on her family's side still brought a sense of quiet pride to her heart.

Xhosa delegations are notoriously difficult to please, but Uncle Lemogang had promised her that he would bring his lawyerly skills to the table and would ensure that she would be well represented.

By the time the negotiations were finalised, she had been relieved that the two families had managed to reach an agreement. She half wished it had been conducted the old-fashioned way, where the bride price was quantified by the number of cattle the groom's family would hand over to the bride's family. With her never-ending list of ambitions, she sometimes wondered whether she had missed her one opportunity at cattle farming. One of her banking clients was a cattle farmer and her eyes had watered on viewing his balance sheet!

After the *lobola* ceremony was completed, his strict Xhosa matriarch of a mom insisted that she *kotiza*, which meant spending time at Soli's home in Umtata tending to all manner of house chores and displaying the demeanour of a respectful and dutiful *makoti*, or bride. Fortunately, Soli's sisters had been around to assist with the daily chores but she had still bookmarked this period as 'The Worst Ten Days of my Life'. She was not a domestic goddess and had been relieved to pack her bags and head back to their shared home where she could apply her labour to her office job instead of toiling away in the kitchen.

She promised herself a life of lavish glamour once she returned to Gauteng, to make up for all the servile tasks she had had to carry out during the *ukukotiza* bridal period.

Within another year, they had put down a deposit for their first home – a duplex in the northern suburbs.

Solomzi then quit his job at a global project management firm to branch out on his own in the construction sector. His charm and ruthless grit scored him many deals, culminating in a five-year construction deal with a multinational company.

His star continued to rise as he scored bigger and more profitable deals, through planning and long lunches with politicians and business influencers.

In the meantime, Moshidi also advanced her career, although her restless nature meant changing jobs and eventually careers, but she remained successful in her endeavours. While she'd started out in human resources, she now worked in purchasing at the same bank where she'd initiated her career.

Each year she and Solomzi acquired more and more assets. Bigger cars, larger homes, never tiring of expanding their fortune. Ten years down the line, they now had three children – twin boys and one sharp-witted girl – three mansions, eight cars and a boat.

In spite of their good fortune, things were starting to look shaky on the ground.

The income from Solomzi's construction business was under enormous strain, the business having lost two of its major clients. With many more players in that market now, construction was becoming extremely competitive. Their holiday homes – in Zimbali and in Knysna – were on the verge of being repossessed. The shame. The utter humiliation of it all!

They were due to host the social club in Zimbali next weekend. It was much too late to change venues without sparking suspicion. That haughty Noma would be the first to ask questions. 'I'm so looking forward to Zimbali again, sweetheart,' she'd said on the phone. 'You and Solomzi are always such perfect hosts.'

Moshidi could just imagine the faux concern in her voice if she told her they would be hosting at home in Joburg instead. Well, she wasn't going to give her the satisfaction. She was keeping both her posh home at Zimbali Estates *and* the home in Knysna, that's all there was to it. If Solomzi was going soft on her, then she would have to man up and save their marriage and their assets.

The Msibis

Lerato never wanted to join her sister's stupid social club. All those pretentious people spending hours showing off their wealth. To what end? What was the point of it all? She'd been disappointed that her husband had fallen for Solomzi's charms and finally acceded to the invitation to join the group despite her own misgivings.

She'd been unfortunate enough to witness them in full display on a number of occasions, but this was the first time she would be joining them as a member. What on earth was she going to talk to them about? She was head of data analytics at a predictive analytics company. She couldn't exactly chat to them about algorithms, now could she?

Maybe Mzwandile was in the clutches of a mid-life crisis, because he'd always been immune to excess in spite of his achievements. A God-fearing man through and through, she was proud of her husband's humility and level-headedness. They were the things that had drawn her to him.

With one son, Lwazi, already at university, and Bongani halfway through matric, Lerato often obsessed about the empty nest. They needed a new life. New interests. Hobbies. My goodness! Did black people actually have hobbies?

Maybe they could start travelling more with the bit of money they had saved up over the years, or even start a foundation at church to solidify their position in their Christian community.

Perhaps they could do both? Surely God recognised their dedication and effort to church ministry over the years. After all, it was their love for God that had brought the two of them together in the first place when they were still students at university.

It warmed her heart to think that, unlike her sister Moshidi, she had fallen in love, married and stayed married to her first love.

Mzwandile was like an extension of her soul, her twin mate on earth.

They had experienced so much of life through each other's eyes and though their marriage may not be perfect, they always knew they could count on each other, no matter what.

'Babe, what do you think I should wear to the social club? I've just realised I've got tons of clothes, but they're only suitable for work or church . . . at least the decent ones are.'

Mzwandile was reading the sports section of the weekend paper and barely managed to look up to view the cause of his wife's distress.

She threw two items on to the bed. A black pants suit that she often wore to important meetings at work, and a long, flowy chiffon dress that she'd wear to garden parties now and then.

'Mzwandile, can you hear me? Please drag your nose out of that paper and look at me. Do I look decent in this dress?'

Mzwandile finally put down the paper. 'Isn't it a bit too much for a *stokvel*?'

She frowned. 'Have you seen how those women dress at these things? They always have this kind of understated glamour. They look fancy without trying to look fancy. I don't even know why they call it a *stokvel*. When I think back to my mom's *stokvel*, all I recall is a bunch of middle-aged ladies meeting every month to contribute towards their burial society.'

Mzwandile shook his head, laughing. 'You're right. My father and mom also belonged to a *stokvel* in our village. They would meet every month, club together and contribute about a hundred rands towards each family's funeral fund. That was it. No pomp, no ceremony . . . but apartheid did a number on us, hey?'

'Yeah . . . cos the *stokvel* culture started because black people couldn't even bank at any of the major banks so short of hiding money under the mattress, they'd resort to that. Which is exactly my point . . . why do we need to belong to a *stokvel* now? It's so archaic . . . I think that the Khula Society only uses it as an opportunity to flaunt the latest obscene set of wheels that someone's just bought or the behemoth of a house that they've just added to their list of assets,' said Lerato.

'Careful there, Mrs Msibi . . . sounds like you're being a hater.'

Lerato scrunched up her face as she held up a maxi dress she'd bought two summers before, wondering whether it would pass muster with Moshidi's band of snobs.

'Do you think this one will pass the Fashion Police's litmus test?'

'Sweetheart, you're just complicating things. Just don't try too hard. It's not a competition. View it as an investment club . . . which is exactly what it is. Works for me. Khula will make it easier for us to plan our holidays, love. Don't stress about dressing up. Just smile at those women, say one or two sentences to contribute to the conversation, then call it a day. I know you're not looking forward to it but think of the ocean. We can go walking on the beach,' he said, picking up the paper once again and burying his nose in it to indicate that he'd exhausted the topic.

'Argh. You just don't get it. After all, you're the only person left on earth who still reads the weekend paper,' she grumbled.

'I heard that,' he said.

Moshidi and Solomzi were hosting this month's gathering at their Zimbali holiday home on the KZN coast. How they could afford that place, beautiful as it was, she had no idea. But Mzwandile was right. They could always go for a walk on the beach if the ladies got too much.

Zimbali

Moshidi had hired a catering company and they had turned the property into a tropical wonderland. In the well-kept garden with its ocean view and swaying palm trees, cream-white umbrellas and multi-coloured woven beach chairs broke the dense green. There were floating canapés and gorgeous floral arrangements.

Lerato went downstairs to greet her sister, who was barking out orders to the waiting staff, something she seemed particularly gifted at doing.

'No. No. Don't put that vase on that cocktail table! Are you insane? I told you it belongs on the table in the lounge—' She stopped abruptly, staring at Lerato with alarm. 'Sis . . . what are you wearing? Is that what you're going to wear to the party?'

Lerato grinned shyly, tugging at her lime-green maxi dress like a bashful schoolgirl.

'No, sis, please. Are you seriously planning to embarrass me?'

'What's wrong with her dress?' asked Mzwandile, trailing behind his wife.

Moshidi covered her face. '*Goodness!* What am I going to do with you two? You look like a farmer going to his first business meeting. No disrespect, Mzwandile, but seriously? And that dress!' she exclaimed, taking off her designer sunglasses to get a better look.

'It really is lime green,' she whispered to an invisible companion in horror, placing her hands on her chest. 'I have no words!'

'What's wrong with my suit?' asked Mzwandile, examining himself to check how he'd missed the brief.

'And what's wrong with this dress? It's the most stylish thing in my wardrobe!'

Solomzi came down the stairs, looking casually chic in shorts, a Gucci top and loafers. 'The question, *sbali*, my dear brother-in-law, is what in heaven's name are you doing wearing a suit in Zimbali on a sunny Saturday afternoon?' asked Solomzi.

Mzwandile shrugged. 'Her sister was making such a fuss about your people that I ended up not knowing what exactly I needed to wear at this occasion.'

Moshidi sighed in exasperation. 'The guests will be here in thirty minutes.' She lifted her head and called out, 'Zozo! Please come and rescue your aunt from being a fashion victim. Soli, you handle the man.'

Mzwandile guffawed. 'Now I'm just known as "the man". Tough life!'

The Jiyas' daughter came bouncing into the lounge smiling with glee. 'I style, no stylist!' Little Zozo belted out the popular tune, grabbing her aunt by the hand and leading her back upstairs to Moshidi's bedroom.

Lerato seethed with embarrassment. 'You're enlisting an eight-year-old to dress me? Moshidi . . . you really don't have any regard for me, hey?'

Moshidi shooed her sister and brother-in-law away. 'Go. Go. Get dressed in something decent while I get everything ready. I can't be dealing with catering and making sure you two don't stick out like sore thumbs.'

The doorbell rang.

The first guests had arrived.

17

Tom and Paul. The social club's first gay couple. They had only joined Khula three months before. Khula Society had needed new members after the Masuabis moved to London amidst fears for South Africa's troubled economy.

Moshidi loved Tom and Paul.

She knew Paul through work. As head of purchasing, she'd been in charge of sourcing a company to furnish three of the bank's new offices. Paul's company had been awarded the contract.

When she told Paul about the social club, he was thrilled at the opportunity for short-term investments, which came with the extra boon of socialising with the well-heeled. He loved Moshidi's tastes and found her fun – if occasionally tedious.

Tom was quieter and more measured than Paul. A financial planner by profession, he often struck Moshidi as too subdued to cope with someone as outgoing as Paul. But then again, people often said the same thing about her and Solomzi.

'I'm so glad to see you, darlings. Please move on to the patio and help yourselves to some drinks and eats. The others will be here shortly.'

The couple wandered around the garden, admiring the stunning view, until a few minutes later the roar of a V12 engine stopped everyone in their tracks. Moshidi, Tom and Paul went outside to greet the new arrivals as two yellow Lamborghinis pulled into the driveway.

Noma Manamela climbed out of the first, and her husband, Julius, aka 'The Duke', from the one behind.

'Woo-hoo! Look at you two. Talk about stepping out in style.' Paul seemed impressed. 'Is this the new V12? Such a beauty! Do you mind if I go for a little spin?'

Moshidi blushed with embarrassment. She knew how snooty the Manamelas were about their cars, and she was still not sure how The Duke felt about the newest couple.

He surprised her by saying, 'Sure. Why not? Trust me, it'll be the best ride of your life.'

And so Paul stepped into the supercar, gesturing to his husband to join him. Tom mock-looked to the right and to the left, then pointed at himself, mouthing, 'Me?' as if he could not believe such a grand invitation.

'Come, you gorgeous thing!' said Paul, laughing.

Tom got into the passenger seat and they revved off, grinning as if they had just been gifted the vehicle.

Moshidi and the Manamelas waved them away, smiling.

'Oh, gosh. Those two are forward,' said Noma.

Moshidi shrugged. 'So, you decided to drive instead of fly this time around?'

'Moshidi, driving a Lamborghini *is* flying,' said The Duke. 'I could really use a stiff glass of whisky. This woman has worn me out.'

'What? Did you guys have sex on the highway?' Moshidi asked, laughing.

'How I wish. We'll add that item to the itinerary next time. She challenged me to a race. She's a demon behind the wheel.'

Noma laughed. 'And a demon in bed as well.'

'Okay. That officially falls under the Too Much Information category. Let me get you guys your drinks. Noma, what will you be having?'

'Just some juice and water for now. I'm really parched.'

Tom and Paul returned, looking flushed.

'Now I know what I want Tom to get me for our anniversary,' said Paul.

The Duke raised an eyebrow. 'How long have you been . . . eh . . . do you, uh . . . are you allowed to marry? I mean . . . is it legal?'

The two men laughed. 'You should see the look on your face,' said Paul. 'Yes, Julius. We've been married for ten years now.'

'Please . . . nobody calls my husband Julius. We both abhor that name. Just call him The Duke.'

The Duke did not abhor his birth name.

The Khathides and the Gumedes were the last to arrive, making up the full tally of the membership.

Food was served, champagne flowed, and one-upmanship drizzled. Lerato longed for her walk on the beach, but escape, unfortunately, was out of the question. The shoes Zozo had her wearing wouldn't have got her very far anyway.

Till Debt Us Do Part?

'Mom! Akhona took my tablet!' screamed Zozo.

'It's school time. The driver's been waiting for you three for ten minutes already. You can't be fighting about tablets right now,' grumbled Moshidi as she placed Zozo's homework book into her rucksack.

Zozo sulked, folding her hands to express her indignation. 'Not fair!'

'Akhona, why did you take this child's iPad? Why is it even floating around the house? You're only supposed to play with your devices on weekends.'

The tall and skinny nine-year-old walked into his sister's bedroom grinning. 'I was trying to help her. Zozo, it's really bad to be addicted to devices,' he said, trying to sound grown up.

Zozo stuck her tongue out at him.

'Where's Kopollo?'

'He's already downstairs.'

'Gosh. At least I have one well-behaved child. Okay, you two, scoot. Off to school you go!'

'But Mom, why don't you drop us off like the other moms?' asked Zozo.

'Because,' said Moshidi, examining herself in Zozo's mirror while straightening her top, 'unlike the other moms, I have to work to make sure you people can afford your tablets.'

She walked out with all three kids in tow. The driver, Sibusiso, stepped out of the driver's seat to open the door for the kids.

'Make sure they're all strapped into their seatbelts.'

'Yes, *sisi* Moshidi. Have a good day at the office.'

'Thanks, Sbu,' she said as she got into her car.

While driving to work, she got a call from Soli.

'Babe, how are you?'

'Good. Are you already at the site?' she answered through her Bluetooth speakers.

A pause. 'Yes. Babe, the bank . . .'

'Oh lord,' she grumbled.

'They say if we don't pay the outstanding balance on Zimbali, they will proceed with repossessing the house and putting it on the market.'

'No,' she said, tears filming her eyes. 'No, Solomzi, we can't allow that to happen. Gosh, couldn't you wait till we got home to tell me this?'

'I'm sorry. I can't deal with this pressure anymore. There've been some . . . uh . . . developments with the Shenzi project.'

Moshidi gestured with her hands as if Solomzi was with her in the car. 'Okay. Stop. Stop, Solomzi. I can't deal with this right now. Let's talk about your bad day when I get back from work. Do you think you can handle that? Can one of us at least have a productive day today?'

'*Thyini!* Moshidi! When I don't tell you about these things, you complain and when I share details with you, you still complain. I don't know what the hell I'm supposed to do with you!'

She felt like screaming. 'Listen, I know you're going through a lot. I'm in this with you but I'm not going to be able to focus on work if I have to stress about every little thing that's going wrong in our lives right now . . . Please. I promise I'll give you my undivided attention when I see you later tonight.'

A deep sigh. 'Okay,' he said softly. 'Let's talk later.'

Nine To Five

The Duke pulled into the security entrance at the office park in his battered Mercedes-Benz, ready for another day at work. To say the vehicle was a wreck would be an insult to the car wrecks of the world. He had had the car since the 1990s. It suited his work image to drive around in the decrepit vehicle.

He'd never thought the day would come when he could actually claim to enjoy his job, but lately he derived an unfamiliar sense of pride in his work. He marvelled at all the years he'd spent at this company, working as a logistics coordinator, which, if he were to be honest, was really a glorified driver.

In fact he had started out as a driver at VNA Trucking, but over time, as the business grew, he had become head of logistics, coordinating the schedules of all the other drivers, ensuring that the fleet of trucks and cars that the company owned stayed in tip-top condition and mapping out the itineraries of all the driving staff well in advance. His role also involved supervising and tracking the drivers through the company GPS systems to ensure they did not meander off route to waste company time on personal errands.

It was perfectly boring, perfectly predictable, and absolutely suitable for a man now nearing his sixties. All in all, it was a good, honest living.

In all this time, none of his colleagues had ever been to his house. They were all under the impression that he lived in Tembisa township with his wife and children. They'd never suspect he'd been living in the suburbs for most of his adult life now.

Once he realised the powerful allure of social media, he had stopped bringing pictures of his children to work as a precautionary measure, relying on time to erase his colleagues' memories of what his children looked like. If anyone saw the real lives his children lived, eyebrows would have definitely been raised and questions asked. The challenge was how to keep his children off social media, which became just about impossible as the years went by.

Fortunately, their mother advanced rapidly in her career to give him a reasonable excuse behind the need for discretion. As head of operations at Zebula Mining, a company that was involved in many high-profile deals, Noma travelled frequently, both overseas and on the continent, and often she was assigned a bodyguard. Children of senior executives in mining could be targets for online predators. Discretion, the importance of family privacy and the dangers posed by Noma's high-profile job were drilled into Khutso and Diamond. Now they were grown – Khutso playing at being a stockbroker and Diamond studying in the States – he could relax a little. But he regularly surfed the internet, going to all the popular apps that the youth seemed obsessed with, to see if his children had established personal accounts. He wasn't sure he always liked what he saw.

At least they were off his hands.

Given his life's circumstances, he was perfectly happy with his perfectly boring nine-to-five job. And if the secrecy slipped and their family's wealth was revealed, he had a reasonable cover because his wife was quite the power player in big business lately.

He didn't mind that image. After all, The Duke was a modern man.

Carnal Thoughts

She couldn't put her finger on it but lately Lerato had started developing a strange, prickling sense of restlessness. Driving to her church cell group meeting she let her mind drift, trying to get a fix on what it was that was bothering her so much.

Seventeen years of marriage. That was a lifetime.

She was turning forty-one next November.

It certainly had to do with the boys about to empty her nest.

For some reason she found herself wishing she had a daughter, although why the thought had just crossed her mind she didn't know. She loved her boys!

Ah yes, she thought, smiling to herself. It was Thembi. Thembi from the cell group. She had a freakishly close relationship with her daughter. No, not freakish. She knew that was her own jealousy talking, but having grown up in an all-girl household, she took for granted the easy female camaraderie that she enjoyed with her sister. Although she and Moshidi were like chalk and cheese, their bond was unbreakable. Her sister was her sounding board, her greatest critic and her most enthusiastic cheerleader.

A smile spread across her face as she recalled the ridiculous 'fashion' intervention that had been staged by little Zozo during the social club weekend in Zimbali. Maybe it was also Zozo who made her long for a girl child. Boy children were differently wired.

They hardly ever thought about calling Mom once they'd sprouted wings and were out in the world. Even Mzwandile, who was a prince among men, had never bothered that much about checking in on his parents throughout their years together. Often Lerato was the one who had to remind him to call his parents, whether it be on birthdays or simply just to say hi.

She sighed. Was she too old for another child?

She laughed at the preposterous thought. First of all, one had to have sex to conceive a baby. Secondly, she was way past her prime in that department, although those Hollywood women were birthing perfectly fine specimens at the age of a hundred.

IVF, of course. Maybe that's what she could do? Because she certainly wasn't getting any. When was the last time she and Mzwandile had done the deed? She stopped at the traffic lights near her church and made a mental calculation, wondering if God would take offence that she was thinking of sex on her way to worship.

Goodness! She actually gasped.

They hadn't had sex in three and a half years! How on earth had that happened?

As she pulled into the churchyard, she started obsessing about the thought. If she were to be honest, they hadn't exactly been swinging from the chandeliers from the inception of their marriage.

Mzwandile's reasoning about maintaining a balance of chastity and sexual intimacy had made sense the first time he'd introduced the topic way back in the early days of their marriage. He had explained that if they became obsessed with sex like all the other couples around them, they would lose the strong spiritual foundation that they had worked so hard to build during their courtship.

After all, it was Mzwandile's strong moral compass that had drawn her to him. She had grown up under her mother's Christian influence so when her father suddenly developed a passion for what he called 'African Spiritualism', she'd felt untethered and clung to her religion to keep her bearings. The clear codes of right and wrong that defined her religious upbringing gave her a strong sense of identity in a world she often found chaotic.

Her cell group comprised mainly women of different age groups and a sprinkling of men, who barely ever attended the meetings. The group usually shared their experiences, good and bad, and shared biblical scripture and prayer to buttress each other emotionally and spiritually in the face of life's ravages. She wondered whether sex was a matter befitting of spiritual reflection.

So, what are your concerns today, Lerato?

I haven't had sex in three and a half years and I think I may be losing my mind.

She laughed to herself.

There was no way she would ever confess to such a dilemma. Not to this group. Besides, she'd been *sort of* resigned to a sexless marriage, so why was it worrying her so much suddenly?

Was she going through an existential crisis? For the past three months, the dry spell in her marriage seemed to have taken on ever greater proportions. Was it a sign that she and her husband were somehow ill-matched? Could spirituality alone sustain a marriage?

No. She was being too hard on herself . . . and her husband.

They shared more than their spirituality. They had their boys, whom they loved fiercely and unreservedly. They'd built a beautiful, calm and peaceful life together, and they'd always been able to count on each other through a lifetime of storms as well as happy sunrays.

He was still a handsome, fit and reliable man. Surely that was enough? Unlike her sister Moshidi, she never had to wonder about his whereabouts. Indeed, of all the men she knew, Mzwandile was the one man who was as consistent as clockwork . . . but was he also consistently . . . boring?

Where did that thought come from?

Surely the issue was only about sex. Everything else about Mzwandile was . . . okay. Better than okay. He was a good man.

She needed to talk to someone. The question was, to whom could she turn, regarding such a delicate issue?

Her husband, of course, since he was the person with whom she wanted to have sex, but Mzwandile had made the topic almost taboo in their marriage.

She wondered bleakly if this was her lot in life.

Like a good Christian, she had gallantly practised the principle of No Sex Before Marriage, which was probably why she and Mzwandile had married so young in the first place. The heavy petting they had engaged in as young lovers had become unbearably hot, at least for her. They knew they were teetering on the brink of committing a carnal sin, so as soon as they completed their degrees, they ran to the parents and promptly sorted out their *lobola* negotiations. They had a quick, painless, no-frills wedding. It had been fun letting off steam after holding off on sex for so long. Small wonder they became pregnant within the first year of their marriage. Now that she thought of it though, she'd always been the one to initiate sex, even then.

It had never occurred to her that after those early years of fun and games, she would find herself practising No Sex After Marriage.

Keeping Secrets

When Moshidi came back from work, she attended to the kids and supervised their homework. In spite of an exhausting day at the office, she planned to get this part of her parental duties out of the way so that she could prepare herself mentally for the difficult conversation she was going to have with her husband.

It was six thirty in the evening. She rounded up the kids to their shared study, which contained miniature desks for each child. Homework time was serious time in her household.

'Okay, do you boys think you can tackle your maths homework without my help?'

'Yup,' said Akhona, who was already scribbling furiously in his homework book.

Kopollo raised his hand. 'A little help, please.'

She went over to his desk to read the maths problem out loud to him. It was a multiplication equation. She explained what was required and Kopollo quickly said, 'Oh. I get it, I get it. I'll be fine.'

She then moved to Zozo who at eight was already a whizz with numbers but still needed help with her reading.

Moshidi looked at her watch. It was almost 7 p.m. Soli would be home soon.

She called him, to find out if he'd already had something to eat. Their cook had prepared a steak and vegetable dinner.

His phone went unanswered.

When the children were done with their homework, she allowed them thirty minutes of television before preparing them for bed. Once they were safely in bed, she went to the basement and picked out a bottle of wine. She poured herself a glass and took it upstairs to her bedroom.

She changed into her night clothes, switched on the bedside lamp and opened up her laptop. It wasn't just the obvious dip in business at Soli's company that was bothering her about their finances – that she could understand; but she had a niggling feeling there was something else. Something didn't add up.

The five-year contract with the multinational had brought in steady handsome revenues over the years, which was why they had been bold enough to acquire so many properties and cars. Even after all these expenses, they had still been able to put away a lot of the money into savings, so why such a dramatic dip in their finances all of a sudden?

Had Soli made some investments he hadn't consulted with her about? Something was off.

She tried calling him again. This time, he answered his phone.

'Moshidi, I'm just wrapping up now. I'll be there in about thirty minutes.'

Slowly sipping her wine, she checked their income and expenditure reports over the past two years. She checked again and her stomach twisted.

Three large sums of money paid out to one company . . . Moreti Investments. Who the hell was Moreti Investments?

She went to the search engine on her phone and typed out the company name. A few companies with similar names popped up but there were no tangible search results under Moreti Investments. Not even a company website or social media page, or even a lousy press release.

Could she check the company owners by going into the registrar of companies website? You needed login details for that, which Soli had.

But why was she being so paranoid?

There was a simple answer to that. Earlier in their marriage, Solomzi had jackknifed them into a truckload of financial trouble . . . twice. First it was his gambling addiction that had almost toppled their marriage. She'd had to threaten him with divorce before he eventually joined Gamblers' Anonymous. His Xhosa pride had been so hurt at having been assigned to group therapy that he'd seemed fully invested in turning that part of his life around just so he could stop talking about his feelings to a group of (like-minded?) people.

And then there was the time he'd had his first taste of real money and started buying Louis Vuitton bags for some girl who couldn't spell. (Funny how her badly spelt texts were all Moshidi could remember about her.)

And now this . . . What fresh hell had she stumbled upon?

Was there no end to the turmoil of raising a man-child? Because it was starting to feel like Solomzi was her firstborn instead of her husband.

Or maybe there was a perfectly reasonable explanation? An innocent business transaction? With a company that didn't have any presence save for a bank account.

No. She was going to ask a lot of questions . . . and this man had better have answers for her, she thought, as she gulped down the rest of her wine.

Still Sweet

For weeks now, Noma had not only been coming home late from work, but she was bringing work home too. Their weekends were no longer dedicated to spending time together or taking trips to visit friends or family.

Things were not the same between them.

The Duke was half watching a tennis match in their cinema when he heard his wife coming up the stairs. He looked at his watch – 9.30 p.m. – and shook his head.

He heard her soft footsteps padding past the cinema, past the pajama lounge on their way along the passage to their bedroom.

Even though he complained about it, Noma's evening routine had seldom changed in all their years of marriage. It always started with the two of them having dinner together and talking about their respective days. After dinner she would take a shower and then begin applying her many creams. She'd once tried to explain her complex beauty regime to him but he'd never been able to get his head around it.

In the earlier days, when he was young, randy and could not wait to pin his wife to the bed, he used to watch her. He'd be lying in bed waiting, only to find that there was still more waiting to be done.

He had asked her once to explain why she couldn't just slap water on her face and apply some moisturiser (he'd actually said Vaseline) and call it a day.

The look on her face! It was as if he'd said a swear word.

That was when she had tried to break down what she called her 'skin routine' for him. He lost concentration at step number four or five because he honestly could not understand how nature could have possibly designed human skin to need so many creams just to get by. How come cavewomen survived without all these creams, oils and things?

His wife was truly a special creature. She wore perfume to bed, which for years he assumed was what all women did before going to sleep. He had never seen her wearing anything other than something sheer and sexy to sleep in. It was either sexy lingerie or nothing at all. Not even through winter. Not even throughout her pregnancies.

He marvelled at how much effort it must really take to be Nomathando Manamela.

'Sugar bean, I'm in the cinema!' he shouted, hearing her footsteps approach a full hour later.

The second level of their house comprised an en-suite guest room, the en-suite master bedroom with a concealed safe in one wall and Noma's vast walk-in closet on another; a pajama lounge; and the cinema. Hence he had to announce his exact location.

Noma walked in and greeted him with a sultry smile. 'I want you, you sexy hunk. Why are you hiding from me?'

He was happy to see that she was in a good mood. He pointed his index finger at himself. 'Who? Me?' She looked irresistible in her long silky nightgown.

She gestured for him to follow her to the bedroom, luring him on with her finger.

Must be his lucky day.

He followed her eagerly, excited to make love to his wife.

It had been way too long.

Sex After Marriage

'Bongani! Bongs!'

'Hey, Ma. You look nice today.'

Lerato looked up at her son who was a few inches taller than her and smiled. 'Really? Thank you, boy,' she said, leaning against the kitchen countertop. 'I'm so exhausted I could pass out. Did *sis* Linda make dinner before she knocked off?'

Her son nodded. 'Very nice. *Sis* Linda can cook up a storm, hey, Mom?'

'Yep. She's a whizz in the kitchen. Small wonder I'm piling on so much weight. Your dad eat already?'

'*Ja*. He was watching the news earlier. He's becoming hooked on that Netflix series *When They See Us*.'

'Oooh. Your dad's so tough. I can't watch that series. It makes me so enraged I start wanting to bludgeon all the white people at work after watching it.'

'Yeah, but you should watch it, Mom. I think it's an important reminder of what can happen to any of us black men. It's not just a US thing, you know.'

Her heart lurched a little when she heard her son refer to himself as a man. A black man. Especially with all the loaded sense of vulnerability and danger that went with the context in which he'd used the words. To the world her little boy was a black man who posed a potential danger and would therefore stay constantly *in* danger.

The microwave pinged. Bongani took out his mother's dinner and placed it on the table. 'There you go, Mama bear. Now go and chill with Dad and . . . um . . . can I please step out for a few minutes? I need to go to KC's house to get my game back.'

'Hmm. Is that why you were being so sweet to me?'

'Ma, you know I'm always sweet to you. I'll be back soon, I promise,' he said, already heading out the door.

Lerato went to join Mzwandile, who was transfixed in his chair, his eyes glued to the TV screen.

'Hey, babe,' she said, pecking him on the cheek.

He looked up for a second and greeted her back. 'How was work?' he asked.

'Argh. Work was work. Is it almost finished?' she asked, seeing that he was indeed watching the series Bongani had mentioned.

'Yeah.'

She ate her dinner quietly. When she finished, she stood up and took her plate through to the kitchen. Then she returned and sat next to him on the double-seater couch, leaning her head on his shoulder, struggling to keep her eyes open.

Bongani came back, announced his arrival, and promptly went up to his room.

On hearing Bongani go up the stairs, she managed to set her gaze on the screen and was relieved to see the end credits.

She nudged him playfully. 'So . . . tough guy. I see you managed to get to the last episode. How are you this composed?'

Mzwandile looked at his wife with a sombre expression. 'Why do they hate us so much?'

She shrugged. 'That's why I couldn't watch it. After the first two episodes, I was rude to my boss for three consecutive days

35

despite that horrific telecom project I'm working on and the promotion I'm hoping for. D'you know what he said?'

'What?'

'He asked me if I was on my period, and I told him I was on a *When They See Us* period pain.'

Mzwandile considered his wife with a serious expression, shaking his head, then suddenly burst out laughing. 'So then what did he say?'

'He kind of looked dumbfounded. Then he reminded me he's Canadian, therefore could not answer for apartheid nor Black Lives Matter.'

Mzwandile laughed some more. 'I sometimes forget there's this side to you. I'm dying to hear what your clever rebuttal was to that cop-out?'

'I bought him the *White Privilege* book the next day.'

They both laughed.

She looked at him with a serious expression on her face. 'Come to bed,' she whispered into his ear.

He looked at her casually and said, 'Babe, can I just watch this last episode with the interviews of the real-life characters? Please?'

She shook her head. 'You're such a sucker for punishment.' She kissed her husband and commanded, 'Meet me in bed!'

He murmured his assent.

She went to their bedroom and started shedding her clothes.

She took a long shower, using a scented shower gel. The drizzle of warm water on her skin felt erotic. She stepped out of the bath and started lathering her skin with an oud-scented lotion. It came to her mind again how long it had been since she'd made love to her husband.

She decided to take action.

She searched her wardrobe for the new sexy lingerie she had purchased a few months before Mzwandile had decided they should give up sex as part of their Lent fast – every year they gave up something as part of their supplication in honouring this period in the weeks before Easter.

Three years ago, Mzwandile had suggested that they give up sex for forty days, an idea that at first had seemed ludicrous to her as they were already having sex irregularly. If she'd assumed they would be tearing each other's clothes off by Easter, she'd been wrong. Not only that, but Lent had come and gone – thrice now! – and they still hadn't reignited their passion. How had that happened?

She wondered whether Mzwandile could be having an affair, but she knew the idea to be preposterous. He was deeply committed to their marriage and his Christian discipline was sacrosanct. Everything he did was guided by biblical scripture. Besides, what kind of mistress would accept such meagre servings of sex; that is, if the sex count in their own marriage was anything to go by? But men could surprise you. Based on her sister's wild stories, a man could have sex with his wife once a month (she'd been shocked that once a month wasn't considered a generous dose) and be a total stud with a different woman.

So what could be the reason behind his utter lack of interest in sex?

Could it be that he had always associated sex with uncleanness? Maybe that's why he'd always preached the importance of chastity . . . even in marriage. But was that even fair on her? Surely God did not disapprove of sex between married couples.

Had she been a fool all along to just accept his dated ideas without question? Upon reflection, she'd realised that she'd been so anxious to radiate the kind of 'purity' that Mzwandile had always prized, that she'd muted any of her own doubts about his unorthodox sexual viewpoints.

At this point though, she was willing to bet that even Buddhist monks had more action than the pair of them.

Recently her libido seemed to have erupted like a volcano so the last thing she needed was a permanent sex drought. Was it her hormones or the realisation that Bongani would be going off to university next year, leaving her and her husband to an empty nest?

They really needed to inject some magic into their marriage, otherwise how was she going to derive any joy from being all alone with Mzwandile in this house?

She turned off the ceiling light and switched on the bedside lamp, then sent Mzwandile a sexy text.

Something curvy, sexy and wet is waiting for you upstairs.
Make your way up for a night you won't forget.

She looked at the text, which was so uncharacteristic of her, and pressed send, giggling with naughty anticipation. She was risking it all tonight! She was starting a new chapter in her marriage and she hoped he'd be ready to come along for the ride!

She lay down on the bed, posing like a lingerie model, and waited.

Waited some more.

She shifted position, determined to get the perfect pose.

Ten minutes went by and Mzwandile had still not made his appearance.

This was ridiculous.

She got off the bed, walked out of the room and called down the stairs.

'Mzwandile, time's up! It's late!' She couldn't exactly tease her husband up the stairs with sexy banter – Bongani would hear.

'Almost done,' Mzwandile called back. 'Be there in a minute.'

She briefly wondered if he'd seen the text. She'd be mortified if he'd chosen to ignore it. Suddenly, all her earlier confidence dissipated and she began to feel silly.

He'd turned her down before . . . she didn't think she could stand another rejection.

She padded back to the bedroom and lay down on the bed, abandoning the lingerie model pose, which was making her neck ache. After another five minutes she got up and went to the full-length mirror, where she examined her reflection. Hearing her husband's footsteps finally coming up the stairs, she quickly combed her afro, sprayed some perfume on her neck and pulse points, and adopted a casual pose beside the bed.

When Mzwandile appeared in the doorway, she walked up to him seductively, doing a little dance. 'Finally. Come here, you sexy thang.'

Mzwandile looked at her and smiled. 'You look nice, babe,' he said.

Nice? Well. That was one word to describe her little get-up. There were more fiery adjectives but at least he'd noticed something.

She draped her arms around him. 'I've missed you . . . so much,' she said, kissing him.

He responded, kissing her softly.

Just as she was getting into the moment, he pulled her arms away.

'My love,' he said, still smiling, 'I'm exhausted. Besides . . . I'm not exactly in a sexual mood after watching *When They See Us*.'

'What? Come on, baby,' she said, stroking his body and starting to unbutton his shirt.

He brushed her away. 'I'm serious, Lerato. That series is heavy. It's emotionally draining.'

So now she wasn't getting some because of *When They See Us*?

'And besides, it's a Monday,' Mzwandile added.

Good God. What about Sunday, Saturday, Friday, Thursday, Wednesday and Tuesday? Not to mention all the years!

She felt like crying.

'Look,' Mzwandile said, sitting on the foot of the bed, 'I know we haven't done it in a while, but I promise to make it up to you. Just . . . not tonight, please. I've got an early morning tomorrow. Mad rush. I just want to lie down, take it easy, okay? Please.'

'But . . . can't we just . . .'

He was taking off his clothes and literally getting into his onesie. Did he choose it specifically because of its lack of access points?

What a cruel man! That was it, then? Case closed. End of discussion.

Lerato sullenly went to her side of the bed, switched off the bedside light and closed her eyes, feeling tears threatening. She couldn't stop them coming. She cried herself to sleep.

She was never going to watch *When They See Us*. Not on any day of the week. She couldn't believe racial discrimination was now being used by her husband to discriminate against her right to orgasm! It was true. A black woman's struggle just never ended.

Debt

Soli had been working late the entire week, so Moshidi had decided to book a table for them at Wombles, one of their favourite eateries in the Parks, a collection of upscale but historical suburbs with stylish restaurants that lined the pavements of some of the main streets.

The couple preferred the area because of its charm and slightly artsy vibe. Marked by grand old houses and cottages with well-manicured lawns and tall trees, the Parks felt like an escape from the busy rumble of their everyday lives.

If anything was going to relax her husband, it was a night out at Wombles with its fine-dining menu and its offering of the very best South African wines.

They settled down to eat and were warmly greeted by the owner, Gregory, who asked after their children and announced the venison that had made its entry to the menu. Soli regaled him with an anecdote about his trip to Botswana, and Moshidi listened as the men went on about all the different types of game and their appreciation of it.

After digging into their starters and making small talk, Moshidi ventured: 'So babe . . . I'm really worried about Zimbali. If we don't settle this month end, we're losing the property. I mean . . . I can barely sleep at night thinking about that. It would be my worst nightmare. I don't think I'd be able to handle it.'

Solomzi reached out and held her hand. 'Moshidi, I know things have been really rough the past few months but there's that Rubicon project I told you about and it's as good as done. We're signing by the twentieth so I don't think you have anything to worry about.'

'But you won't get any money from that before month end. This is serious, Solomzi. For some reason, you don't seem to appreciate the gravity of this situation. Imagine how humiliating it would be to face the social club and tell them we've lost the property. I can't go through that. And what about the kids? We've always said it was an investment for them in the long-term. How the hell did we end up here in the first place?'

'Take it easy, baby, and don't stress. It's just the normal ebbs and flows of business, that's all. I borrowed some money from one of my associates because I thought that Correctional Services deal was a sure thing but when the minister landed in the papers over his dealings with Khoza Construction, all the deals he'd signed were put on ice, including ours. But by that time, I'd invested a lot in our greenfield projects through the borrowed money.'

'Who did you borrow the money from? Who's this associate?'

He shifted in his chair then, casting his eyes downwards, and responded: 'It doesn't really matter but I'll pay off the debt and we'll be back on our feet again.'

She wasn't satisfied with his answer. What was he hiding? 'Is it Moreti Investments?'

He bore the same expression he'd worn when she had first confronted him about his texts with the bad speller. First the eyes pop, then a downward shift of the eyebrows as if they were about to descend to a basement of lies.

'How do you know about that?'

'Because unlike the hoochies you used to date, I can read and write . . . Honestly, Soli, how did you think you'd hide that from me? And what's so shady about these people that you can't tell me who they are?'

Soli stood up and marched to the restaurant patio.

What on earth?

He returned more than five minutes later. 'I've paid the bill. I thought we were supposed to use this time to relax, but clearly you just want to aggravate me. As if I don't have enough on my plate already! I'm ready to go home,' he said, still standing.

Some of the patrons were now staring at them. She hated causing a scene, so she just looked at him, dumbfounded, then picked up her bag and joined him in the walk to the car.

The drive back home was silent and laden with tension.

How could she find out more about this Moreti Investments? And what was so mysterious about this loan or whatever it was that was going on between Soli and the owners?

She was going to get to the bottom of this, whether Soli liked it or not.

The Dress That Caused All The Trouble

Noma woke up in a hurricane of haste. She felt her heart beating fast . . . too fast. She must take her blood pressure medication. Such a long to-do list today!

She had asked Tshidi, her domestic worker, to pack clothes for her trip to the conference in Durban – a three-day mining *indaba*. She examined the four luggage bags Tshidi had packed and bristled with irritation. Where was her Vera Wang gown for the gala dinner? Where were the chic golf pants and top she'd asked to be packed for the golf day? And her lingerie?

Arghh! You truly could never rely on the help, could you?

She stepped into her walk-in closet, rifling through the hanging pieces of various sizes, patterns and shapes, searching frantically for the Vera Wang dress. It had this amazing spaghetti strap that snaked down her back, exposing the toned body she had worked all her life to maintain. That dress was a showstopper. Nothing screamed wealth, drama, elegance and sexiness like that dress. How could Tshidi even think of omitting it from her luggage?

As she smiled triumphantly, having located her prized garment, The Duke strolled in whistling 'Love and Happiness'. He had a tone-sharp whistle – she loved his musical ear.

When he saw the dress, he stopped in his tracks. 'You're not wearing that dress to that conference.'

Noma shrugged nonchalantly. 'Of course I'm wearing it. It's Vera Wang.'

'I don't care if it's Vera Wang, Jackie Chan or Kung Fu. I let you flaunt your body every day at work and every fucking other place, but that dress . . . you might as well be naked, Noma. Why would you parade yourself to all those immoral men at that *indaba*? I heard they are the biggest spenders at the brothels in Durban during that dirty mining conference.'

Noma stopped fussing over the dress, threw it on her bed and faced her husband. Hands on her hips. '*Hey wena ndoda ndini!* You've fucked around on me throughout our entire marriage. Do you really think you still have the right to tell me what I must or must not wear?'

He wagged his finger at her. 'Listen here, Noma, you may be a boss in those dusty offices of yours but you're still my wife. Have some self-respect, woman! What do you think all those dirty bastards think of you flaunting your body every day, huh? You're a fucking old woman! Give young girls a chance. Dress appropriately. You have plenty of beautiful, decent dresses in your wardrobe. Why choose that one? Can't you see it's too revealing?'

Noma threw her arms in the air. So typical of Julius. He couldn't seem to make up his mind whether he wanted to be a progressive man or whether he wanted to keep her barefoot in the kitchen with an apron and slippers on. Mr Price slippers, at that, not Gucci.

This was one aspect of him that infuriated her the most.

'I've worn this dress before. I wore it to Thebe's sixtieth birthday. I wore it at the Zoha fundraising gala. Why has it suddenly become a problem?'

'Because, you foolish woman, you were with me on all those occasions. You were wearing it *for me*. Who will you be wearing it for in Durban? Who will be fucking you?'

'Argh! I hate you when you're like this. When are you going to stop being so bloody insecure? I'm wearing this dress and you can just go fuck yourself! I'm old enough to decide what I do or don't put on my body.'

He grabbed her by the wrist. '*Hey wena*, Noma. I'm not arguing with you about this. You're not taking that dress with you.'

Noma took the dress off her bed and placed it gently inside a suit bag, folded it and put it on top of the neat pile of clothes already in the open suitcase. She added lingerie and her golfing outfit. Then she lifted her head and called out, 'Tshidi! Tshidi! Come and take my bags downstairs!'

It seemed Julius still thought she was the eighteen-year-old girl he'd met in her father's lounge all those years ago. Solomon Mahlangu had been a notorious gangster in Diepkloof Soweto and The Duke had been one of the 'rising stars' of his criminal empire.

Back then, The Duke's leather jackets, Pepe jeans and sexy swagger had left her swooning in admiration. And of course, the defiance of carrying on the affair right under her father's nose had been staggeringly thrilling. She still found her husband sexually appealing, but she wasn't his little doormat anymore.

Just because he was older and had managed to boss her around for the early part of their marriage, did not mean he could dictate anything to her – least of all something as personal as her dress sense. She was a forty-four-year-old woman and could dress any way she pleased. She'd worked damn hard to rise above his domineering attitude. Gone was the little girl who'd idolised his bad-boy image.

Noma could not believe there was a time when she and her friends thought that a boyfriend's jealous (and sometimes violent) rage was sexy.

Being a gangster's girlfriend had really messed with her head but that was all in the past. That Noma had long left the building, but it was clear this old man needed reminding of that important fact!

The Duke grabbed the dress out of the suit bag and started tearing it apart with as much force as he could muster.

'*Hey, wena*! What the hell do you think you're doing? Do you know how much that dress cost?' she screamed with fury. This was the last straw. She could not believe he could stoop so low! He knew how much the dress meant to her. She had bought it during their twentieth anniversary trip to New York. Seeing Julius tearing at it like this felt like a physical assault.

'I don't give a damn what it cost. These small pennies you're earning are swelling your fucking head. No wife of mine is going around looking like a prostitute. You want to be chowed by those diseased mining miscreants, then fuck you!'

Fuming, Noma tried wrestling the dress from his hands, but The Duke stood strong, ripping at it forcefully. Noma sank her teeth into his arm and The Duke slapped her repeatedly till she fell to the ground.

He hadn't dared touch her since their last altercation more than ten years ago when she'd pointed a gun at him and almost pulled the trigger. Memories of the incident flooding back amped up her adrenaline and she kicked him in the groin with her Louis Vuitton stiletto till he screamed in pain.

She scrambled to her feet, grabbed a lamp and threw it towards his face.

He ducked to the side, the lamp missing him by an inch, while Noma ducked into the walk-in closet. She emerged brandishing a wooden hanger, flailing wildly with it.

'I told you to never mess with me, you old bastard!'

As The Duke rushed towards her, the hanger connected with his forehead with a sharp crack, but he kept coming, tearing at the blouse she was wearing. He grabbed her by the neck and began choking her. Noma managed to knee him hard in the groin and he let go, swearing in pain.

47

She passed Tshidi on the staircase coming up as she was running down. What had taken her so long?

'Madam! Are you okay?' Tshidi gasped. 'Oh my God, madam! Is everything okay?'

'I'm fine. Fine,' said Noma, waving her off irritably.

She went to the kitchen and took a packet of frozen peas from the fridge. She held it first to her left cheek, then her right. Then she went to the dining room to examine the damage in the mirror there. Thankfully her dark skin was a strong camouflage. She looked unharmed.

She smiled sardonically, thinking of the hanger, which would almost certainly have left a mark on The Duke's face.

She flashed back to the day that she had pulled a gun on him; The Duke had gone on his knees and pleaded for his life . . . she'd sworn that if he ever touched her like that again she would end him. Today's incident was a clear sign that he needed a reminder of who he was dealing with. Noma never operated on fear, not in business and certainly not in her own home . . . that was not how Solomon Mahlangu had raised her. In fact, her father was the one who had told her to fight back when she had finally confessed to The Duke's fiery temper.

Solomon had warned The Duke that if he continued lashing out at his daughter there were only two ways he would meet his end . . . either Solomon would put a bullet through his skull or Noma would do it herself.

After she almost shot him, Julius had been reduced to a puppy in the subsequent years of their marriage. She hoped today's incident sent a clear message to never mess with her again.

She thought about the Vera Wang dress and shed a tear. All the spectacular moments she'd enjoyed draped in that dress. Transient but indelible moments etched in the memories of others, distinguishing her as That Unforgettable Woman. Now all gone.

She wouldn't be able to even fix it at the tailor. She made a mental note to hold a memorial service for the beloved dress on her return from the mining *indaba*. She'd light a scented candle and bury it in the yard next to her favourite tree.

She took a deep breath, went back to the kitchen and made herself a cup of chamomile tea, but her rage could not be abated.

She went to the study, surreptitiously checking if Tshidi was in sight. Closing the study door, she tiptoed like a cat to open the hidden safe. She unlocked it and took out the beautiful Sig P238 that her father had gifted her on her thirtieth birthday. After tracing the gun with her fingers, she placed it in her bag and walked upstairs to face her husband.

She found him staring at the full-length mirror on the bedroom wall, rubbing his forehead. With great satisfaction, she noted that the wound had bulged to an impressive size.

She closed the door and sat on her bed, took out the gun and started stroking it.

'Julius' – she spat out his name – 'in all the time that we have been married, have you ever known me to go back on my word?' she asked, still caressing the gun like a lover.

He turned away from the mirror, saw the gun and held up his hands. 'Noma, put that thing away. You know I hate guns.'

'Ha! A cheap criminal who hates guns. What a joke,' she said, pointing the gun at him with her legs casually crossed on the bed.

'Come on babe . . . I just lost my temper . . . it's just that . . . I love you so much I still get jealous over you. Put it down, please,' Julius pleaded, his hands shaking.

'I wonder if you are aware how many of us poor, weak women end up having to kill our husbands in self-defence because the cowardly bastards keep thinking they can get away with using their considerable brawn against us,' she said, pouting and still pointing the gun at him.

'Sweetheart . . . come on. Put that thing away . . . you're going to miss your flight, please. Let's just . . .'

'I'm not afraid to kill you, you know that, Julius, *neh*? I'd mourn your death, of course . . . you were the love of my life after all . . . but it still doesn't mean I wouldn't kill you if I thought you were a danger to me.' Her finger flicked towards the trigger.

You *were* the love of my life? Why was she speaking in past tense?

'Babe! Babe, stop that!' Julius yelled, panicked.

'Hmm,' she said, glancing at her watch. 'I am running late but I need some assurances. If you're contrite about using me as a human punching bag, you're going to get on your knees and atone for your sins.'

'Tshidi!' screamed Julius.

Noma laughed. 'Really? You're now calling on the maid for help. Tsk, tsk, tsk. Come on, on your knees!' she barked as she stood up and pointed the gun at his forehead.

Julius quickly got on his knees and steepled his fingers. 'Baby . . . I really am sorry. I love you more than I love myself. Please . . . please forgive me.'

She laughed, placed the gun carefully back in her bag, walked up to him and pinched him on the cheek. 'There . . . that wasn't so difficult now, was it?' she said in a chirpy tone.

A visibly shaken Julius stood up frowning and said, '*Mxm*. You're such a crazy bitch.'

She looked at her watch again. 'Damn. I'm going to miss my flight,' she said, sprinting to the shower as if nothing had happened.

Some minutes later, Noma stepped out of the shower and reapplied her make-up.

The Duke was still shaken. He was sitting heavily on his favourite armchair, hands covering his forehead. He could not believe what he had just gone through. He was married to Satan!

As Noma put on her make-up, he looked at her with disgust and, admittedly, fear. He shook his head and dragged himself to the walk-in closet where he undressed and put on his trackpants. He needed to go for a walk . . . clear his head.

Noma heard the front doorbell chime. 'Tshidi? Will you get that?'

No reply from Tshidi.

Annoyed at the disturbance and at Tshidi's non-responsiveness, Noma went downstairs. She pressed a button on the keypad beside the front door.

'Hello. How can I help you?'

'Police! Please open, ma'am.'

The police? What on earth were the police doing here?

Suddenly she felt paralysed by fear – that old fear, the one she hadn't experienced in a long time. Her father's worst nightmare. Her husband's greatest dread.

'Ma'am? Can you open the door?'

She looked upstairs anxiously. 'Um . . . okay,' she said meekly, pressing another button to release the outside gate and opening the front door at the same time.

Two policemen walked briskly up the path. One tall and lean and the other short and stocky.

'Ma'am, are you Mrs Manamela?' asked the tall one.

She nodded, pulling her dressing gown protectively close to her chest.

'We received a report about a domestic disturbance?'

For a moment she was confused. Had Tshidi seen her with the gun?

'A what?'

'Ma'am. Was there an incident between you and your husband this morning?'

She laughed unconvincingly. 'Oh. What? An incident? Ha! No. I mean, yes, but it's nothing to worry the police about. It was just a minor disagreement.'

'We received a call saying that there was some violence that took place here, ma'am. Is your husband in?'

'Yes, but he's . . . busy. He has to rush to work and I'm rushing to the airport. Please . . . sorry for wasting your time. My silly maid must have just gotten excited.'

'Do you mind if we come inside? We will need to talk to your husband.'

She rolled her eyes. 'Oh *bethuna*! Really? Eh . . . officer . . . we are very busy people here. I'm sure there are more pressing issues you should be attending to. We're fine. Really. Sorry to worry you.'

The short officer interjected. 'Ma'am, we're going to need to hear your husband's version of events.'

'Gosh! This is really annoying,' she mumbled, now starting to worry about her little gun stunt. But Julius had started it!

She showed them into the visitors' lounge off the hallway and made her way upstairs.

'Honey! Hon!' she called out. 'Julius?'

'Yes?'

'The police are here.'

The Duke stepped out of the walk-in closet, pulling up his trackpants. 'Shit. What's going on, Noma?' he asked, pure panic in his eyes.

Noma shook her head. 'It's the stupid maid. She must have called them when we were arguing.'

'Fuck! What? I don't want police in my house!' he said, despite himself. He wondered whether Tshidi had seen his wife pointing a gun at him. His life had really been in danger . . . or had it? Surely she wouldn't have pulled the trigger on him.

She looked at him worriedly. 'You know I wasn't going to shoot you, right?' she whispered.

He looked at her, raised his hands in exasperation and said, 'But why must you always be so dramatic, hmm? Now I have to deal with the police in my bloody lounge!'

Noma shooed him away. 'Just go. Go and talk to them, please.'

On his way out of the room The Duke caught a glimpse of himself in the mirror; he touched the lump on his head with his fingers and winced. Great. Just great, he thought, as he limped his way down. He was battered, bruised, and had had a gun pointed to his head and yet *he* had to be the one to do damage control. His groin throbbed like a voodoo curse.

'Hello, gents,' he said, moving delicately into the visitors' lounge where the two men were seated. 'Have you been offered something to drink? Tea, coffee?' he asked brightly.

The two men shook their heads. 'We're fine, sir, thanks. Please sit down. We just have a few questions.'

Amarhada. Bloody cops!

Imagine a cop offering you a seat in your own house? He'd always hated cops. Here was another reason why.

'No, gents. I'm good. I need to head out to work. How can I help you?'

'We got a call regarding a disturbance here in this house. We just want to check if everything is okay?'

The Duke chuckled. 'Argh. You know *bo-ausi* . . . domestic workers. They panic about every little thing. The madam and I were having a little argument but as you can see – there's no drama here. Everyone is okay.'

'Hey . . . but it looks like your madam got you there,' said the short police officer, pointing at The Duke's forehead.

He chuckled again. 'Ey, what can I say? She's a feisty one, my wife.'

The three men laughed and the two officers stood up to leave.

'Anyway, gents, thanks for coming through to check up on us. It's good that our cops still care about us. Now I know I'm in good hands.'

The men laughed again. 'Yes, you are,' said the tall cop. 'And next time you drive by in one of those beautiful Lamborghinis, please give me a ride.' He nudged his colleague. 'You know, I've always seen that car around the neighbourhood. I was curious who it belonged to. I never dreamed I'd be in the owner's house one day.'

The Duke faked a laugh, cursing himself for not putting the Lambo in the garage last night.

'When you invite my colleague Prince here, for a ride, please don't forget me, sir,' said the other policeman.

'Of course, gents. Of course. Any time,' he said, walking the officers to the front door.

He wanted to *murder* Tshidi . . . and his wife.

Summer Body

Debt is not sexy, thought Moshidi.

After the fight she'd had with Soli over their financial situation, she would not let him touch her until he came clean about his business dealings. That was three weeks ago. She had not let Soli anywhere near her, such was her rage and fury. And he still had not provided a plausible explanation for the hole in their fortunes. He'd said the Rubicon deal would sort out all their problems, but the main investor had been travelling and seemed to have other priorities than signing with Soli's company.

Meanwhile, the bank had proceeded with taking over their Zimbali property as they had not paid the mortgage for over eleven months.

Absolutely unbelievable! Zimbali had been her dream home.

What infuriated her the most was that she was going to have to suffer the humiliation of having lost the house without knowing the real reasons behind their financial predicament.

She had not even had the courage to tell Lerato about Zimbali, such was her embarrassment. She hated keeping secrets from her sister, yet her pride would not let her reveal the true extent of their financial troubles.

She knew Soli was lying about something here. She'd been with him for a decade. He had a way of shifting in his seat and casting his eyes downwards when he was fibbing so that had been a dead giveaway.

What was really happening in this man's life?

It was Friday morning and she was due for her session with her new personal trainer. She always signed up with a trainer for the last month of winter – she was a staunch believer in attaining the perfect 'summer body' – and this young man was a stunner. Just thinking about the session made her catch her breath.

He was so sexy!

He was sculpted like a perfect ebony statue. Tall, broad-shouldered, narrow waist, long lean legs, muscles from torso to toe. She hadn't known they still made men like that.

She changed her gym outfit three times before she settled on a leotard that showed off her toned butt and tiny waist. She wore a top over her sports bra but intended taking it off the minute she walked into the gym changing room.

At their last session, he'd complimented her on her beauty and she'd floated on a cloud the entire day – at thirty-nine she was grabbing every compliment she could get. After all, Soli was so lost in his cloud of debt that he barely noticed her.

She wondered what it would be like to be with a man like that. She had made love exclusively to Soli over a period of ten years. Amazing. She'd never thought she'd be capable of such a feat.

She'd been mostly in steady relationships throughout her life but they only ever lasted about six months, then she would get bored and come up with an excuse to end it. She had discarded Ludwe the minute she met Soli, so taken was she by the charming Xhosa man. She had thought it was just another sexual attraction that would not amount to much. It was only when they had been going out together for six months that she realised she'd not tired of him and actually wanted to spend more and more time with him. She had not necessarily been poised for a steady relationship, but she and Soli had so many shared values and goals it was almost inevitable that they would end up settling down together.

She scolded herself for overthinking things. Of course, she was not going to do anything inappropriate with the hot personal trainer.

Chance Encounters

It was two months to her church's annual fundraiser and Lerato was already having a busy week. As lead organiser and treasurer, it was up to her to ensure that the women's organising committee raised enough money to host the *Sisonke* Charity lunch for the people in the neighbouring township, which was supported by various projects run by the church. One of South Africa's greatest ironies is that oftentimes, the poorest neighbourhoods live cheek-by-jowl with the most affluent suburbs. Alexandra township, which lay on the banks of the Jukskei River, comprised row upon row of shacks and neighboured South Africa's most affluent suburb, Sandton, where Lerato's church resided.

Fortunately, the church was only five minutes from her workplace but she still had to rush to get there on time.

Her women's group championed the *Sisonke* lunch and Back-to-School projects. Over the years, they had been successful in meeting their targets, but with the constrained economy, parishioners were becoming ever more frugal in their spending, even though the Alexandra community needed their financial support more than ever, due to the rising unemployment rates in the country.

'Ladies, thank you for coming at such short notice. We have good news from Thembi, which we thought we'd share with everyone.'

She handed over to Thembi to address the group of twelve women who were gathered in one of the church's smaller conference rooms.

'Yes. I wanted to update everyone on our fundraising initiatives,' Thembi said, smiling broadly. 'Yesterday I received an email from the chairman of the company I work for. They will be contributing R100 000 towards the Alexandra High Back-to-School campaign.'

Everyone clapped and ululated with excitement.

'Thembi, you've really eased the load for the rest of us. Thank you so much for your hard work,' said Mama Grace, the chairperson of the women's committee.

Driving home after the meeting, Lerato felt elated – whole and uplifted. Maybe the gift of giving was the ultimate pathway to true joy and enlightenment.

Work was so stressful at the moment. The telecom project was proving more complicated than she and her team had anticipated and they were all putting in long hours. She had taken to working after dinner at night, just to keep up. Mzwandile, it seemed, was bringing work home in the evenings too; he was always on the internet doing some research or other.

Suddenly she remembered that she'd left her laptop at work so she made a quick dash to her office block. It was going to be too late to start cooking by the time she got home so a couple of Woolies' ready meals and some vegetables would have to do for her and Mzwandile. She drove to the food store, which was close to her office, luckily getting a parking space right outside. Picking up a shopping basket at the entrance she headed for the fruit and veg section.

Lost in her own world, daydreaming about how well things were going with the fundraising and projecting for a higher revenue given the generous donation from Thembi's company, she bumped into another shopper, her grocery items spilling on to the floor. She couldn't believe how clumsy she could still be after all these years – when she was younger, she was always teased about her butterfingers. In fact, that's how she'd met Mzwandile.

She'd been motioning towards the queue at the university registration office after collecting her textbooks when her then bespectacled self clumsily launched into Mzwandile, who'd looked bewildered at the sight of her. Unfortunately, neither age, contact lenses, nor maturity seemed to have done anything for her poise.

'Oops. I'm so sorry,' she said now, bending down and chasing after a couple of onions.

The stranger bent down, too, and helped her load her things back into the basket.

'Thank you. You're too kind,' she said, rising to her full height. She looked up to see a tall, dark man with slight dimples and a kind-looking face.

'You're welcome. Actually, I think I've met or seen you before . . . ?'

She appraised him again and innocently shook her head.

'Don't you work at Optima Data just around the corner?' he asked.

She widened her eyes in surprise and nodded. 'Guilty as charged.'

He offered a handshake. 'I'm Lawrence, by the way. In case you were wondering . . . or dying to know,' he said with a glint in his eyes. 'We work in the same building. I always see you in your power suits looking very serious.'

Lerato laughed. 'Well, us data scientists have never claimed to be the most fun people in the world.'

He laughed. He had a nice laugh. 'Is that so?'

She nodded.

'Funny. To me you've always looked like the life of the party.'

'Ha ha. Yes. I believe you. Anyway, thank you for your kind-ness. Hope you have a good evening,' she said, holding her basket firmly to indicate that the conversation was over.

'I'm glad we got to chat. See you around.'

She gave him a little wave and made her way to the checkout line.

Domestic Realignment

Noma had returned from her Durban trip feeling like she'd been run over by a steam train.

There had been far too much drinking, schmoozing, deal-making and, to confirm her husband's worst fears, too much flirting as well. But she was a woman who could handle herself.

The company driver had dropped her off at her home late on a Thursday afternoon and as she was busy taking out the keys to open the door, it was flung wide.

'Madam. You're back!' said Tshidi with a big welcoming smile. 'Let me take your bags.'

She looked at Tshidi, her mind suddenly buzzing with details of the drama with the police on the day of her departure.

'Hi, Tshidi. I'm exhausted. I'm going upstairs to take a shower. Please bring me a glass of water for my medication and some peppermint tea in exactly thirty minutes. I need it piping hot,' she said.

'Yes, madam. I know exactly how you like it.'

In her bedroom Noma immediately started stripping off her clothes, eager to shed the weight of the conference from her slim shoulders, and stepped into a scalding hot shower.

She thought about the conversation she had had with Marewe, Zimbabwe's mining minister, who wanted to woo Zebula Mining into investing in chrome mining in his country. Then she thought

about the young Zimbabwean mining entrepreneur he had introduced her to. If he was part of the minister's pitch, she thought,
it was a clever move. The man was ambitious, devilishly attractive
and very persuasive.

It was a potentially good opportunity because she knew many
investors were reluctant to go into Zimbabwe. She wondered if
taking such a step would reap good returns, given the country's
chaotic governance issues.

When she finished taking her shower, she checked her texts.

Ping!

A text from The Young Man.

Ping!

Another.

'Oh no,' she groaned, allowing the ghost of a smile to linger on
her face. So soon. He was nothing if not persistent.

She put on a silky red negligée and matching gown and dabbed
on some perfume, then she lay down on her bed and closed her
eyes. For some reason, visions of The Young Man's mouth, his deep
voice and his enigmatic eyes came into her mind. She sat up with
a start when Tshidi knocked on the door and presented a tray with
a glass of cold water and peppermint tea in Noma's finest china
teapot.

She took out her pill case and popped her hypertension medication in her mouth, downing it with the water, then she closed
her eyes again and took a deep breath.

She felt compelled to discuss the incident that had occurred
before she left for Durban, but at the same time she knew that she
was not going to fire Tshidi for having called the police.

Things had tensed up between her and The Duke since the
dress incident.

On the phone, he had been curt with her, only speaking to
her in three-word sentences. 'Yes, I'm fine.' 'It's okay.' . . . But she

had no regrets. He knew not to push her. There would always be consequences when someone did that to Nomathando Manamela.

Thankfully, he seemed more concerned about Tshidi having called the police than he was about the gun. She shrugged. Her father had been the same. Of all things the two men detested in life, the men in blue always ranked highest.

She was secretly thankful for this aversion. Part of her wondered if she had gone too far with the gun . . . but no. It was a necessary evil. Her father had always told her not to cower under any kind of threat, and in that moment, Julius had been a threat and she'd had to deal with him.

Julius had sent her two texts while she was in Durban, reminding her to have a talk with Tshidi. She couldn't believe how cowardly he'd become in his old age – he was literally waiting for her to return all the way from Durban to fire Tshidi while he'd been with her daily in her absence.

One thing was certain: she was doing no such thing – Tshidi had withstood her moods, her exacting demands, her detailed attention to all elements of housekeeping without so much as a single complaint.

'Thanks for the tea, Tshidi. Don't go. Take a seat,' commanded Noma.

Tshidi hesitated.

'Go on. Sit. There – on the occasional chair.'

Tshidi folded her apron beneath her bottom and sat down as instructed.

'Listen . . . what happened earlier this week, the day I went to Durban . . . between me and Mr Manamela. You must know that we were just having a normal couple's disagreement. It was nothing serious. Understand?'

Tshidi looked a little surprised but she nodded.

'Mr Manamela was very unhappy you called the cops on him. In future, please don't.'

Tshidi looked at her quizzically. 'Um . . . I'm not sure what you are saying, madam. You mean . . . even if you or he is in danger, I must not call the police?'

Oh lord! How to explain?

She sighed again. 'You know what? Never mind. Apologise to *ubaba wasekhaya* and let's just forget about the whole thing, okay?'

Tshidi nodded, even more confused now. 'Okay,' she said, standing up to take her leave. When she was at the door, she said, 'Madam, I'm sorry if I caused trouble between you and Mr Manamela.'

'It's fine. It's fine,' Noma said, waving her away dismissively. 'Just don't do it again.'

Distress In The Quarters

Tshidi always arrived at the Manamela mansion at 5 a.m. on Monday morning. Today she wasn't alone. Using the remote to unlock the main gate, she and her companion quickly walked through the pedestrian gate that gave access to the maid's quarters, which were tucked away at the back of the house.

She put a warning finger to her lips.

It was not the first time she had brought thirteen-year-old Nthabiseng to work, and Noma would not be happy if she knew, but there had been violent protests in Mamelodi involving a lot of looting, burning of stores, shootings and necklacing. Protesters were literally burning foreigners by draping tyres around their necks, then dousing them with petrol or paraffin.

For three consecutive nights her daughter had woken up screaming from terrible nightmares after she had witnessed their foreign neighbour, Mr Mzilethi, being kicked and bludgeoned to death by members of the community – neighbours who had shared the same space, the same drinks and a few rare jokes with the Zambian man who had run the street *spaza* shop, where the community had bought their everyday necessities such as bread, condiments and toiletries.

The fireball of xenophobia had escalated to high voltage amongst even the most docile members of the community and

Nthabiseng was not sure what to make of it. She and her mother were from Lesotho, which marked them as foreigners, but because they spoke Sesotho like most South Africans, somehow the hatred had not spread to them . . . yet. But the attitude of their neighbours was changing by the day and hatred had become the language of choice against any black person who did not speak 'South African' and their general indignation at foreigners, especially in the townships, included an endless litany of complaints: 'They steal our jobs.'; 'They drug our children.'; 'They sleep with our wives.'

Her mother Tshidi was a domestic worker for a wealthy family. Did this mean she fell under the category of 'job thief'?

Probably, Nthabi thought.

The township was a ticking time-bomb and Nthabi lived in constant fear of being 'found out', because South Africans spoke loosely and openly of their hatred for foreigners whilst in her company. She kept waiting for someone to point out that as a Lesotho national she fell in the category of the *hated*. She was relieved when her mother told her she was bringing her to the fancy mansion where she worked. She loved it here. Here she could relax a little bit. It was like paradise. So different from the shack that she shared with her mother and her aunt. When her aunt lost her own job as a domestic worker in one of the suburbs and decided to go to Lesotho for four weeks this left Tshidi and Nthabiseng with a problem.

How she was going to stay unnoticed for four weeks, Nthabi didn't know. But one thing she and her mother both knew was that she couldn't stay at the shack all alone while her mother was safely nestled here in this castle.

She didn't think Tshidi had thought it through, but it was enough to know she was sheltering her from the storm that was swirling in the township.

She smiled at her mother and put her finger to her lips to show she understood.

Lerato

Horny. She had to admit it. She was horny. All the time.

She'd prayed about it, but horniness was a difficult subject to pray about. It felt like complaining to a parent about not having enough sex.

As a devout Christian, finding the right words to address the issue with God was challenging.

At first, she prayed for intimacy with her husband. Then, when she started getting so horny she thought she was losing her mind, she started praying for the easing of carnal desire.

When she started eyeing petrol attendants, car salesmen, her boss and the guy behind the cafeteria counter, she struggled to find the vocabulary to talk to God about the issue.

The final nail in the coffin was the Mr Bean saga. That was when she knew . . . when she truly realised that her life was awful.

When Bongani was about ten years old, they had become ardent Mr Bean fans. They'd watched all the series, and as Mr Bean had made movies so, of course, the fanaticism continued. Last Saturday, they'd stayed up giggling their lungs out as they enjoyed his last offering.

To her utter humiliation, that night she had a very erotic dream involving . . . Mr Bean. Mr Bean was kissing her and fondling her . . . it was all so dire. No offence to the guy acting the role, but surely having wet dreams about Mr Bean fell under 'abnormal' on the psychology spectrum . . . no?

She was embarrassed. There's thirst . . . then there's Mr Bean proportions of thirst, and it wasn't pretty. She had never thought this was the kind of subject matter she would need to address with the Almighty.

Was it the change of season? Spring was a time of renewal after all. Maybe her body was responding to an ancient genetic code to procreate?

Or maybe it was the devil?

Age?

Ageing?

What the hell was it?

She had to do something. The drought had gone on for long enough. She'd worked it out exactly. The last time they had made love was after Moshidi's fun and very lively birthday party three years ago. Twentieth of February. In another three months, it would be four years of a sexless marriage. How on earth had she survived?

They had tried to have sex a month later, on the twentieth of March, but she was on her period and Mzwandile had been too disgusted to indulge. Then Lent rolled around and he came up with the idea to abstain from all sexual activity.

Last November she had turned forty. She couldn't remember how they had celebrated but it definitely hadn't been in the bedroom.

Recalling the sexy lingerie evening three months back, her attempt at seduction a humiliating failure, Lerato felt despair rise. Despair was the only thing rising around here.

Mzwandile, however, seemed completely at ease.

She looked at him lying in bed peacefully. How could he be so calm? Why was he not feeling what she was feeling? Was there something wrong with her? Was the devil playing tricks on her?

She fished out her phone.

'Does turning forty make you horny?' she asked Google.

She thought she'd read something like that at some point in her life. Oh yes. In one of Moshidi's wild women's magazines. Could that be the reason? Some kind of biological trick?

Google came up with a smorgasbord of search results confirming her suspicions. So, if that was the case, what was she supposed to do with her sex-resistant husband?

It was time to call on the experts. She hated talking about sex, but she feared that she would lose her mind if she bottled her frustrations for a minute longer.

By experts, she meant Moshidi. She needed some serious sibling time.

Tomorrow was Saturday, Solomzi's golf day, so she hoped her sister would be at home and not too busy with the kids.

In the morning she woke up, took a shower and got dressed in her old track pants. For the first time in years, she took out her running shoes and went for a jog. She enjoyed the beat of her feet on the tarmac, the kiss of the sun on her face, the breeze whipping past with each stride of her legs. There was something hopeful about this simple exercise. It felt like sprinting forward towards something. A shimmering possibility.

On her return home, she found Mzwandile doing some gardening, trimming the apple tree in their front yard with his spanking new garden shears.

'Where's the offspring?' she asked her husband.

He stopped what he was doing, rubbed the sweat off his forehead and shrugged. 'Not sure. Soccer practice maybe?'

'Oh, okay. I'm going to get some orange juice. Do you want some?'

'Sure, babe. Come here,' he said. He kissed her lightly on the lips. 'Are you starting a fitness programme like your crazy sister?

Summer body?' he said, bouncing on his feet and shaking his skinny bottom.

She laughed. 'Don't do that. You look insane.'

He bounced again, then wiggled his head left and right like an old-school hip-hop dancer. 'Summer body, summer body! *Ayeye!* Summer body!'

'You're ridiculous.'

She went to the kitchen and poured two glasses of orange juice. So strange that everything felt so normal yet off-kilter at the same time.

Was sex really that important?

She went back outside and handed Mzwandile his glass. He was clearly feeling very playful. Spring was his favourite season. He'd always had green fingers, thanks to growing up in the Natal Midlands. His dad had been a farmer for most of his life.

This was one of the things she loved about Mzwandile – his industriousness. He rarely stayed indoors on spring and summer weekends. If he wasn't attending church meetings, he was happy either in the garden or *braaing* for friends and family.

She left him to his gardening and went into the kitchen to talk to her sister.

Moshidi answered the call after two rings.

'Hey, Moshidi. What are you up to today?'

'Nothing much. Soli's playing golf, then he's going somewhere with his friends. I have to drop the twins off at a birthday party and then Zozo's friend's mom is coming to pick her up for a playdate.'

'What time do you think you'll be done with the mommy duties?' she asked, reflecting that the playdate and birthday drop-off days were a thing of the past for her.

'Hmm. Around twelve. Wanna come over?'

'Yes. I miss chatting to you.'

'Okay. Sure. Do you know what I need today?' asked Moshidi.

'What?'

'A crazy, boozy weekend with a friend . . . like my sister.'

'I can do crazy, but I can't do boozy.'

'How are you surviving middle age without wine?'

'First of all, we're not middle-aged . . . yet. Second of all, you don't need wine to be an adult.'

'Yes, you do.'

'Whatever. You're so middle-class.'

'And you're so middle-aged.'

Loved Up

She loved going down on him, but lately she'd noticed his penis had become wrinkled with age.

Why had nobody warned her about this? That penises give way to atrophy?

And aren't penises muscles? So why would they just succumb to ageing like that? Was it not getting enough exercise? And wasn't that a bit sad?

Was it even a muscle?

Maybe she could get an anti-ageing cream for it. It was more attractive when it was smooth and unlined . . .

An unbidden image of The Young Man suddenly sprang to mind. She raised her head to look at The Duke, worried that her thoughts might be audible.

His eyes were closed and he was doing that strange thing with his mouth. A sign of bliss.

Shame. She loved her old man.

The tension following the dress incident had lingered for more than a month. She had hated how he had started looking at her with something akin to fear. She wanted her tough and sexy gangster back. Ever a woman of action, she'd launched a campaign to win back her husband and the one way to do this with The Duke was with hot, wild, scintillating sex.

That was his love language.

She rose to kiss him passionately on the lips and allowed him to flip her over and enter her from behind. They went on forever. Loving each other, feeling the warmth of their bodies, their uncontrolled passion and desire rhythmically guiding them towards shared bliss. It never got tired. When they were done, she rolled over to her side and went into a deep, contented slumber.

He woke her after about an hour, walking around naked, looking as blissful as he used to do during their earlier days.

'Mr Manamela . . . I'm famished. You soaked up all my energies,' she said. 'What time is it and what are we going to eat?'

He closed the curtains. 'Ready for another round?' he asked.

'Are you sixteen years old? What's going on with you lately?'

Of course, she knew what it was. Her *Fifty Shades of Noma* campaign was a success! She'd even taken him to a strip club and ordered him a saucy lap dance from a sexy buxom stripper.

He smiled and puckered his lips, then went to her dresser and picked up some tablets. He showed her the packaging. 'I got these from my friend at the joint next to our offices.'

She took the box of pills and read the packaging. 'Cialis. What is it?'

'Penis motivator.'

'I thought I was your penis motivator.'

'Enhancer.'

'Oh. Okay. Tell the makers of this product that we love them and we are willing to sponsor them for a lifetime.'

He laughed gleefully. 'I'll be happy to let them know. Proudly sponsored by Zebula Mining.'

'Indeed. I'll use all my stock options to advance the cause.'

'I love you,' he said to his wife, kissing her softly on the lips.

Sister Talk

Lerato showered, then dressed in jeans, a T-shirt and sneakers.

The estate on which Moshidi and Solomzi had lived for more than five years was a quick drive from her house, and by the time she stepped into her car her sister had already sent her a gate code to access the entrance.

Driving in to the immaculately preserved estate, Lerato sometimes still could not believe how wealthy her younger sister and her husband were.

Three homes in some of the most exclusive addresses in South Africa . . . and yet she and Solomzi were both still fairly young. As much as she often worried about their opulence, the couple seemed comfortable and confident in their financial status. And Zimbali was Moshidi's pride and joy.

When she finally got to the house, she found Moshidi waving off a Bentley – Zozo's playdate, she presumed. She went and hugged her sister.

'I remember when parents used to pick up my boys in Toyota Tazzes to take them on playdates. You guys roll around in Bentleys now?' she said.

Moshidi laughed her off. 'That's little Lindiwe's mom. She's the CEO of some financial services company. I just admire her for still managing to arrange playdates while running a blue-chip company.'

Lerato shrugged. 'Yup. I guess there's definitely something to be said for that,' she said.

'Come out to the patio. I've fixed us some platters.'

Lerato followed her sister into the spacious lounge area and proceeded through the sliding glass doors that led to the patio where Moshidi had set out savoury and sweet platters, a jug of juice for Lerato and a bottle of champagne in an ice bucket for herself.

'Wooowee, Shidi! Are you going to finish that whole bottle by yourself? *Leya tagwa*, man!'

'*Hayisuka!* You teetotallers are so boring. Leave my champagne alone.'

'Where's Soli?' asked Lerato.

'He's upstairs. He'll be down in a few. He was on the golf course all morning. Now he's joining some friends for lunch.'

'Okay. Good,' said Lerato, biting into a fruit kebab.

'So, when did you last speak to Papa?' asked Moshidi.

'Two days ago, actually. His left leg is acting up again. But Mama said she took him to the doctor last week and he's been given some painkillers to manage it.'

'Oh. Poor Dad. That leg's been bugging him since that accident when he was visiting at Tlhabane.'

Lerato murmured in agreement.

Solomzi came down the stairs and out to the patio to greet the two sisters.

'Hey! How's my favourite sister-in-law?'

Lerato stood up to hug him. '*MoXhosa!* Where are you going, looking so fine and all? Hmm?'

Solomzi laughed happily. '*Hayi mani wena.* I need to go out with the boys. Discuss business. You know how it goes.'

'Hmm. As long as you behave. You, Xhosa, are notorious flirts!' she said, giggling playfully.

'Don't worry. I promised my wife here I'd be back in good time,' he said, pecking Moshidi on the cheek.

'Bye, Soli,' Moshidi said dismissively.

'Enjoy, ladies,' said a retreating Solomzi.

'Hmph! Why are you acting all cold and distant towards *sbali*? Everything okay?'

Moshidi rolled her eyes. 'Things are critical but stable . . . as usual,' she said, sipping her champagne. 'Have some juice.'

Lerato pondered her sister's words. 'Hmm. You know how we laughed when you first used that term to describe the state of your marriage?'

Moshidi did not want to think of that period in her life so she chose to sip her champagne like it was the ultimate gift of life. Soli's affair with the girl who didn't know how to use spellcheck had dented her self-esteem.

'Mm-hmm.'

'But I think it's the general state of most long marriages. You know?' offered Lerato.

'I actually don't know. Look at Noma and that dodgy Duke character of hers. They always look like they've just had sex, yet they've been married since the Mfecane war. Nothing "critical but stable" there. All the vital signs are in perfect range with those people.'

Lerato shrugged, poured herself a glass of orange juice and gazed at her sister. 'Speaking of sex, sis . . . tell me something . . .' She cleared her throat. 'How are things between you and *sbali*? I mean, in the bedroom?'

'Ha! Lerato Msibi! Are you asking me about my sex life? I have never heard you broach the sex subject – ever! What's this about . . . hey?' asked Moshidi with genuine curiosity.

'*Eish,*' Lerato sighed, fidgeting with one of Moshidi's unnecessary napkins. 'Frankly, Moshidi, I ain't getting any. Not for a long, long, long while.'

'Long like how? A month? Three months? A year?'

Lerato raised one finger, then two, then three. 'And counting.'

Moshidi sipped on her champagne glass, then raised both hands up in a prayerful steeple. 'Please say those fingers mean months not years . . . or God forbid . . . decades,' she said, her almond-shaped eyes bulging exaggeratedly.

Lerato opened her mouth to respond, then stopped in her tracks and looked at her with a cross expression on her face. 'Now how on earth could it possibly be decades? This is serious Moshidi!'

'Sorry sis . . . but what? Three months? Three years?'

'The latter,' responded Lerato.

Moshidi shrugged, hardly believing her sister's revelations let alone the fact that this was the first sex talk Lerato had initiated since she started her periods nearly thirty years ago. Moshidi, on the other hand, had told Lerato almost everything about her own sexual encounters. Of course, she'd been careful to omit the ones she thought would make Lerato turn to salt because of the saucy details involved.

'*Shoo!* What's happening? Is it you or him?'

'It's him. Why would you think it's me?'

'Just asking. So . . . what exactly is the problem?'

'That's the thing. I don't know. I've tried everything, sis. It's driving me insane!'

'Do you think he's seeing someone else?'

'The thought did occur to me, but you know. It's Mzwandile. I just can't see him cheating. It just seems so far-fetched.'

'Every single man on this earth is capable of cheating, sis. Just take those rose-tinted glasses off your pretty little nose. When it started . . . I mean three years back, do you recall noticing any changes in his behaviour? New cologne? Press-ups? Viagra? Had he started taking extra care with his body, more vain pursuits suddenly? Working late at the office? Anything like that?'

'Wow. Where did you get that list?'

Lerato entertained the saner of Moshidi's questions, then shook her head. 'Nah. It's never been anything crazy like any of the stuff you mention. If anything, he's even more available physically. Not sexually but just his physical being. He's more homebound. More present than in the earlier years but I just can't access him sexually.'

Moshidi sipped some more of her champagne. 'Well. This gets curiouser and curiouser.' After a while, she ventured another possibility. 'Do you think he's gay? It could be the case, you know. I mean . . . I always found it weird that he was so patient when you guys were still dating. He wasn't pressuring you at all during that whole no-sex-before-marriage thing. A lot of closeted guys entertain the straight act for a while in marriage but eventually tire of it altogether, maybe that's what's happening with Mzwandile.'

Lerato looked at her incredulously. 'Are you insane? Of course, he had to be patient. Mzwandile and I are *practising* Christians. We've always been that way. Don't turn something that's beautiful and pure into something nasty, Moshidi. I seriously need your help here.'

'No, I'm serious, Lerato. Most guys wouldn't have waited five years before banging.'

'I really wish you'd take this seriously.'

'Okay. Okay. What do you want me to help you with?'

'I want advice on how to deal with this. He somehow finds ways to avoid the topic. I've tried everything. Sexy lingerie. I've set the mood a thousand times . . . nothing seems to work. It's like his sex switch is off for good.'

'Oh, my word! I wouldn't be able to cope with that. What about counselling? Maybe there's some deep psychological issues he's dealing with.'

Lerato looked at her sister and fiddled with the cheese sticks on the platter, then she frowned. 'I've suggested all of that before. How do I survive in the meantime?'

'I know!' said Moshidi, clapping her hands with glee. 'The rabbit!'

'What?' asked Lerato.

'The rabbit, dear sis. Don't you know? That's the only way to get sexual satisfaction if your man's not delivering the service.'

Lerato's eyes were popping out of their sockets. 'I'm supposed to have sex with a rabbit? Isn't that bestiality?'

Moshidi giggled uncontrollably. 'Lerato, *maar wena*, you're living in the Dark Ages. The rabbit, my dear sister, is a sex toy. It's a vibrator. The difference between our generation and that of our parents' is that we have options. You don't have to endure months of drought when you can have orgasms on tap.'

Lerato looked sceptical. 'I'm not sure if a sex toy would do the job for me. I need passion, that masculine touch. I want to feel loved. I just need my man to be a man.'

Moshidi shrugged. She went upstairs and came back with something in a pink satin package.

'What's that?'

'My latest rabbit order.'

'We can't have sex with the same rabbit!'

Moshidi looked at her sister as if she were missing a few brain cells. 'Of course we're not going to have sex with the same rabbit. I just bought this vibrator. Never been used before and ready to perform!'

Lerato took the beautifully wrapped package and slowly opened it. It was smaller than she expected, compact, with a diamond stud and . . .

'Why is it so small?'

'Oh, ye of little faith. That thing is proof that size doesn't matter. It's about technique. Get some triple-A batteries, get into a warm bath and have fun. You'll thank me later, believe me.'

The Observer

The old couple who owned the mansion fascinated Nthabi. The old man was always relaxed, doing the garden, going to work during the week in his dilapidated car, then driving out in one of the many fancy cars at night when his wife was away on work trips or on weekends.

She did her best to keep out of sight, but sometimes she couldn't resist sneaking occasional peeps at the goings-on in that household.

They seemed like a very strange couple.

The wife was forever rushing off somewhere, and she was always dressed in fancy clothes. Nthabi thought she wanted to live this kind of life one day. Without fear of being called a *kwerekwere*. Eating different kinds of food every day, dressing fancy just to go out to the shops. These people really had it all sorted out in life.

Why did they have all the luck? Why did God favour so few and discard so many? You could just tell by looking at them that these people never worried about school fees or clothes or money in any way.

But how come they had so many cars? Couldn't they give some of them away to the needy? She shook her head. She decided that either she was not going to be a rich person when she grew up or she'd just have to be a different kind of rich person if she became successful.

They were two people and they lived in a house with more than ten rooms. They hardly ever had any visitors, yet they had enough groceries delivered to feed a village. Did they ever share? There was something wrong with the way they ran their lives, for sure.

She'd taken to peeking out of the window whenever she heard movement in the yard or in the driveway. At about six o'clock she saw the old lady come out of the house in such high heels Nthabi didn't know how she could walk in them, long artificial hair flowing to her shoulders. She'd never seen an old lady like this one before, but she could tell that she was really old. Definitely much older than her mom, yet she seemed determined to look as young as possible. She was talking animatedly on her phone as she used her remote to open the garage to go to her car. One of her cars. Which one would it be today? These two had the biggest garage she had ever seen.

Nthabi opened the window ever so slightly so she could hear the old lady's conversation.

'Yes, darling. I can't wait to see you! What time are you landing?'

A pause while she listened to the person on the other end of the line.

'Wow. That's wonderful.'

Pause.

'Of course I'm dressed to the nines. Is there any other way to show up for one of your visits?' She laughed and laughed as she spoke to the person on the other end of the line.

Nthabi wondered who she was talking to. It couldn't be Mr Manamela because he was inside the house. His cars were all parked in the garage.

The old lady hadn't been gone long when she heard another of the cars revving and she peeped out of the window again. Mr Manamela was on his way out now, a soft cap on his head and a maroon scarf round his neck. Even though it was cold outside he still had the top down.

Hmm! Rich people were so strange. And why did they act so much like white people?

What was wrong with them?

Déjà Vu

A night out with the boys at Busy Corner, his favourite drinking hole in Tembisa township, was just what The Duke needed. Nothing cheered him more than drinking whisky with some old timers from the old *kasi*. Being in the township was always an enriching experience for him. After all, that was where his roots lay. In the township he was not pressured to act bourgeois and did not need to adopt any of the Western affectations that seemed so important to Noma. Here, he could just be himself with *his* people. Simple, streetwise, and down t0 earth. Best of all, they all remembered him for what he'd been, and they loved, feared and respected him for it.

Bra Force was in fine form, regaling the group of friends and old acquaintances with wild and often preposterous tales from his youth back in Sophiatown. Just as Bra Force was getting to the climax of his tale, The Duke's phone rang.

'Julius. How are you, my friend?'

A white man.

The voice had a haunting cadence to it.

Like déjà vu.

Who was it?

'Excuse me. It's a bit loud here. Who's this?'

A pompous laugh. Arrogant. Self-important. 'I see you don't recognise my voice. I guess it's been a long time. Rockefeller Diamonds. Ring any bells?'

Ah. Of course. The old bastard. But where on earth had he got his number?

'Mr Wiese. How are you?'

'Come on, Julius. What's with the formality? It's Danie to you, man. We go back a long way, you and I. I hope you've been staying out of trouble.'

uMthakathi Womlungu. White Sorcerer, this one. Sounded like he hadn't changed one bit. The Duke picked up his glass of single malt and moved away from the group to continue the call outside. He was slightly shaken.

'Yes. I'm a man of my word. In fact, I've kept the same job for over . . . *Jislaaik*. Almost twenty-five years.'

Raucous laughter from the other end of the line. 'I know. Can't fucking believe it!'

The Duke was completely lost. Why was this conniving old geezer calling him on a Friday night after more than twenty-five years?

'Good to hear from you, sir. How are things going with you?'

He didn't really need to ask. The old goat was often in the media these days. The sea changes in the country's political environment were placing him and his ilk – those old, white elites – under enormous pressure. They were finally being challenged about the wealth they had amassed during apartheid and were being questioned about their complicity in that evil system of oppression.

'Ah. I told you to stop it with the sirs already. I really miss you, Julius. Remember the times you used to take me to Soweto and Alex back in the nineties? How we used to *jol* in the shebeens and taverns? Man. Remember that one time we ended up at Mzi's in Pimville, then Bra Hugh Masekela just rocked up and started playing the sax? Until dawn!'

The Duke couldn't help but laugh. 'Ah! *Jislaaik*. Ha ha! That was a crazy night. One crazy night!'

'*Ja*. Then your beautiful wife showed up and found you with that girl . . . what was her name again?'

'Hey, Danie, man. Ha ha. You're bringing up crazy memories.'

'*Ja*, man. What was her name? The girl with the sexy round lips. You loved that girl.'

'Lovey. Her name was Lovey!' exclaimed The Duke, the whisky elevating his pitch more than he would have liked.

'Ha ha ha. You and Lovey. I thought you two would go on forever.'

Lovey.

The old bastard was actually reminding him about Lovey. He always did know how to get to the very bottom of his soul. What the hell did he want from him?

'Listen, Juls. I'm getting sentimental in my old age, hey? I know we didn't end our friendship on the best of terms, but . . . I'd love to meet up with you, man. Just us old timers. A fine bottle of whisky. Some great grub. Catch up on old times?'

What?

To say they did not end on good terms was the understatement of the century.

Now he came to think of it, he did not wish to go back to those times. He had not expected Danie Wiese to ever talk to him again, let alone invite him out for a drink. Had the old man finally lost his mind?

'Ah . . . hey. I'm very busy these days, Danie.'

A beat.

'Too busy for an old friend? We've done big favours for each other, Juls. Life-saving favours,' he added meaningfully.

Shit. He should have known this day would come. The old bastard was far too cunning to let him off the hook that easily.

But fuck. How conniving would you have to be to save a favour for this long? Twenty-five. Fucking. Years?

The Duke rubbed his eyes disbelievingly.

What on earth did Danie Wiese want from him?

Confrontations

'Solomzi Jiya. We have to talk! I've had it! You can't keep running away from me like this!'

Soli stared at the approaching figure screaming words at him and picked up his golf clubs. His wife looked deranged in her ghostly face mask, silk negligée, gown and slippers as she marched towards where he was standing, transfixed, in their home gym.

'*Hayibo. Yintoni ke ngoku?* I'm just going golfing,' he said.

'No! No! No! You're not going golfing. Last night you said you were too drunk to talk. The other night you were too tired and now you're sneaking off at seven in the morning just to avoid talking to me?'

'What do you want from me? What the hell do you want from me, woman!' The veins in Solomzi's neck popped out in purples and blues.

Zozo walked in on her parents' row and rubbed her eyes, gazing at them with concern. She looked precious and fragile in her little Planet Afrika onesie.

'*Tata*, why are you shouting at Mom?'

'*Nana*, go back to sleep. It's nothing,' said Moshidi.

'But I heard *tata* screaming at you. I don't like it when you guys fight.'

Solomzi slumped his shoulders and walked over to his daughter. 'Don't worry, my girl. Just go back to sleep. Momma doesn't like me to golf early, that's all. But I promised Uncle Thami and Uncle Zwide.'

Zozo looked at her mom, waiting for reassurance.

Moshidi walked over to her and gave her a kiss on the cheek. 'Your dad is right. It's nothing major,' she said.

'Okay. No more fighting, you two,' said Zozo, pointing her finger at each parent.

They both laughed.

'Okay, sweetie,' said Soli. 'We promise.'

When Zozo had retreated to her bedroom, Moshidi looked at her husband and said, 'We can't go on like this, Soli.'

He sighed, walked out of the gym and began making his way down the stairs.

Moshidi followed him downstairs and went to the kitchen to make a pot of tea, then joined him outside on the patio.

'Have some tea,' she offered quietly.

Soli looked at his watch and reluctantly poured himself a cup.

'Why is it so difficult to talk about this issue?' said Moshidi. 'You and I . . . we talk about everything. We're a team. That's what makes us work. That's the magic of our relationship. Why are you shutting me out?'

Soli sipped his tea in silence, looking out into the distance. 'I don't really know what you want me to say. What exactly do you want to talk about that we haven't addressed already?'

'Our finances.'

'Jesu,' he murmured.

'Why won't you fill me in on the whole picture? I know there's something you're hiding from me. You've not started gambling again, have you?'

'No! Come on. Give me some credit. Moshidi, I've drawn a fucking diagram for you. The whole encyclopaedia of our fucking money issues. What more do you want? Is that all this marriage is for you? A fucking business plan? Are we in a marriage or a bloody corporation here?'

Moshidi covered her face with her palms. 'Gosh, Soli, you know exactly what I'm talking about,' she said in exasperation. 'I'm just as good at figures as you are. It still doesn't make sense that we're missing so much money after the great financial run your business had for so many years,' she said, trying to keep her voice down in case their little busybody of a child walked back in.

'My business,' said Solomzi with a stern line furrowing his forehead.

'Phew. Say what now?'

'*My* fucking business. You said it. It's my business so why don't you leave it the hell alone?' he responded, throwing his hands in the air and standing up as if to walk away.

'Soli, sit back down!' she commanded, pulling him back to his seat angrily.

He looked at his watch and said, 'I have a meeting.'

'Forget about your meeting! Is that where we are now? Your business? The same business that I cashed out my pension to fund when you started it on a wing and a prayer?'

'I paid it all back and some change.'

'So, who's all about the business plan now?'

'I'm not the one who's seeped out the last morsel of passion in this marriage by draining it in money, houses, cars and things!'

'You're not going to shame me for being ambitious. If I recall, that's what you said attracted you to me in the first place.'

He sighed. Looked at his watch again. Fidgeted. 'Fuck. Okay. If you must know.'

Moshidi gazed at him in anticipation.

He rubbed his eyes and looked at her. 'It's . . . it's a business deal that went wrong.'

She sipped her tea and nodded, eager to make him feel at ease to continue.

'It's uh . . . this guy . . . *eish*. I don't know. I don't want to stress you, Moshidi. That's the thing.'

'Moreti Investments?' she offered.

He shook his head, looking exasperated, then dropped his shoulders like a man burdened with the weight of all the world's troubles.

She stood up and walked over to him. She rubbed his shoulders and kissed him on the cheek. 'Babe, I actually prefer stressing *with* you. I love shouldering some of your worries. And let's face it,' she said, smiling cracks in her face cream, 'we've solved most of our biggest challenges together. Trust me, my love, please. Trust in me.'

Soli raised his head heavily and said, 'Moreti Investments. Edward Serame. I'm sure you've heard of him.'

She'd never heard of him. 'So, you owe this person, one person . . . the entire two million rand? That's the amount that's missing from our account.'

He kept silent. After a while he sighed again and said, 'More.'

Her legs fluttered inwards like feathers. A strange motion that felt overpowering but, fortunately, was not visible from the outside.

'More? How . . . how much more?'

'More, Moshidi. Almost another R250 000.'

She went back to her chair and slumped down in it. She was trembling with a primal fear. An ancient instinct to protect her family and all that they had.

'How did you get to owe this man so much money?' she asked.

He shook his head. 'It was a stupid trap. A combination of . . . of a set of circumstances. Partly financing . . . of the greenfield projects in the early days. We agreed on monthly instalments of R200 000 plus interest – as in twenty-five per cent interest.' He chanced a glance at his wife, clearly embarrassed at his own gullibility.

Moshidi remembered seeing the payments of R250 000 to Moreti Investments. She was trying to mentally calculate how many R200 000 monthly fees plus twenty-five per cent interest amounted to a two-million-rand loan. How dumb was this man that she'd married?

'Why didn't you go to the bank? That's a ridiculous payment plan!'

'I'm sorry, babe,' he said, still looking like a shamefaced school-boy. 'When I agreed, I was expecting to make a huge profit from the Correctional Services deal, so I was sure I'd pay the whole thing off in months.'

She felt sick to her stomach. So, the gambler in him prevailed. So much for group therapy. 'How come you never mentioned this man, this . . . Serame . . . before?'

'Ah Moshidi . . . I didn't want you to worry . . .'

Were those tears she saw in his eyes? This whole business wasn't making sense.

'He's just . . . we play golf together sometimes,' Solomzi said.

'Ha! The sacred golf course.' Moshidi clicked her tongue impatiently.

'It was a ridiculous trap to fall into, but things were going so well that I got all excited, thinking if I was more liquid, I could have access to bigger projects. I made some unsound investments . . . stupid stuff that men convince each other about on the golf course.' He gave her an uneasy look.

'So, what happens now?' Moshidi asked. 'How can we fix this? Do you have a plan?'

Solomzi shrugged.

'I'm good with budgets,' Moshidi said. 'Would it help if I talked to him? Does he know I'm in banking?'

Soli sneaked another glance at his watch and as he was doing so, Moshidi stood up, grabbed his phone and sprinted over to the adjacent lounge, all the while scrolling down his list of contacts.

Solomzi ran after her to get his phone back, but she was already on the line, talking to someone.

'Moshidi! Give me my phone back. You're being so juvenile!'

'Mr Serame? Edward Serame,' she said, almost breathlessly speaking into Soli's phone.

Soli stood staring at her, a look of horror and anguish on his face. He mouthed to her to give him back the phone.

Moshidi shushed him and continued. 'This is Moshidi . . . Solomzi's wife and business partner. Sorry to bother you so early in the morning, but I was wondering if it would be possible to invite you over for dinner at our house some time?'

She paused, listening to what the man was saying on the other end of the line.

'Mm-hmm. Okay. I'll take down your numbers and call again on Monday when you get back from your trip. Yes. That's perfect. Thank you.'

She dropped the phone and gave Soli a sly smile. 'He doesn't sound so bad.'

Solomzi looked like he was about to explode. 'What the hell do you think you're doing?'

'Soli, I'm tired of letting the future of my children hang by a thread because of you and your reckless decision-making.'

'This is humiliating. That's my business associate. What's he going to think when he starts getting unsolicited phone calls from my wife?' he said hysterically.

Moshidi was unfazed. 'I've invited your business associates countless times to our homes. In fact, most of your deals used to be sealed right there in that dining room,' she said, pointing at the space in question.

Their home was an open-plan space with the patio's folding doors leading to the lounge which flowed into the dining area.

'This is different,' he said.

'Yes, it's different and more urgent because if we don't handle it like adults, this debt will just keep on expanding and swallow us whole,' she said, as she clicked on Solomzi's phone and sent herself Edward's contact details.

Reunion

Danie Wiese had booked a private table at The Grillhouse in Rosebank, proving just how stuck he was in his ways.

Although he spent most of his time at his lavish estate in Knysna, Wiese had enough business interests in Johannesburg to entrench him among the city's affluent set. This meant that he had several favourite haunts in the city. The Grillhouse, with its smoky lounge seating, earthy tones, and understated glamour, was a firm favourite, but he never dined where other patrons could see him. He would get an assistant to book one of the private dining lounges for him.

The Duke was not surprised that he'd foregone all the swanky new restaurants in the Sandton Square Mile for this particular restaurant. Danie, for all his wealth, frowned upon places he felt were cloaked in ostentation.

When The Duke joined him in the private dining area, he found that Danie had already ordered starters and a bottle of wine. As he walked in, the old man stood up and embraced him warmly.

'Ah! Look at you, Julius! Or should I say "The Duke". They still call you that, right?'

Julius returned the embrace guardedly. He felt like a little fish who was being courted by a piranha.

He sat down and placed a napkin on his lap, eager to show Danie that he was at his level of sophistication. The truth was that he hadn't the faintest idea how to behave around the man.

Danie had become decidedly rounder over the years. A double chin stretched out like an amoeba towards his neck. Big meaty shoulders with an equally fleshy belly. The Duke had seen pictures of him in the media, but he was still alarmed at how much weight the businessman had amassed over the years. He wondered how many kilograms Wiese had gained per billion rand he'd made over this time. Julius liked turning people's idiosyncrasies into algebra formulae. Life was a mathematical problem that required solving. He'd hated school but always loved numbers. At least he'd managed to put this love to good use.

'My friend. I ordered us springbok carpaccio for starters. Love the stuff. You know, whatever happens in this country, there are certain things this new government can never change. And the springbok is one of them. That's our national talisman. We love its beauty and grace. We love to have it on our rugby jerseys, and we love to eat it. That's a true South African iconic emblem. Cheers, my friend.' Danie raised his glass and Julius mirrored the action.

'You're quiet. Why? It's not like you to be like this?'

Julius shrugged. 'I'm just surprised. And curious, of course.'

Danie smacked his hands together. 'Ha! My kind of man. Straight to the point. You want to know why you're here.'

Julius nodded. 'Yes. I'd love to know why I'm here, but I am not a rude man. How is *ausi* Lydia?'

'My wife is the same as always, Julius. She still loves her horses, although she can't really ride anymore. Lower back problems. My daughter Sunette takes after her. Always out riding. She can't get enough of horses. Owns forty of her own now. Breeds them. Feeds them, gets them into the races. She's a great girl.'

The Duke smiled. 'I remember how she was when she was just a baby. So beautiful. I'm sure she's a good-looking young lady.'

Danie nodded with pride. 'Great girl. Lousy taste in men, though.'

'Nobody's good enough for our little girls.'

'Nobody,' concurred Danie, laughing. 'How are your kids? They must be grown up by now.'

'Yes. Khutso is a stockbroker and his sister Diamond is studying film at UCLA, can you believe it?'

'Rare among your people.'

'What do you mean? My people? Really, Danie?'

Danie laughed. 'Come on. Don't be so sensitive, man. That's actually very good. Very good.'

A long pause followed as Danie drank his wine.

He checked his phone.

He made two phone calls.

Julius took out his own phone and started scrolling through his messages.

Finally, Wiese returned his attention to Julius.

'I have a company listing in London in a few days' time,' he explained. 'Had to check in with my CFO.'

Julius nodded non-committally. Usually people apologised when they made phone calls during dinner, but he guessed Wiese had a billion reasons not to care about social niceties.

'Julius, my friend. How's it going with the heists these days?'

The bastard. He knew Danie was up to something.

He frowned. 'Heists?' he said. 'What heists?'

Danie laughed uproariously. 'You should see the look on your face. Can't keep secrets from your old friend, Julius. And if I were you, I wouldn't even try.'

Julius looked at his watch. 'How long are we going to be? I have to fetch my wife from the airport.'

Danie swung his head slowly . . . left, right. This was his signature gesture of arrogance. 'I told you about this meeting two weeks ago. I'm sure your wife can make other arrangements.'

Julius looked at him irritably. 'So why are we here?'

'Redemption. You know that word?'

The Duke shrugged.

'Julius, my friend . . . remember when you stole from me after I had practically made you part of my family? What did I do? I let you go. Didn't press charges. Nothing. Remember that?'

The Duke looked away, then looked back at the man. 'So? What is this?'

'I need you to return the favour.'

The Duke laced his fingers. 'You know, you must be getting really old. You used to be so direct. Am I going to have to wait until the main course before you tell me what you want?'

Danie poured himself another glass of wine and also poured for Julius. 'My family built this nation. Your people have gained more employment from my family than any other business in this country . . . for decades and decades. We employ more black Africans in good paying positions than any other company in South Africa.'

Julius clapped his hands slowly. 'Congratulations.'

Danie shrugged. He did his head-swinging thing . . . left, then right. 'The arrogance of blacks these days in South Africa just boggles my mind!' he exclaimed, frothing at the mouth. 'Everything is about making us whites feel guilty about everything we've done. The good is lumped with the bad. Now we are all made to feel like the bloody architects of apartheid. It makes my blood boil! Do you know who used to fund Steve Biko during apartheid? Hmm? This man. This man right here' – pointing his finger at his chest – 'but now all we hear is White Monopoly Capital this and White Monopoly Capital that. Empty catchphrases with no meaning. Fucking ungrateful lot!'

The waitress came and asked if she could bring the main course.

This man! He had pre-ordered every course. A natural-born bully. Even the meal had to be a display of who was in charge at this meeting.

'Hey, Danie. Look. You can save your politics for those EFF boys. I'm just a family man living my life in peace. I have nothing to do with how people are attacking you and your rich friends in this country.'

The waitress brought their food. A lavish display of cholesterol. Noma would lose her mind at the sight of it. She was on a new crusade to get them eating green and clean. In spite of himself, he looked forward to tucking into this rib-eye steak.

They took up their utensils.

Danie was silent as he devoured the steak.

Then, with Julius only halfway through his own meal, he started his narration again.

The Duke sat patiently waiting for the one-man tirade to end, which it eventually did.

'So, listen,' said Danie, downing his eating tools. 'I'm leaving this country and I need you to help me.'

Julius continued enjoying his meal. He gave Danie a non-verbal cue to continue.

'I have some jewellery, in fact a lot of jewellery. I wanted to move it quickly, but with the disaster of an economy that your political leaders have saddled us with, I'm stuck with millions of rands' worth of gems that are not making me a dime.' Danie's chest heaved with frustration. 'I need you to move it for me. Fast.'

Julius scratched his head. 'I don't understand. How do you want me to move it?'

'I want you to steal it from me,' said Danie softly. 'The same way you did twenty-five years ago.'

Julius stopped eating. Put down his utensils and gaped at the man. Then he began to laugh. 'Danie, is this some kind of joke?'

'Do I look like I'm playing games with you?'

Julius picked up his knife and fork again and slowly resumed eating his steak. He made a show of enjoying it, savouring each bite. Inside his mind was racing.

No, no, no. Think, Julius. What if this is a trap?

When he'd finished, he wiped his mouth on his napkin and said, 'Danie, you've been complaining all night. Black people this, black people that. I hope you're not trying to live out your racist wet dreams through me. If you feel bitter about the money I took from you, I can repay it. I know the insurance paid you, but I can repay you, no problem. Just don't bring disgrace to my family. I beg you, please. Somehow my ancestors allowed me to get away with some naughty things in the past. But I'm an old man now, I can't land up in jail. If you want to settle old scores, be straight with me.'

'Listen, you fucking bastard!' Danie slammed his wine glass on to the starched tablecloth. 'First you betray my trust – did you really think I'd allow you to get away with that?' His lined face still trembling with rage, Wiese took out a standard-sized white envelope, looked around to see if any of the waiting staff was in sight, then laid out sepia-coloured pictures side by side on the table.

Instinctively, Julius knew what was in the pictures.

As he glanced down, there stood a younger Julius wearing a leather jacket, cap tilted over his eyebrows, baggy jeans and Caterpillar boots. With him were two other men. Each held a loose cotton bag and were stuffing various items into them.

They'd thought they'd switched off the CCTV cameras in Wiese's jewellery storage room at his downtown offices in Mayfair. He'd been working for Wiese for five years and needed a financial boost as he and Noma's luxurious life was starting to collapse from the strain of debt. The money he'd made from his past criminal activities was running out and he and Noma had two babies and a huge mortgage bond hanging over them. He'd hated stealing from the Wieses but at that time, it had seemed like the only way out.

He wasn't surprised that the bastard had been saving these pictures for a rainy day.

'Listen to me and listen good. The value of the physical items you stole from me doesn't come close to the hurt you caused me. I hate hyenas who break my trust.'

He took the photos and carefully placed them back into the white envelope, taking his time to seal it back with his tongue, a gesture that looked both ridiculous and vaguely threatening.

He looked at Julius with a wry smile, then took out his phone again. 'I have the head of police on speed dial right here, on this phone. There's no statute of limitations on theft in this country, my friend, and I'm not here to negotiate. I need you to stage the biggest heist of your life. I've kept tabs on you, I know you never stopped. Logistics manager! Hmmph!' he said with a dry laugh.

Julius tried to hold the man's gaze, wishing he hadn't drained his wine glass with the last mouthful of steak, but he knew Wiese had him.

He shrugged. 'I should have known you'd not let this go,' he said, frowning resignedly.

'Relax. What's the big deal? If I were you, I'd consider this a fucking favour. Those ancestors of yours still have your back . . . if you play your cards right.

'I'll give you all the information and all the resources you need to get it right,' Danie went on. 'This is your lottery ticket, you lucky bastard. You won't get caught. Do I look fucking stupid? I just want to claim on insurance like I did back then and get the fuck out of this shithole country. Do you understand? Or must I draw stick figures for you?'

Revelations

Lerato had experimented with the rabbit several times but was still on the fence about its ability to fulfil its intended mission.

Maybe she was doing something wrong because women on the internet waxed lyrical about vibrators and their astonishing abilities to bring them to orgasm. Thus far, the rabbit had only managed to make her feel *something* but had failed to deliver her to the proverbial promised land.

Today she decided to employ a different strategy. So far, she had been using it in the bath as per Moshidi's instructions, but she had learned via an online search that some women watched pornography while pleasuring themselves with their rabbits.

Perhaps this could be the missing link.

The rabbit needed to be let loose in the wild.

Bongani was sleeping over at a friend's and Mzwandile was at a men's church meeting, so she knew he wouldn't be back till later in the evening as the men often sat around discussing social matters after they were done with the church agenda.

So she had the house all to herself.

She switched off her bedroom light, took out her tablet and mounted it at the edge of her bed. She lay down on her back and googled 'black pornography'.

The videos that came up were awful. Didn't pornography have a storyline these days? She recalled the time she and Moshidi came across a porn DVD underneath their parents' bed when they were teenagers. They'd waited for a quiet day when their parents were away and watched it. Although they were both repulsed by what they saw, it had started out like a love story, and had been much more tasteful than the material she was viewing online now.

Maybe porn directors were all men? Just like in the dreary action movies, this porn stuff was low on storyline and high on action. How disappointing.

She took a deep breath and tried to suspend her irritation by focusing on the task at hand: achieving orgasm.

She settled on a video of a classy-looking black woman and a black man who looked decent enough, given the circumstances. She took out her vibrator and closed her eyes, imagining the man doing to her what he was doing to the woman in the online video.

She was momentarily lost in the fantasy . . . coming close to climax, when she opened her eyes to find a shocked Mzwandile staring at her as if she were some character straight out of Sodom and Gomorrah.

She threw the rabbit off the bed and pushed the tablet down, muting the volume clumsily – the bumping and grinding of the actors was now in full throttle. Much to her humiliation, the vibrator kept buzzing away on the floor. It *was* certainly running loose in the wild. She sprang out of bed like a skilled hunter and hurled herself at the offending object, finally managing to find the off switch. Then she hid the vibrator behind her back like a naughty schoolgirl.

'Mzwandile . . . I can explain. This is not what it looks like, I promise,' she said, feeling guilty, as if she'd been caught in bed with Idris Elba . . .

But was it really so bad? It was more like being caught making out with Bugs Bunny, wasn't it? Surely it was just harmless fun? That was why it was called a sex *toy*, right?

Mzwandile regarded her with disgust. 'Not what it looked like? Lerato, this is . . . it's fornication! Dear God. What on earth is wrong with you?'

'I'm sorry. I'm so, so sorry. I don't know what got into me . . .'

What got into me? Had she just said that?

'Lerato, imagine if Bongani walked in on you with your legs spread out for a . . . a machine. An inanimate object. I have never witnessed such depravity in my whole life!'

Lerato began to weep. 'But . . . honestly, Mzwandile, what do you expect me to do? I really don't know how you are managing to live without sex but I, for one, am struggling. How am I supposed to feel your love for me when you barely ever touch me?'

Mzwandile sat on the edge of the bed and looked at her. He was silent for a long while, lost in thought, as if measuring how to react to his wife's words.

Lerato gathered herself up, pulling closed the silky black gown she had on to cover her naked body. She went and sat next to Mzwandile at the foot of the bed.

'You're the love of my life, Mzi. All I want is to be able to express this love by sharing my body with you. Is that not part of marriage? There's no shame in it. Why have you always felt that it's taboo for us to have sex with each other?'

Mzwandile buried his face in both hands.

Lerato was not sure if he was deep in thought or crying.

He shook his head. 'Okay. Okay. Okay-okay-okay. Look, I think I need to share something with you, and I hope you'll keep an open mind because what I'm going to say . . . well, I don't know how you are going to take it.'

Lerato's heart started thumping against her chest. A thousand thoughts raced through her head. Was there something Mzwandile had been hiding all this time?

She took a deep breath and mentally prepared herself for the worst.

He took her hands in his and rested them on his lap. Then he started talking.

'Lerato, I've been trying to understand why I don't feel the same way that you feel about . . . intimacy . . . desire. It's not a new thing, by the way. I've never been truly able to get as excited about sex as everyone else.' He sighed.

Lerato looked at him quizzically. 'I don't . . . I don't understand. You lack sexual feelings for . . . women?'

He shook his head. 'This is the thing. This is what I knew you would battle to understand. I am not sexually attracted to women . . . or men . . . or animals, or anything. I'm not a sexual deviant of some kind. Unless you regard asexuality as sexual deviancy.'

'A what?'

'Lerato, I'm asexual. It's a rare sexual preference or whatever you want to call it . . . a sexual category, I guess. I've been doing my research because it's been eating me up inside. I've felt like I've been living a lie all my life, so I needed to know that I'm not alone in the world. And . . . hah . . .' Mzwandile gasped. 'I . . . apparently I'm not the only one. Very few people are like me, but they certainly exist. For the past few months I've been part of an online chat group of people just like me and I tell you . . . it can be debilitating. A lot of the people suffer from depression because they feel so isolated. Imagine living in a world where everything is about sex and you're the only one who has no sexual feeling whatsoever?'

Lerato shook her head. 'No. This makes no sense. You and I . . . we've been having sex. Okay, I know it's always been sporadic

104

but . . . it was sex. We were intimate with each other. How can you say you have no sexual feelings?'

He looked her in the eye. 'Think about it, babe. For the entire first five years of our relationship we were not having sex at all.'

'That was because of our vow to God.'

'Yes. And I believed wholeheartedly in that vow. But I wasn't pushing you like most men would. My peers were constantly complaining about blue balls when their girlfriends were unwilling to sleep with them, but I never had a problem with our abstinence.'

'No,' Lerato persisted, 'you can't diagnose yourself via the internet. I think you're just going through a downtime sexually. I refuse to believe that you are . . . what? Asexual? Only animals and micro-organisms are asexual. We're born with a sexual instinct. It's as natural as breathing.'

'You know, I've thought about this from a spiritual point of view and I think maybe this is a blessing, not a curse. Think of all the couples who are now ill because the husband is always chasing skirts and brings diseases to the home. Or the countless women who discover that their husbands have made children outside marriage. You will never have to worry about that, sweetheart. I see people in my support group moaning every day, wanting to cut themselves, feeling disheartened, but I tell them that we are the chosen ones. Just like Jesus Christ, who never defiled himself, we are an example of true spirituality and connectedness to our Maker. The world has become so filthy with all this sexual obsession and depravity. But we are proof that man can live beyond the flesh by looking inwards into the soul. That's why I was so disappointed to catch you defiling yourself with that . . . object.'

Lerato drew in a deep breath. She felt like she'd been swept up in a tsunamic tide. How did they go from her husband confessing that he never enjoyed sex to a spiritual lesson on the virtues of abstinence?

She let the breath go.

'But none of this makes sense, Mzwandile,' she said. 'I mean . . . we have two children born out of this marriage. What was going on the entire time we were having sex?'

'It was always a mammoth effort on my part . . . and don't take this personally. I really need you to understand that I love you and I'm devoted to you and I'd choose you over and over again. I don't want or prefer to be alone. It's just that my expression of love and affection is different from most other people's. And in many ways, I would say it's the best kind of love because it doesn't diminish when I see the next attractive woman. It's constant as day and night.'

Lerato's head was spinning. She felt like she was in a nightmare. Was this some kind of cruel joke? Did this mean she would never have sex with a man for the rest of her life?

Goodness. She was only forty years old. What if she lived to eighty? She wouldn't have sex for the next forty years!

'So . . . so how do you suggest we move on from this point, Mzwandile?'

He looked at her in shock. 'Well, there's nothing drastic that needs to be done. I mean, I'm not going to divorce you because I caught you having sex with that . . . thing. But I think we should pray about the situation so that you are also spiritually strong enough to resist carnal desire.'

Did this man hear what he was saying? He was condemning her to a lifetime without sex because *he* had no desire. Why didn't he tell her all those years ago so she could make a conscious decision whether she was willing to marry an asexual or not?

She took both his hands and placed them on her thighs rubbing one hand slowly towards the opening between her legs.

He pulled both hands back, gasping as if repulsed by what she was doing.

Lerato bowed her head in exasperation. 'What is wrong with you?' she cried, covering her eyes in shame, despair and humiliation. 'What kind of a person are you? Are you punishing me for something?' she asked, her body shaking with uncontrollable sobs.

He came closer to her and hugged her. 'It's okay, baby. Nothing is wrong with me and trust me, nothing is wrong with you either. Only prayer will get us through this. Trust me and trust in the lord,' he said as he bowed down next to her.

He steepled his hands in prayer and said: 'Father, forgive your child for surrendering to the weakness of the flesh. Make her strong enough to resist carnal desire. Banish all temptation from Your blessed lamb and bless this marriage by fortifying it against evil spirits. Amen.'

Lerato did not respond. She just continued weeping quietly until she somehow managed to cry herself to sleep.

Moshidi

Moshidi had woken at 6 a.m. to get to her appointment with her personal trainer. He'd been texting her throughout the week, checking to make sure she had not derailed from the meal plan that he'd set out for her.

His texts were professional, but with a hint of flirtation in them. She had to admit, she enjoyed the attention; after all, the only game she'd been playing with her husband over the past few months was hide and seek.

She was slightly apprehensive about meeting her trainer because she'd had a very strange dream about him just the night before. It was set around her house but instead of her husband being Solomzi, it was the trainer who was the father of her children and keeper of her smiles. He was so attentive and romantic in the dream, her heart swelled when he was near her.

She'd woken up just as they were enjoying a passionate kiss . . .

She laughed at herself. This was so juvenile. Of course she was not about to run off with her personal trainer, despite their constant flirtations. Maybe she should consider exchanging him for a female alternative.

As she lay in bed, agonising over her upcoming gym session, she felt an arm wrap around her waist.

'Hey, sexy. How are you this morning?'

She turned around to face her husband. 'Good. Just getting mentally amped for the session with my trainer.'

Solomzi smacked her bum under the sheets. 'Judging by your delicious-looking posterior, I'd say this guy knows what he's doing,' he said, rubbing her bum seductively. Before she knew it, he had turned her around, groping and kissing her.

Things had been much better between her and Solomzi since he'd come clean about the loan. Besides, seeing as he'd proved incapable of reining in the situation with Edward Serame, she'd decided to use her own wits to manage the disaster.

She'd called Serame on Monday as per his instructions on that stolen phone call and was relieved when he agreed to meet with her separately from her husband. Judging by how Solomzi had handled the situation thus far, she'd decided a different approach would be required to salvage it.

She hadn't needed to call on the rabbit's services for a while . . . which reminded her to check in with Lerato and see if things had improved in the bedroom for her. With a warm body like Soli's in bed beside her, she still couldn't grasp how her sister had managed to go for so long without sex. Lerato and Mzwandile's anniversary was coming up. Perhaps as a gift she and Solomzi should give them a night in the honeymoon suite at a five-star hotel.

Solomzi's kisses had intensified, sweeping her into a maelstrom of passion fuelled by a combination of her love for him and her earlier fantasies about the trainer. She briefly wondered if this qualified as a threesome.

As they gently pulled apart, still feeling awakened by the rush of intimacy, she heard a knock on the door.

'Mom! Kopollo ran away with my iPad charger!'

'No! It's not true! Akhona's the one who stole *my* charger!'

Nkosi! Never a moment of peace.

At least they had knocked.

A New Menu

Lerato was standing by the office cafeteria staring ahead at the light-box with all the 'new and improved' items on the menu board that had been installed just a week ago.

Since the rabbit incident and Mzwandile's ridiculous announcement, she had decided that a few lifestyle changes, like exercising and eating more healthily, might take her mind off what wasn't happening in the bedroom and reduce her stress levels. Her blood pressure was worryingly high and the pressure she was under at work only added to her stress.

This work project was challenging. Pulling data from two recently merged telecom giants that needed their data synched to optimise their CRM systems was going slowly. The data was not well organised because the companies had operated differently, which meant she had to put in a lot of work in finding patterns to create algorithms that would enhance their systems.

What she needed right now was a quiet (healthy!) lunch to get her back to her desk with a calmer mindset. She deliberated over the items on display, trying to decide whether tuna salad on soft rye counted as healthy.

'Are you studying for the latest data science exams?' she heard a voice mock-whisper behind her.

Startled, she looked up to see a young man smiling down on her. He looked familiar . . .

'Um . . . hi,' she said uncertainly. She could not quite place him, which made the too-friendly tone of his question slightly uncomfortable.

Realising it was her turn to place an order, she looked up at the fancy new menu again and felt so distracted that she just decided on the beef lasagna and a garden salad – hoping vaguely that the salad would somehow neutralise the lasagna. She would make up for it with a vegetarian dinner. She quickly shifted to the left to wait for her lunch, feeling suddenly nervous about the tall stranger hovering nearby. He still seemed familiar though she couldn't place him.

'You don't remember me?' asked the stranger.

She scrunched up her face. 'Sorry . . . no . . . though I know I've seen you somewhere before,' she said bashfully.

He extended his arm and introduced himself. 'Lawrence Moyo. Think spinach and assorted vegetables spilling on a floor somewhere not far from here . . . ?'

Now she was completely lost. 'I'm sorry,' she said. What had he said again? Something about assorted veg . . .

He was quite good-looking and had a great voice. Certainly a step up from Mr Bean. Not that she was on the market or anything like that. She was a married woman after all.

She glanced at him as he placed his order and half hoped he'd continue chatting with her, though she also feared the prospect with an alarming ferocity.

He came to stand next to her in the collection queue as if it was the most natural thing in the world and did exactly that – continued chatting.

'So, as I was saying, I've met you before, but you obviously don't remember anything about it.'

Lerato smiled. 'I know we've met,' she said. 'It's just that I have so much going on I can barely recall what happened in my life just last week.'

'That sounds hectic.'

She nodded.

Her food arrived and she collected her order, but something held her to the spot, and for some reason, she found herself standing next to him instead of going off to enjoy her lunch.

'What did you order?' she asked.

'Steak and chips.'

She laughed. 'How on earth are you going to get through the day with a heavy lunch like that?'

'Says Miss Beef Lasagna.'

She laughed again. She was actually more *Mrs* Beef Lasagna, she thought guiltily, wondering if he'd noticed her wedding ring.

They found themselves heading for the same table and chatting away as if the words glued them together. Thirty minutes later, it was time for them to go to their different work destinations.

'So, you still haven't figured where we met before?' asked Lawrence as he cleared his plate.

She looked at him naughtily. Of course she remembered him. Woolworths man.

'Nope,' she smiled.

'That's the shakiest "nope" I've ever heard in my life. Meet you here. Tomorrow. Same time. Expect a quiz on the vegetable drop meeting from a few months ago. If you answer the questions correctly, then lunch is on me.'

She laughed. 'And if I can't?'

A pause. Then a smile. 'Then lunch is still on me.'

After this first enjoyable encounter, they met almost daily at the canteen. At first it was nothing more than exchanging light banter, weaving their way around each other's personalities, careful not to encroach on any delicate points.

Lerato made no attempt to conceal her marital status and Lawrence never brought it up. She also confided to him that she was a devout Christian, signalling that this could only ever be a platonic relationship.

'So, how do you navigate the cold, hard, factual world of science with religion?' he asked one lunchtime.

'You mean with Christianity?'

'Yes. Of course. Christianity . . . my bad. You know . . . my dad is a Methodist minister, so I guess I *should* be more specific.'

'Ha! No way your dad is a minister! Really? So how do you balance being a flirt with Christianity?'

He laughed. 'Clever one you are, right?'

They both laughed.

'Hmm . . .' said Lerato. 'I'm the only believer in my entire company. It could be tougher, but I get away with it because I'm also the only woman in my department. All the data scientists are either agnostic or atheist, but they leave me alone because I'm already an anomaly.'

'Ahh. You don't fit into a pattern. Which for people who are always looking for patterns must be either annoying or intriguing.'

She shrugged. 'We're all too fascinated with data to be interested in each other.'

'That makes me happy,' said Lawrence.

'Why?'

'Because I'd like to be the only one fascinated with you . . .' he said, his eyes flicking briefly to her wedding ring. 'Around here, I mean . . .'

Anniversary

Lerato was enjoying a fitful rest after a long week at work when she was awoken by a kiss on the lips. For a moment, she thought it was Lawrence's lips that had finally touched hers. This past week they'd shared lunch every day at the cafeteria; she'd never made eating there a daily habit but somehow visiting the humble eatery had become something exciting to look forward to.

During their chats, she found herself opening up to him more and more about both her work and her personal life. Talking to him felt like talking to a kindred spirit. She had started having fantasies about him, but their relationship remained what it was – platonic, which was probably for the best.

When she opened her eyes, she found her husband kneeling next to her with a large bouquet of flowers in his hands.

'Happy anniversary, my sweetheart,' he said with a smile.

Her eyes widened. 'My word! July twentieth! Eighteen years today,' she whispered.

He nodded. 'I asked the florist which flowers represented a long-lasting marriage and she said asters are the perfect symbol for our anniversary. They are believed to have magical properties that impart knowledge and wisdom. I couldn't have been blessed with a kinder, wiser, more beautiful and thoughtful partner to share this incredible journey with. You truly are everything I could have dreamed of in a wife. I love you now more than ever before,' he said.

She smiled and kissed him on the lips. 'Thank you, darling, but aren't asters meant for a twentieth anniversary?' she asked as she propped herself on one elbow, taking the flowers from Mzwandile and admiring their beauty.

'Trust me, I'll find something even better for that day . . . that's a big one!' he said, smooching her playfully on the cheek.

She sighed. 'Aren't you worried you'll jinx it?'

'By getting asters two years earlier than our twentieth? Nope. I live by faith. The man upstairs always has my back,' he said confidently.

'He does. It's amazing, isn't it?' she said.

Just then, her husband's phone buzzed. It was a video call from their eldest, Lwazi.

'Hi, *Baba. Uphi u* madam?'

Mzwandile smiled. 'She's right here.'

Lerato leaned in so their son could see her face.

'Happy anniversary to the best parents on the planet!' he said.

Her eyes moistened. 'Thank you, boy. You're so sweet. I'm so blessed,' she said, crying.

'Mom! Why the tears now? You should be celebrating. Where's the old man taking you tonight?' asked Lwazi.

'*Hey wena.* Keep out of my business. That's for me to know and for you to find out.'

'Where's Bongani?'

'Downstairs. Probably still sleeping,' said Mzwandile. 'You know how he is.'

Lwazi laughed. 'He'll probably wake up after all the celebrations, especially with this cold weather. Anyway, I've gotta go. Love you guys. I wish you many, many more happy years,' he said, beaming.

'Love you, my darling boy,' said Lerato.

'Bye, big guy. Thanks for the call. Don't break any hearts out there.'

'Bye, *Baba*. Bye, Mom. Say hi to Bongs for me.'

As it turned out, Mzwandile had really pulled out all the stops for their anniversary celebration. In spite of the winter chill in the air, he'd booked dinner for two at an exclusive restaurant, one Lerato had always been curious to try out. He'd also surprised her earlier with a gorgeous long-sleeved cocktail dress that hugged her curves and accentuated her complexion.

Even though she had to don a long coat over the dress, she felt sexy and beautiful and was grateful to have such a thoughtful partner. Mzwandile was dressed in a black polo neck, a long winter coat and black formal pants. Tailored clothes looked good on his tall, slim frame. She'd always loved how they looked together. She was proud that they'd both taken good care of themselves through the years.

When they arrived at the restaurant, the maître d' led them to their reserved table.

'This is gorgeous, babe. Look at you . . . so fancy,' Lerato teased.

'Well, I'm not just a pretty face, you know. I happen to know how to put on the charm when necessary . . . and only for a certain special someone.'

She laughed happily.

The waiter came over to take their drink orders. Mzwandile ordered passion fruit with lemonade while she asked for a club soda and lime.

They chit-chatted casually throughout the three-course meal, reminiscing about their earlier days and laughing at some of the mishaps and foibles on their journey.

After they'd enjoyed their meal, Lerato asked casually, 'So what lies ahead for us Msibis in the years to come?'

Mzwandile took her hand in his, turned it over and kissed the palm. Then, gazing into her eyes and giving her the dimpled smile that she had fallen in love with when she was a young woman just approaching adulthood, he said, 'I see more adventures along the way . . .'

She sighed, imagining.

'Now that the boys are both coming into their own,' Mzwandile continued, 'we'll have more freedom, more time for ourselves.'

'But—'

'The main reason I wanted us to join the social club was to start putting away money for that great travel adventure we've always spoken about. We both work so hard. Actually, Lerato, I worry about the stress of your job. I think we both deserve a sabbatical. Just to travel and see the world.'

She nodded. Mzwandile was right about the stress. 'It's really affecting me, love,' she admitted. 'Last time I checked my blood pressure, it was sky high. The doctor even wanted to book me off work.'

Mzwandile frowned.

'It's the telecom project,' Lerato said. 'It is just so much work. If I take time off, I'll never catch up. And I may end up not getting that promotion I've been working so hard for.'

'Do you need that promotion though? I mean, we've saved up enough for both boys' educations. We don't really need the money and I worry about your health.'

She shrugged. 'It's not just about the money. I mean . . . I don't really enjoy the environment at work, but I do get a kick out of the challenge. There're very few data companies who're on top of the game as we are. Where would I go if I were to quit?'

'You don't have to quit. Just take things a bit easier.'

She rolled her eyes. 'Babe, let's not ruin this beautiful evening by talking about work. Let's talk about the great travel adventure!' she said, circling her arms demonstratively.

They traded wish lists of top countries to visit, enjoying the dream and feeling excited about their prospects.

He leaned over to kiss her and for a little while she allowed herself to get lost in the moment. Allowed her lower body to dissolve into liquid, knowing full well that this was where the passion ended. If only this evening could end with their bodies merging into each other, so that two could become one, just as they had said during their wedding vows. If only, if only, if only; then this would be the perfect anniversary date.

◆ ◆ ◆

On Sunday, they went to church with Bongani, then went out on a family lunch date.

By the time Monday rolled around, Lerato felt deeply contented, refreshed and ready for the new week.

At the office she checked her mailbox and found three emails, each marked urgent. She knew the drill. The project was rearing its now familiar ugly head.

She made herself a cup of coffee and greeted Mark and Thabo, who were also having their morning caffeine boost.

'Hey, guys. How was the weekend?'

'Super cool. I went to the Rage Gaming weekend. Epic time. Thabo popped along yesterday,' said Mark.

'Yeah, bro, but I still can't believe you only told me about it on Saturday night.'

'It's cos you'd said you were working through the weekend,' said Mark.

'*Ja*, but anyway. Did you check the Nag Lan this year . . . flippin' next level, man!'

On and on they went. The funny thing about Thabo and Mark was that one was white and the other one black, but if she closed her eyes, she wouldn't be able to discern which one of them was talking at any given time.

She left them, knowing that they'd barely registered her departure.

When she got to her desk, she saw a text message from Lawrence.

Lunch outside the cafeteria today. I think it's time we tried something new.

Oh no. She'd tried not to think about him the whole weekend. Her husband had been so amazing that she felt guilty even entertaining any thoughts of this man. What was she going to do?

Her heart was racing. She had to cut down on the caffeine.

What to say to Lawrence?

Hey. Lots of work to catch up on. Lunch at my desk today.

Aww . . . can't even come out for half an hour? I'm going to be away for work next week for a whole month!! Pretty please?

A pleading hands emoji.

This wouldn't do.

Sorry. I'll be chained to my desk all week.

She hoped that was the end of it. She put her phone on silent, put on her earphones and listened to classical music as she started focusing on work.

When she took a break two hours later, she saw that she had four missed calls from Lawrence.

Frowning and feeling deep regret, she took a big breath and blocked his number.

It was for the best.

Planet Mystique

July month end and it was Noma and The Duke's turn to host the social club. As usual, Noma planned to pull out all the stops.

Ordinarily, these meetings were the highlight of her social calendar. She was a woman of great taste and she viewed these occasions as an opportunity to showcase her style and panache – but something was different now. Her thoughts kept drifting to The Young Man.

He had been staying in his Bryanston townhouse the past two weeks, which had been absolute bliss for her. She'd even started surprising him at his office with mid-morning coffee dates. She had never met a man so brilliant, so exciting and energetic. There was just something about him that made every day seem brand new. As if he gifted her with a new lens through which to see the world. And he never failed to compliment her choice of outfit. His was the reaction she found she was thinking of every morning she went into her walk-in closet.

Her phone pinged, bringing her back to the present and signalling the arrival of Chef Rico, who was booked to cater for the event. She had sent him an access code for the entrance gate and at 8 a.m., he was there. Punctual as ever.

Her guests would start arriving at one but there was much to do.

She was looking forward to hosting the group and dying to catch up with everyone, especially Moshidi. There was something off about her lately, but she couldn't put her finger on what it was exactly. Maybe they needed a girl-to-girl talk, away from everyone. She didn't know what to make of Moshidi's sister. She was a bit too . . . simple for her tastes. She liked Paul and Tom, though, the new couple. She smiled to herself, remembering Paul's delight in taking Julius's Lamborghini for a spin at Zimbali.

Which reminded her.

The Duke had been in the study all morning making calls to God-knew-who. She hoped he wasn't mixed up with some low-grade slut as per usual. She had beaten the daylights out of that Lovey woman he used to flaunt like a second wife. If The Duke hadn't learned his lesson then, she still had enough balls to deliver a cool reminder of the woman he'd married. She was not the daughter of Soweto's most notorious gangster for nothing. The small scar she could still see on her husband's forehead from his encounter with the wooden coat hanger still made her smile.

Tshidi ushered Chef Rico inside and showed his crew through to the kitchen, where she began to help them set up.

'Rico!' Noma exclaimed, air-kissing the chef.

'Today, Ms Noma, I make an exquisite meal for you and your guests,' said Chef Rico.

'I know! I know! You're the best, Rico. The menu-tasting last week was perfect. I know I'm in safe hands with you. I'm just going to the garden to make sure the décor team has set up everything before my guests arrive, okay?'

'Ah yes. You handle the beautiful things . . . I handle the cuisine.'

Tshidi fussed around the catering team, all the while stealing glances out of the kitchen window. Nthabiseng had been feeling restless of late and she was excited with all the activities going on around the house. Tshidi prayed she would stay put. The xeno-phobic attacks in the township had subsided, but she had enjoyed having her daughter around so much that they had taken to sneak-ing her in on Friday afternoons after school when both Manamelas were still at work. Weekends with her daughter had made such a difference in her life. Mrs Manamela was a difficult boss because of her mixed messages and exacting standards, which sometimes seemed impossible to meet. As for Mr Manamela, he was just one big puzzle. The more you thought you knew him, the more you realised you didn't know him at all.

Nthabi's presence made it easier to deal with her strange employers. She would take her a plate of some of this nice food later.

Noma had transformed the garden into an Arabian-themed landscape. Four intimate nomadic tents were set up at a discreet distance from one another. Each could comfortably seat about six people. Inside were different-coloured ottomans with intricate stitching for the guests to relax on, and scatter cushions in silky rich materials. Low tables adorned with ornately patterned vases, and soon to be laden with platters of delicious food, completed the look.

The first to arrive were Paul and Tom. Dressed in cool shades and matching Polo outfits, they walked straight out into the garden and stood taking in the scene. Waiters dressed in baroque waist-coats, beautifully textured pants and fezes immediately offered them refreshments.

Noma, wearing a silky kaftan with silver and gold embroidery, waltzed towards the couple.

'Darling, why didn't you tell us this was a themed party?' asked Paul, as he hugged the hostess.

'It's a surprise. I wanted to do something different. What's wrong with a bit of mystique?'

Tom was delighted. 'I must say, I have no regrets joining this group if this is the kind of fun we can look forward to. I'd thought Zimbali was unmatched, but now this!'

Over the next hour, the social-club couples drifted in, with Lerato and Mzwandile being the last to arrive. Soon the party would be in full swing.

The society made their monthly contributions via electronic transfer and only spent a few moments dwelling on the financial aspects of the gathering.

Solomzi was the group treasurer and quite ceremonial about presenting the monthly contributions of the group. Paul, as a new member of the group, had introduced the ringing of a dainty golden bell to signal the start of formal proceedings, which included the announcement of the accounting of the month's bounty for the couple whose turn it was to benefit from the contributions.

At the insistent tinkling the members gathered expectantly, ready for Solomzi to begin.

'As treasurer of the group, I am happy to announce that all members have deposited their contributions towards the Manamela household. Per custom, the main contributors deposited R20 000 towards the host, and the partners each contributed R10 000 to the kitty. In total, the Manamelas will be receiving R240 000 from the club this month. May they spend the money wisely, may they grow their households, and may we see progress in their homes and their family's general wellness,' announced Solomzi, to wide applause.

Tom raised his hand. 'And if anyone is looking for financial planning advice – for a fee, of course – don't hesitate to call on your accountant in residence.'

The group laughed uproariously, enjoying the convivial atmosphere. The Khula Social Club prided itself as a foundation for wealth and progress amongst its members.

After the formalities, the couples unfurled to different spots in the sprawling yard in order to enjoy the rest of the day's entertainment. Most of the men gravitated to one tent, while the older ladies in the group commandeered another, where they sipped gin and tonic companionably together. Mzwandile and Tom were chatting casually in the third tent, which left Moshidi, Paul, Lerato and Noma in the fourth.

Moshidi was happily smoking a hookah, having consumed copious amounts of alcohol. She stared up from her ottoman at Paul and Noma, who were equally soaked in the sweet nectars.

Moshidi was always outrageous after one too many glasses of wine, Lerato knew. It was as if alcohol turned her into some controversial talk show host. And today she feared it had turned her into Jerry Springer.

'So, tell me, Paul, how often do you and Tom have sex, hmm?' Moshidi drawled, feeling wanton and free from the wine and hubbly-bubbly.

Lerato felt utterly mortified on behalf of herself (as Moshidi's sister) and poor Paul, but Paul just shrugged.

'As often as possible,' he said, grinning. 'You see, Moshidi, when I chose my man, I knew the kind of beast I am. And honestly, there's so much cheating going on in our world that I wanted us to be a bit different. I've fucked everything there is to fuck, so when I decided to settle down, I knew I was looking for a different life.'

'Everything?' asked Lerato, incredulously.

Moshidi laughed. 'Even a lawnmower?' she teased.

'I fucked a lawnmower and sent it flowers the next morning. I've been with a toilet roll, a drainage pipe, even a plug point . . .'

'Can your thing fit into a plug point?' asked Lerato.

The other three burst out laughing.

'Moshidi, does your sister live in a borehole? Seriously, I'm worried about you, Lerato. You sound like a virgin!' exclaimed Paul.

Lerato blushed. 'I mean . . . I've read about these things online, but I honestly didn't think that people actually did them,' she said, now reassessing the bizarreness of Mzwandile's recent confessions.

Tears of laughter streaming down her face at Lerato's serious expression, Noma took pity on her. 'You do realise Paul is just joking, right?' she said.

Lerato stared at her, then started laughing bashfully. 'Of course I knew he was joking.'

Noma sipped her champagne to get her amusement under control. Then, growing thoughtful, she said, 'But it's sad how many of us are ignorant about sexual pleasure. Especially those of us who married our first loves. Do you know I only discovered oral sex about ten years into my marriage?'

'A sexy fox like you?' said Paul, then added, 'Heterosexual marriages sound awful.'

'They *are* awful,' mumbled Lerato, but no one registered her sentiment.

She looked across to one of the other tents and saw Mzwandile talking to Paul's husband Tom. They seemed deep in conversation. She wondered what the two men could possibly have in common. Once again, seeds of doubt germinated in her head. What if he was lying about being asexual? Maybe he *was* gay, like Moshidi had suggested.

She moved closer to Paul and whispered in his ear, 'Are our husbands flirting?'

Paul looked in the direction of the two men. 'Don't you find flirting sexy?' he asked. 'It's perfectly welcome in my relationship.'

'What?'

He looked at Lerato pityingly. 'You see, this . . . this is why so many relationships fail. Women don't understand men. Do you really think you are the only creature that your husband is sexually drawn to?'

The comment was a stab in her heart.

She sighed. 'Never mind.'

Paul shook his head. 'You know what you need? You need a drink. Let me pour you a glass of champagne.'

'No, thank you.'

'Come on. Everyone likes bubbles.'

'No!'

'Yes! You are far too uptight. I've only met you twice now, but you always seem so stressed. Are you even getting enough sex?'

Lerato tossed her head. 'The world doesn't revolve around sex,' she said.

'Maybe not, but we all deserve a little fun.' Paul held up the champagne bottle invitingly.

'No, thank you,' she said again. She felt uncomfortable, as if Paul could see through her. 'Let me go join the older ladies. You guys are too wild for me.'

Lerato half-sprinted towards Mrs Gumede and the three quieter members of the social club.

'You know, marriage is entirely about sacrifice,' Mrs Gumede was saying as Lerato crouched into their cosy set-up.

Oh no . . . from the frying pan into the sacrificial lair?

'Hi, Lerato. So good to have you join us. Here . . . sit right here next to me,' said Mrs Gumede, patting the cushion next to her. Then she picked up where she'd left off. 'I remember earlier in our marriage, when Sizwe used to come back in the wee hours of a Sunday morning reeking of alcohol and some woman's cheap perfume. I don't know how many times I threatened to walk out on him. But you know what? I always went back to the sage wisdom my aunts shared with me during my *lobola* preparations.'

The other three ladies nodded patiently.

'They always said that marriage is about tenacity. Patience. *Ukubekezela.* These girls today bring Western ideals to make sense

126

of their marriages. It's a recipe for disaster! One thing's for sure,' she said, wagging a finger like a headmistress, 'those Western ideas don't work in African marriages.'

'You're right, MaGumede,' said Mrs Khathide. 'The reason so many of these younger couples go through divorce is because they don't understand that we have to submit to our husbands in order to sustain our relationships. Men are like children. If you don't let them feel their power as head of the household, then you're finished. They go to the mistress and turn her into a second wife.'

Lerato thought she was dreaming. Which planet were these women living on?

'What do you think, Lerato?' asked Mrs Gumede. 'Don't you believe we've become too Westernised in our attitudes towards marriage?'

Lerato patted down her skirt, feeling strangely ambushed into voicing her opinion. 'Um. Well . . . I mean, so much has changed now. Even the Bible, which is my own reference point, acknowledges the idea of transition . . . you look at the Old Testament and how much it differs from the New. I think the changes in the way men and women relate to each other challenge all of us to review gender roles. I don't think a woman should just submit to a man unquestioningly.'

An uncomfortable silence descended around the tent.

Mrs Gumede shrugged. 'I feel sorry for you younger people, because you'll struggle to find happiness. You want too much. But men are not capable of giving you everything you see in the movies. By the way, what are you drinking? Do you care for a gin and tonic?'

Mrs Khathide snapped her fingers, summoning the waiter.

As the waiter approached, Lerato quickly shook her head.

'No gin and tonic for me, thank you. A virgin mojito, please.'

'Why are you having a non-alcoholic drink? Are you on medication?'

'No,' Lerato smiled shyly. 'I'm a teetotaller.'

'You poor thing. How on earth do you survive marriage without alcohol?'

Mrs Gumede and her friends laughed uproariously.

If Lerato had a penny . . .

Even the old Stepford wives had an obsession with alcohol.

She clearly did not belong anywhere in this group of people. At the rate things were going, maybe she belonged nowhere on earth.

The Duke

In spite of himself, The Duke had to admit he was getting a buzz from putting the wheels in motion for Danie Wiese's unorthodox heist, even though the circumstances around it still stung.

Wiese had taken him back to a cruelly uncertain time in his life.

After he and Noma had had their lavish wedding, living off the vast amounts of money The Duke had made from his cash-in-transit heists, things had started moving in a significantly different direction in their lives.

When the money started running out, making Noma increasingly irritable, The Duke had tried to seek counsel from Noma's father, Solomon Mahlangu, who was the heist kingpin of Soweto and The Duke's personal mentor in the criminal underworld.

Julius could not understand how Noma had transformed into a prissy suburban superwoman; one minute signing up for university correspondence classes and completing her commerce degree in record time, the next, birthing two children in between said studies!

He had started to feel misplaced in his own life. Where was the gangster's moll he'd adored? The one who could kick and punch any man or woman who tried to come between them, swirl a bottle of Crossbow cider, all the while swearing like a miner?

Who was this studious mother figure who'd replaced her? This suit-wearing minx who hardly uttered a word of *tsotsi-taal* – the beloved street language that distinguished the kings and queens of ghetto life?

When Solomon died, The Duke had looked forward to taking over the reins, but Noma swiftly pointed out that her father had been on the police's most-wanted list and that Julius would fall straight into their lair if he took centre stage in her dad's operations.

She convinced him that between the two of them, with The Duke's own money from his criminal operations and the sizeable stash that her father had left her, they'd survive a strait-laced life in the suburbs; especially given the fact that they were now parents.

That's when The Duke had done the unthinkable . . . gone job-hunting. He'd landed the job of head of security at Danie Wiese's company.

With Noma clinching important-sounding job titles, while The Duke woke up every day to stare at security cameras, his testosterone levels plummeted day by day.

It was only when their fortune dwindled to a point that even Noma's job in the corporate world could not finance their mortgage and pay for the children's exclusive private schooling, that he felt his masculinity rising and felt ready to take centre stage again.

He'd been thinking about how he was guarding the exact kind of wealth that had dizzied him in his gangster days and reckoned that it was his ancestors who had placed him in this cushy position.

When the idea landed to steal from Wiese's jewellery store, all he needed was to manipulate the security cameras and bring in old Quicks Tshabalala and Tim-Tim to help him carry out the heist. Unfortunately, Danie had an in-built system to counter such attacks and The Duke's fail-proof plan had backfired.

But as luck would have it (or the ancestors, of course), it turned out that Danie had been going through financial troubles of his own. He chose to hike up the value of the stolen items and claim the insurance instead of ratting out The Duke and his crew. All

Danie did was swear to the high heavens that Julius would get his comeuppance and, of course, he fired him on the spot. At that time, he had truly been grateful to his ancestors for their abiding love and support for him.

Twenty-five years later and the proverbial chickens had come to roost. All he could do was pray that this was truly only about another insurance-fraud scam, and not something more sinister.

Just a few weeks to go before the big hit.

He felt energised by all the planning he needed to do for this job. Besides, Noma's gun stunt had dented his ego. To think she'd had him begging . . . on his knees! Yeah . . . Nomathando was truly a witch. He loathed the fact that as much as he wanted to hate her, Noma's nerves of steel seriously turned him on. That's why even Lovey couldn't hold a candle to her.

In any case, this project was making him feel like a man in control again.

The Duke had been in retirement from the business for eight years now, but he couldn't deny it was exciting to feel the all too familiar rush that came with every new heist.

His last job had precipitated Noma's promotion to chief of operations at the mining company. That had been a beautiful, clean professional job if ever there was one. And the money! *Jislaaik*, he'd never seen so much money in his entire life!

His crew had comprised sharp young men who were not only hungry for the big time but were also smart and efficient. He'd never worked with a crew like that before. In the olden days, all you needed in a team were good contacts, one or two 'inside' guys and then maybe a few tough guys to help rough up any resistance along the way. But first, you needed a mastermind like The Duke to put all the pieces together. After that you were more or less on your way to riches.

In the modern age, though, muscle and experience were not enough to pull off a big job. With all the new technology, you needed men who knew their way around digital security systems. You needed smart guys who could outsmart the latest security technologies. And you needed pure genius to think three steps ahead of the game.

This Trojan horse delivered by Danie had been both a blessing and a curse. Why were things always so complicated when it came to him and Danie?

He'd consulted with his spiritual healer – his *sangoma* – and he had been told that the ancestors would protect him on this mission and that he would gain insurmountable wealth!

Lately, Noma was getting too big-headed for her own good. Sure, he loved the fact that his young bride had blossomed into some kind of business titan, but as proud as he was of her success, he remained an old-fashioned sort of guy. From day one, he'd been the one to bring home the bacon. Scratch that. He'd brought home the whole piggery and some change!

Noma's burgeoning success made him proud, but he also felt belittled sometimes. It was even hard to charm the young ladies without feeling guilty about how Noma would feel about his escapades . . . and yes, there was an element of fear lately whenever he was tempted to double-cross his wife. He hated to admit it, but he needed this job. It made him feel alive, in charge and, best of all, if all went well, he'd reassert his role as the breadwinner in his home.

And he'd finally get his pants back.

Confessions

Lerato's life was a turbulent quadrant of agony, ecstasy, angst and guilt.

Work – torturous and high-pressured.

Home – awkward and distant.

Church – guilt-ridden.

Thoughts of Lawrence – joyful bliss.

This was not who she was. Living a double life was taking its toll on her. All her life, her spirituality had been central to her existence. But with Lawrence in her life, it was becoming impossible to locate her Christian self in this whirlwind of attraction. At least she'd managed to contain the situation by blocking him, but it didn't stop her from obsessing about him every minute and hour of every day.

He was travelling for a few weeks but she kept getting tempted to unblock him so she could check if he was well.

She'd withdrawn from the fundraising committee at church, citing work pressures. She was also no longer a regular attendee of the cell group meetings, although she did attend Sunday service. Though she often prayed about her situation, she still needed to do more to free herself of her guilt.

Lerato had even considered visiting a Catholic priest for confession, but she knew very little of the ways of the Catholics and had only seen Catholic confessions in mafia movies. Those gangsters made it all look so easy: you throw someone into a cauldron of acid on Friday, turning them into soup, then you visit your local priest on Sunday (or even the same day!) and say: 'Forgive me, Father, for I have sinned.' And then the priest, bless him, will say something like, 'Confess your sins, my son.'

My son. To the head of the Mob.

Those words alone must be reassuring to those gangsters.

She was certain they left confession feeling light and free of sin. But she was a Protestant. *Dololo* confession. So her guilt was hers to bear alone.

A little while ago she had decided to confide in Moshidi, so she casually dropped in on a Saturday afternoon, having checked that Solomzi was out on one of his golf jaunts. Was that man ever home?

She worried about her sister's marriage sometimes, but since Moshidi seldom confided in her about any chinks in it, she knew it was best to wait for her to raise the subject . . . if she ever felt it necessary. She wondered how she survived. For Lerato, a problem shared was a problem halved, but Moshidi seemed to think that talking about any negatives meant that her life did not live up to the perfect façade she worked so hard to maintain.

When she got to Moshidi's, she found her sister, wearing a sunhat and short denim overalls, bent over in the garden plucking rosemary and parsley from her compact herb garden.

'Wow. I can't believe you do stuff like this,' said Lerato. 'I'm taking a picture to send to Papa.'

Moshidi stood to her full height, hands on hips. 'Why are you this person?' she asked ruefully, striking a pose that she clearly associated with farmers.

Click, went Lerato's Samsung phone. She immediately sent a WhatsApp to their father.

See your daughter. She's on the front page of *Farmer's Weekly*.

Their dad responded right away, with laughing emojis.

Moshidi walked over to see the messages. 'I still can't believe Papa sends emojis.'

They both laughed.

'You know he leaves no trend unturned,' said Lerato.

They accessed the house via Moshidi's entertainment area, Lerato trailing behind her sister.

'Come with me to the bedroom while I get cleaned up and changed.'

They continued chatting as they walked upstairs.

'How're my nephews?' asked Moshidi.

'Lwazi called us on our wedding anniversary. He looks so grown up it's scary.'

'I miss him so much. And Bongani? He promised he'd take the twins to Laser Tag last weekend. Why did he stand them up?'

Lerato couldn't remember anything about such a date. She shrugged. 'Sorry. That doesn't sound like him. He loves the twins. I'm sure he'll make it up to them. Something must have come up.'

At the mention of the twins, they came scurrying down the stairs, chasing after each other.

'Hey Akhona! Come give me a hug! And stop running – you'll trip and fall,' said Lerato.

The boys came for a hug from their aunt, then broke out of her embrace and pounded down the stairs.

'Poor Zozo. How does she keep up with these two always attached at the hip?'

Moshidi laughed. 'That's the last person you should worry about. She's at a playdate as we speak. She and her friend say they want to start a kids' fashion accessory range.'

'I swear your daughter was born two decades ago.'

'I know. Sometimes she sounds more grown up than me. Anyway, I've been meaning to ask, how was the wedding anniversary?'

'It was amazing,' Lerato said, sitting down on the bed while Moshidi went to the en-suite bathroom to wash her hands. When she came back and started going through her closet, looking for a change of clothes, her sister added, 'Thank you for the present, by the way. So gorgeous.'

Moshidi had decided a night for Lerato and Mzwandile in a five-star hotel was a bit extravagant given her and Solomzi's current financial straits. It might also be insensitive, she realised, and only add to her sister's stress. In the end she'd settled for a set of cut-glass fruit bowls. 'You're welcome, sis. So . . . does that mean you guys have resolved your bedroom issues?'

Lerato sighed. 'Hmm . . . not really. He finally confessed what's really happening with him.'

At this, Moshidi stopped mid zipping up her jeans, and regarded her sister with curiosity.

'Zip up your pants. The revelation won't escape while you're getting dressed.'

'*Mxm.* You're so boring,' she said as she fastened the button of her jeans and pulled a T-shirt over her head.

'Mzwandile says he's asexual.'

'A what? Like what . . . is he attracted to plants or something?'

'Nope. Not attracted to plants. Attracted to nothing.'

Moshidi folded her arms in disbelief. 'What the hell is that supposed to mean? Give me your phone.'

Lerato did as instructed.

Moshidi busied herself typing something into Lerato's search browser, then read out loud: '"Asexual. Without sexual feelings or associations. Asexual individuals may still experience attraction but this attraction doesn't need to be realised in any sexual manner."'

She stared at Lerato. '*Mxm*. This is rubbish. In this horny South Africa, do you really think such a thing exists?'

Lerato shrugged. 'I thought it's sunny South Africa.'

'No. It's horny South Africa.'

They laughed.

'Well,' continued Lerato, 'it probably affects like . . . one per cent of the population.'

'You're saying there could be 600,000 South Africans who are asexual?'

'Okay, maybe 0.001 per cent.'

'Hmm . . . so he's one of, like, 6,000 asexual people in this country?' She shook her head. 'Why are we even focusing on statistics? I don't believe him. I'm sure he's hiding something. Anyway, how does he propose you proceed, given his supposed asexual orientation?'

'He prayed for me. To stop me having carnal thoughts.'

Moshidi laughed incredulously. 'Are you kidding me? Like prayed, prayed?'

Lerato nodded.

'Talk about narcissism. So you're supposed to turn yourself into a frigid shrimp because he doesn't have sexual feelings. The nerve of these men!'

'And you know his confession is messing me up. I keep going over our sexual history, noticing things that I took to be normal but now I have to actually question every single thing.'

'Like what?' asked Moshidi.

'Well . . . I mean . . . the sex itself . . . I always had to be the one who initiated it, you know. And it was never really regular.'

'So before The Great Drought, how often would you guys have sex?'

Lerato shrugged. 'I don't know . . . in the early days, maybe once a month. And then . . . it just started happening less and less often.'

'*Yho*. You must be growing cobwebs down there . . . and you only discovered the rabbit this year. You poor thing.' Moshidi came to sit next to Lerato on the bed. 'Sweetheart . . . jokes aside, how on earth are you going to continue in this marriage?'

Lerato started wailing as her sister took her in her arms and hugged her.

'I don't know . . . But, Moshidi . . . I've done something very bad . . . So, so bad.'

Moshidi squeezed her tight. 'What is it? You can tell me.'

Lerato released herself from the hug and started wiping her eyes. 'I met someone, Moshidi. At work. I've been kind of seeing him for a few weeks now, though I'm trying my best to cool things off.'

Moshidi couldn't believe the words were coming out of her sister's mouth. She frowned. Was this the time to also confess that she thought she, too, may have feelings for someone else? The last session with her personal trainer had been . . . What had it been? Well, a bit steamy maybe – and not in the sauna.

But, no. This wasn't about her. Lerato's problems were bigger than hers.

'When? How? I don't think it's wise to date someone at work, Lerato. Affairs can be catastrophic. They can ruin you.'

Lerato shook her head. 'We don't work together,' she said. 'Just in the same building. He's amazing, Moshidi. He's so attentive and sweet and exciting. I'm really trying to resist him but . . .'

'So you haven't been physical yet?'

'No! Of course not. I don't think I even have it in me to take things that far. I'm really trying hard to resist him. I even blocked him on my phone. But I can't stop thinking about him. Even *thinking* about sex with someone is sinful. Isn't it?'

Moshidi shook her head in pity. She honestly didn't know how to advise Lerato, especially given her strong moral compass. She steepled her fingers, deeply concerned.

'Look, I understand what you're going through . . . and I get it, you know. I get it. Gosh, if it were me in this situation, I probably would have strayed long ago. But you are you, sis. I don't know if you can handle something as messy as an affair.'

Lerato started weeping again. 'I don't know either. When I'm with him, everything is perfect. I'm happy . . . over the moon with excitement. I've never felt like this about a man. Even in the earlier days with Mzwandile it was never like this. He makes me feel swept up in a cloud . . . like my feet can barely touch the ground. It's just amazing. But when he's not there . . . when I'm at home especially . . . I feel wretched. I look at my son, my husband, and I wonder what I'm doing. And then God – I can't even pray anymore because I feel guilty all the time.'

The two sisters sat quietly in contemplation.

Finally, Moshidi took Lerato's hand. 'Look, I can't judge you here. I know you've been unhappy for years now. In the end, it's you who has to decide what do with this situation. You're only human – don't forget that. So try not to be too hard on yourself. But promise me you'll be careful, sis. Till you figure out what you want. Do you still love *sbali*?'

Lerato nodded. 'Yes. I actually do. That's why this hurts so much. I just wish things were different, you know . . . because for as long as he's sticking to his asexuality, the future is very grey for me. I can't really envision what the rest of our life's going to look like.'

'And do you think you're in love with this new guy?'

Lerato shrugged. 'I don't know. He's been travelling for work for a few weeks. I blocked him because I was worried about the intensity of my feelings towards him.'

'Do you intend to rekindle things when he comes back?' Moshidi looked at her sister with concern in her eyes.

'I don't know,' said Lerato.

Invitations

The invitation had come hot on the heels of the Manamelas' social club event. It was as if the ebullient new members Moshidi had recruited couldn't wait to stake their claim.

A chauffeur-driven black Chrysler had drawn up outside their house and out had hopped an extremely handsome gentleman in a tight-fitting tuxedo. He struck a distinctive pose and, reading from a gold-embossed invitation card, which he flourished with style, he announced:

'Good morning, lady and gentleman of the house. Misters Paul and Thomas seek the pleasure of your company at their Great Gatsby Supper Club event on the thirtieth of August. Dress Code: Old-School Glamour. Please present yourselves at Shangri La no later than eighteen hundred hours on the designated evening.'

Oh brother, thought Moshidi. What had she unleashed on the social club?

Just when she and Solomzi were sinking in debt, she'd gone and recruited the most extravagant people on the planet to join Khula. As if the Manamelas weren't enough to keep up with!

Her meeting with Edward Serame was supposed to take place the week before but he'd sent a lengthy email apologising for having to shift the dates as he'd had to travel for business. The email was all manner of weird and she was surprised that he'd penned it himself instead of delegating the duties to his secretary. All things considered though, it made her feel better about their whole ordeal – at least he seemed like a decent human being. But waiting to resolve the situation was driving her crazy. When she'd forcefully taken the phone from Solomzi to talk to Serame, she'd made a mental note to keep all future communication with him under wraps until she was sure she could meet with him in person to present her case. Solomzi was far too jittery about the situation. Maybe he was intimidated by this Serame person? One thing was for sure: when it came to the safety and stability of her family, nothing and nobody could lead Moshidi to submission. There was both an art and a science to negotiation and she had mastered both elements through years of practice.

In the meantime, Solomzi's behaviour was not helping the cause.

He had taken to keeping late nights, which made her worry even more. She hoped he'd not gone back to his gambling ways to try and cover their debts. Then, to top it all, he had casually told her that he was going on a golfing trip to Cape Town next weekend – Women's Day weekend! – and she wasn't invited. She couldn't believe the cheek of it!

'Babe, why are you frowning? Isn't this the coolest thing we've experienced since joining Khula?'

Moshidi just blinked her quiet alarm. If this was how their invitations looked, what new level of grandiosity were they to expect at the couple's soirée?

She felt her stomach tie up in knots. The pressure was on. Thanks to the arrival of this wealthy pair, whoever's turn it was to host the social club next would be expected to outdo the extravagance of the last. She didn't know how *she* was going to cope, let alone Lerato, whose turn it would be next.

Solomzi, on the other hand, seemed tickled by the over-the-top invitation.

As the walking telegram left their home, Soli was beaming from ear to ear. 'Hey, man, I love these guys! This is gonna be a frigging rocking party!' He bounded up the steps, snapping his fingers happily.

Moshidi watched him then folded her arms and shook her head. '*Mxm*. You don't even have the budget for a walking tuxedoed invitation-card person . . .' she murmured.

'What's that, babe?' he asked.

'Nothing,' she replied.

Not only was Solomzi away living it up in Cape Town with his golfing buddies over the long weekend, but it was also a school holiday. Taking the rare opportunity of her father coming through to Joburg from Phokeng to visit a friend who wasn't well, Moshidi sent the kids back with him so that they could spend time with their grandparents. And give her a break.

She thought she and Lerato could spend Women's Day together treating themselves to a decadent lunch out, then work it off – along with her frustrations – at the gym on Saturday. Her personal trainer had said he would be going away for work – she couldn't remember what his day job was, something in an office – for a few weeks and she didn't want to let her summer body training schedule slip.

Unfortunately, the first part of her plan was scuppered when Lerato informed her that Mzwandile had persuaded her to go on a church weekend somewhere. That left her with a gaping public holiday, Women's Day, all by herself.

On the off chance she fired off a text and within minutes, she received a text back.

As it happens, I am free today. Come on over to the gym.
Let's get you those abs!

She grinned at the phone screen and hurried out of the room.

She hopped into the shower, lathering her body with a coconut shower gel, then got in to her athletic gear, checking out her body before stepping out to go to the gym.

Moshidi walked briskly through the gym's neon-lit entrance and made her way straight to the studio. He was already there, waiting for her, greeting her with that confident smile of his. Those brilliant white teeth against his dark skin, his long sinewy body and rock-hard abs . . . hmm . . .

As usual, he acted businesslike for the first few minutes of their session, but then . . . the way he touched her legs, guiding her movements . . . She couldn't help it. He set her pulse racing. Focus, Moshidi, she told herself. Think of your summer body. *Your* summer body – not his.

When the session ended, she stood up to leave, only to hear him say, 'Listen . . . are you busy after this? I thought maybe we could have brunch? On me?'

'But it's a public holiday,' she said. 'Don't you have somewhere to be?'

'I do,' he replied. 'I'm having brunch with a beautiful woman.'

Oh. A beat.

'Say yes?'

Moshidi laughed lightly. She knew he was aware of her marital status. Then she thought of the brand-new golf shirt she'd seen Solomzi packing into his bag yesterday. And how lonely and off-kilter her own marriage had started to feel. Other than debt, kids and business, what else did she and Solomzi really talk about?

Maybe she should say yes? Say yes to adult conversation. Say yes to being heard, seen and adored . . . say yes to easy jokes and lovely flirtation.

'Sure, why not?' she said. 'My kids are with my parents.'

'Ah, yesss,' he said, doing an irresistible fist pump.

He was so cute. And that smile!

'So I'll hop into the shower real quick and meet you back at reception in about fifteen or twenty minutes?'

She nodded.

As she walked into the changerooms, Moshidi started panicking.

What the hell am I doing?

She started shedding her gym clothes.

Do other people have brunch with their personal trainers when their husbands are out of town?

She knew the answer to that, but she wasn't other people. Or was she?

What if someone sees us?

So what if someone saw them? It was just brunch, wasn't it?

She realised she was trembling, on the verge of panic.

She took a deep breath.

It was just an innocent outing. What could go wrong?

Unblocked

She'd been dreaming about Lawrence almost every day since she'd blocked him. She missed their chats, hearing his sexy voice, seeing his smile, listening to his crazy stories . . . but she knew she'd made the right decision. Her marriage was sacred. She was not about to allow any third party into it, regardless of the challenges ahead.

Her talk with Moshidi had only made her more resolute. She was not some flaky woman who melted from the attention of a younger man. She just needed to push away all thoughts of desire and she'd be fine. She wasn't the first person to be in a sexless marriage (she'd googled it) and neither would she be the last.

Back at her desk after a tough meeting with her boss, who'd complained that she and her team were dragging their feet on the project, Lerato slumped her full weight on her chair. Hmmph. Dragging their feet when they were pulling late hours and weekends too? The man was impossible to please.

The last time she'd seen Lawrence, he'd said he'd be travelling to Kenya then Nigeria for business but as she looked at her calendar, she realised he would have been back in Johannesburg for a few days now.

She needed some air. Maybe she should just go to the coffee shop across the road in order to avoid bumping into him at the cafeteria.

Just then her landline phone rang.

'Hi.'

That was all he said, and she felt her body instantly responding. First it was a rush of panic, then a warm sensation in her panties, then an apparent inability to breathe.

'Um . . . hi.'

'So . . . you blocked me?'

'Um . . .' she said, rubbing her eyes and biting her bottom lip.

'Look, I know . . . this may be complicated for you. But please. Can I just see you? Even for a moment? Please, Lerato . . . I miss you . . . so much.'

A long pause.

'Lerato. Are you still there?'

She nodded. Then realising he couldn't see her, she said, 'Yes. Where are you?'

'Um . . . at work. But I can see you now, if you like . . . ?'

'Okay. It's my lunchtime.'

'Come out of the building. I . . . I desperately need to see you.'

'Okay,' she said. She could barely get the words out, such was her ache for him.

She took her bag, told Thabo that she was stepping out for lunch, then went to the bathroom where she put on mascara, foundation and lipstick. Brushed her afro, smiled at the mirror. Then pouted for some odd reason. Laughing at herself, she spritzed some perfume on her neck and pulse points, then took the lift downstairs.

Outside in the fresh air, she phoned Lawrence. 'I'm outside. Where are you?'

'Just driving out of the basement. I'll be there in a few minutes.'

Lerato was standing awkwardly in the parking lot, clasping her handbag to her waist, when she saw a long, sleek black Mercedes-Benz with tinted windows coming towards her.

The car stopped beside her. The back passenger window shifted down. 'Hi, Lerato. I thought that was you,' said a voice in cool, silky tones.

Noma Manamela. Wearing designer shades and a rouge lipstick.

Lerato felt like a schoolgirl caught playing truant. She looked nervously around, willing Lawrence's car not to appear.

'Um . . . hi, Noma,' she said, touching her face. 'What brings you here?'

'Oh, I had a meeting at Red Marketing. They're in this building. Is this where you work?'

Lerato nodded nervously. What a small world.

Lawrence was an account director at Red Marketing. She knew they ran social responsibility programmes for corporates, including some of the big mining companies. Feeling mortified for no reason, she managed a smile.

'Yes – this is where Optima Data's office is,' she said. 'Fifth floor.' Red Marketing was on the fourth. 'I'm actually just running to a meeting. It's so great seeing you, Noma. Bye for now.'

She gave a nervous wave and took off for the other side of the parking lot while the Mercedes lumbered towards the exit gate of the building complex.

Phew. This was bad. It was so, so bad. Noma's company was one of Red Marketing's clients. What were the chances?

Definitely too close to home.

Maybe she should just bail out . . .

Before she could finish her thought, she saw a grey Nissan Navara coming out of the basement parking. She instinctively knew this was Lawrence. The car drove up to where she was standing.

'Step in,' said Lawrence.

She went around to the passenger seat.

'Where are we going?'

He drew into a parking bay close to the gate, then turned off the ignition.

Before she could think of Noma – or anything else – he turned to face her. Looked at her with such deep longing she felt as though his eyes were piercing through her soul. Then he reached out to cup her face and leaned in to kiss her. She felt her whole body release a fiery, warm glow of passion. She had never been kissed like that before. He opened her legs and touched her most private place, stroking her till she felt her body explode.

She wanted him. Right there . . . she wanted him so badly.

When they broke off their passionate embrace, he looked at her and gasped. 'Wow.'

She widened her eyes and laughed shyly.

'I've missed you . . . I thought I was going mad! Oh Lerato . . .' said Lawrence.

'I've missed you too,' said Lerato.

Their lips met again, this time with more urgency than before.

After they broke away from each other again, Lawrence started the engine.

Lerato sat back. She knew where they were going. She had subconsciously known this since the first day at the cafeteria.

There was no closing the door they had just unlocked.

Shangri La

The couples drifted in one by one.

It was a huge, sprawling property, with a massive house – Tuscan villa style – and a large water-spouting fountain in the yard, among many other extravagant features. The name 'Shangri La', which was inscribed in calligraphy on the front wall beside the gate, said it all.

The garden was formal in design, with symmetrical, geometric beds and delineated hedges and walls. Shrubs were manicured into neat geometric topiaries. Trellised foliage vines, several water features, each more gorgeous than the next, and sculptures completed the garden's Italian theme. Tonight, the couple had draped the trees in fairy lights and outdoor chandeliers to add glamour to the evening.

Everyone had honoured the Great Gatsby-themed invitation and the couples were decked out in ritzy outfits befitting of the 1920s' jazz era.

The Gumedes and the Khathides were the first to arrive. They were escorted to Paul and Tom's bar, where they were greeted by a stunning hostess adorned in a champagne tower dress. They each treated themselves to a glass of bubbly from the human champagne tower and drifted off to the loungers by the couple's infinity pool where cocktail tables and lounge chairs were set out in the yard, with floating candles illuminating the pool.

An eight-piece jazz band welcomed guests with a snappy rendition of Billy Holiday's 'Summertime' belted out by a talented female vocalist.

The evening promised to be a magical one.

Lerato and Mzwandile shared an Uber with Solomzi and Moshidi to take them to the venue. Paul was on hand to welcome them as they arrived.

'Wow! This looks incredible!' said Moshidi, as Paul linked his arm through hers.

'You know I never disappoint, my darling!' responded Paul.

He turned to compliment Lerato, Mzwandile and Solomzi.

'Love, *love* your outfits!'

'Where's Tom?' asked Lerato.

'Come with me. I'll take you to my hot husband,' Paul announced. 'I swear, tonight he looks *edible*.'

Julius and Noma were the last to arrive as usual, thanks to Noma's arduous grooming routine. As expected, they arrived at full throttle in their matching Lamborghinis.

As Moshidi watched the extravagant entrance while leaning on Solomzi's shoulder, she wondered what their combined carbon footprint might be. Why did they even need to arrive in two cars? Did they not know the Earth needed healing?

Was it the Earth Mother in her talking or was it jealousy? she wondered. She'd never questioned it before, had she?

With all the members of the social club now gathered, Tom and Paul allowed them to settle down with starters and welcome drinks before Paul lifted his little bell and tinkled them into silence.

As treasurer, Solomzi ran through the financials for the evening, recording all the members' deposits, which had been transferred a few days before.

'Judging by the lavishness of this event, I'd say our hosts have already blown our contributions for the month,' Soli added, much to the amusement of the guests.

The décor and catering certainly seemed extravagant, and the eight-piece jazz band just added to the opulence. Everyone relaxed, tapping their toes, taking in the ambience and the beautiful evening.

Then Paul stood up and tinkled a spoon against his champagne flute. Once he had all the guests' attention, he stood straight and gestured for Tom to come and join him.

'We've actually been a little bit naughty,' he said, 'because this evening is more than just about hosting our supper club.'

Supper club?

Lerato blinked. So did Moshidi. They exchanged a look. If they could have read each other's thoughts, they would both have smiled.

When did people stop calling these things *stokvels*? thought Lerato.

When did they stop calling it a social club? thought Moshidi.

Phew. They both sighed to themselves. Life had become so complicated of late.

Tom walked up to Paul, looking dashing in a David Tlale cream-white tuxedo. They linked arms and Paul continued with his speech.

'Tonight marks ten years of my union with this wonderful man. We took the bold step of committing to each other when it was taboo for gay people to so much as be seen with each other in public. We braved all the whispers and ignored the raised eyebrows because our love blazed with such intensity that even the judgement of others couldn't extinguish it,' he said, his eyes beginning to moisten.

'I'm proud to stand here before you as we toast a decade of magic, messy fights, tears of joy and pain and, more importantly, a love that we hope will endure for many more years to come!' He raised his glass, sniffing away the sentimentality of the moment.

Tom kissed him on the lips, much to The Duke's utter shock. He had accepted the nature of the couple's relationship, but he wasn't quite sure if he was ready to see two men kissing. He gulped down his glass of champagne and stopped the waiter to ask for another.

Noma side-eyed him with amusement.

It was Tom's turn to speak. 'I met this fox of a man during a time when I was troubled . . . I was in denial of who I was and was desperate to fit into the mould. He took one look at me and saw me for what I truly am. And he's never stopped seeing through my soul . . . and loving me anyway. Here's to you, my love,' he said as he raised his glass to toast his partner.

Moshidi couldn't help but shed a tear. She was touched by the couple's love for each other and she now realised that there was more to Paul than his cheeky banter. Their chats were usually superficial and flighty – everything outside of work seemed fodder for comic relief when it came to Paul. It felt good witnessing him in this moment of such tenderness and vulnerability.

After their sentimental speeches, one of Paul's friends stood up and said, 'Are we at a wake or are we here to party?'

At which cue the jazz band came alive and started mixing favourite African jazz classics like 'Phatha Phatha' and modern *amapiano* tracks to liven up the party. Soon everyone was on the floor. Even Lerato was throwing in some funky moves, to the surprise of a few people.

All in all, the event was a glorious celebration of love and friendship, and everyone left the party knowing that the warm memories would remain like indelible ink in their collective consciousness.

If they'd known what awaited them, they might have held on to those carefree moments just a little bit longer.

A Spring In The Step

September – it was officially spring and what was even better was that The Young Man was back in town!

Noma wasted no time making reservations at their favourite Michelin-starred restaurant as she excitedly recalled their last meeting. She so enjoyed his company. The man was a fireball of ideas; when she was with him, the world felt limitless in its scope of possibilities. She had read of business mavericks, but The Young Man epitomised everything she had ever ascribed to the ideal of a Renaissance Man.

Not only were his business ideas energising, but he could speak at length about almost any subject. Why was The Duke not like this? Sure, they had met when they were very young, but she had spent the years elevating her knowledge and exploring all the new avenues that their wealth opened up to them, whereas Julius . . .

The Noma of today was radically different from the young woman who had fallen in love with the rough, rugged, ruthless but charming Julius 'The Duke' Manamela.

The origins of their success may have been somewhat dubious, but through education and exposure to the finest networks of businesspeople, they had made a clean break from their past. They were successful and respected in their own right. They had made it.

But for some reason, The Duke was still quite rough around the edges. She wished he was a bit more worldly and sophisticated. Like The Young Man.

Her mind suddenly flashed to The Duke's annoying habit of sticking a toothpick in his teeth just for sport. Such a typical *tsotsi* move! If she had a penny for every time she had to admonish him for that annoying habit!

And then there was his gold tooth. She'd begged him to have it taken out, but all he would say to that was that he'd remove it when she agreed to stop wearing designer labels. So the gold tooth stayed.

She loved him but he really annoyed her sometimes – especially lately, with his late-night phone calls and mysterious meetings. She was certain he was up to his old tricks again.

Well, the new Noma was not taking things lying down. She'd spent her whole marriage fighting off The Duke's various entanglements. Maybe it was finally her turn to entangle herself with someone.

Her phone buzzed.

'Hello? Yes . . . I'm getting ready. I'll meet you there in an hour. Yes, yes. Veritas. Seven o'clock. Can't wait . . .'

She knew from previous experience that The Young Man was always punctual and did not brook tardiness at meetings. She couldn't afford to spend an hour getting ready so chop, chop, chop and within twenty minutes, she was on her way.

In the car she reflected on what he'd said on the phone yesterday. What were his exact words? Oh yes.

'I have a proposition for you,' The Young Man had said. 'And I know you're going to love it!'

She sent Julius a quick text.

Don't wait up.

He didn't reply.

154

◆ ◆ ◆

D-Day was on the horizon for the jewellery heist. All the guys were on standby. They'd be a crew of nine in total, six of The Duke's old team members and two new guys who had come with Quicks Tshabalala. He was never too keen on new guys, but he'd been inactive for a while now and some of the guys he'd had in mind were untraceable. It was as if they'd just disappeared off the face of the Earth, even though he'd spent weeks trying to locate them. He hoped they were fine.

This type of life wasn't ideal for an old man like him. People just vanishing like that . . . yet there was an unmistakable adrenalin rush that charged through his body each time he thought about the upcoming job.

For once it suited him that Noma was so busy. She was always rushing off to meetings, even at night – fancy dinners at fancy restaurants, mining clients from out of town needing to be entertained. They hardly saw each other. Sometimes all he knew of her presence was a waft of her perfume left in the air.

Danie Wiese had been true to his word. They had met a couple of times but these meetings had been brief and professional. All the meetings were arranged via the burner phone, which The Duke would dispose of as soon as the job was done, and all of them were held at discreet places where no one would witness their interactions. Danie had given The Duke a detailed plan of the office park and the building where the jewellery was kept in a vault. He had the location of the security cameras, inside and out, and the schedules of the security companies' guards – those on duty at the boomed entrance to the office park, as well as those from Royal Guards, Danie's security company, who would be on-site on the day. Everything.

And, as an extra precaution, most of the staff were scheduled to be away for the day at a team-building event so there shouldn't be anyone in the office. In any case, The Duke and his team would be in and out long before offices opened and the roads were full of commuters.

It was going to be so easy it was almost too good to be true.

Those were the words that kept ringing in his head at night. Too good to be true.

But it was true. In and out. Easy.

Even so, The Duke knew not to be complacent. He acknowledged that he was a bit rusty, and this wasn't a tried and trusted team. But what choice did he have?

When Danie Wiese called in a favour, he didn't mess about. And who the hell wanted to end up in prison at sixty years of age? Not him. Nope. That was not what the ancestors had aligned for The Duke.

I job yi job. The very last one, for sure.

A Business Meeting

Solomzi watched Moshidi pull different outfits from her walk-in closet, trying to choose an outfit for her meeting with Edward Serame.

When she told him she'd scheduled a meeting with the man, he'd been unable to eat for two days. Part of him wanted to stop her, but another part felt almost resigned to the whole thing. After all, he knew his wife. Once she set her mind on something, there was nothing he could do to stop her.

Or was that what he told himself?

He was pacing like a jaguar in their bedroom. The two glasses of whisky he'd stealthily consumed did nothing for his nerves.

'Babe, please, don't wear anything flashy. Just be conservative,' he said now, coming closer to inspect her apparel.

'What about this dress? It's chic yet understated.'

He inspected the dress carefully and shook his head. 'Too revealing. It's a business meeting, hon. Can't you wear a pants suit or something? You want to show the man that you're a serious negotiator.'

Moshidi frowned. 'But it's a Sunday evening. Must I really be so formal?'

Solomzi gazed at her.

'Soli?'

'What? Oh. Yes, I think formal is better. Serame won't take you seriously if you look like a little kitten.'

She laughed. 'Oh no, babe. I ain't no kitten. I'm a tigress! Hear me roar . . .' she said, growling playfully for effect.

Soli took a step back. 'Be serious, Moshidi. Just be yourself. But be formal . . . and tough,' he said.

'I got this, man. This is what I do with my eyes closed. Like . . . every single day,' she said.

She took off her clothes and stepped into the shower.

Soli went downstairs.

When Moshidi came out of the shower, he was sitting on their bed drinking whisky. It looked like it wasn't his first glass.

'Baby, take it easy with the booze, okay? I'll work out a good deal for us, I promise. I'll be back before you know it.'

Solomzi stole a glance at her and gulped down the drink. 'Okay, look. I think I'm going to head out to Fridays. Meet up with Khehla and the boys. Be good. Be strong at this meeting, okay?'

He gave her a quick peck on the cheek and was gone. A minute later Moshidi heard his car starting up.

He really was behaving a little strangely, she thought. No doubt the burden of the debt to Serame was stressing him. It was understandable. He was the one who'd gotten them into this financial mess. He should have come to her sooner, but still . . .

She would talk to this man, draw up a feasible repayment plan.

As bad as Soli's judgement had been in acquiring so much debt, when it came to numbers, Moshidi's was sound and she could be very convincing, as well as practical. They would pay the man back but right now what they needed was some breathing room. Their current overheads were overwhelming. There had to be a better way.

She considered the pants suit laid out on her bed and decided she'd feel ridiculous looking so formal on a Sunday. She settled for the black dress she had initially intended to wear.

She went to inspect her children, who were in their playroom, sucked in by the various gadgets they were allowed on weekends.

'Hello, little people. I'm stepping out for a while. *Sisi* Lizzie is taking you to bed at nine, okay? No misbehaving. Agreed?'

'Can't we stay up a little later, just for one night?' said Kopollo, chancing his luck because both parents were going out.

'Tomorrow's a school day,' said Moshidi. 'You are already getting an extra hour. Unless you want to sleep at eight as usual . . . ?'

They all groaned.

'Okay. So let's be happy with the nine o'clock curfew then. Good ni-ght,' she said, sing-song.

In the car, she started reciting the key points of her speech to Mr Serame. She was confident this was going to be a good meeting.

It was serendipitous that the meeting was taking place in The Parks area – her and Soli's favourite dining district. Almost as if that first confrontation they had had at Wombles about Moreti Investments was coming full circle.

As she drove up the hilly incline leading up to the majestic Four Seasons Hotel in Parkview, she wondered once more who this Edward Serame was and why he would choose such a swanky meeting place. A man of means, obviously, which explained how he was able to loan her husband such a hefty amount, but that wasn't much to go on and Soli had been reluctant to talk about him. She'd looked him up on the internet, but there wasn't much info there either, apart from a not very good photo of the man. Enough to recognise him though.

If she was honest, she was irritated about the whole arrangement. But she had resolved to support Soli and help unburden him of the heavy load he'd been carrying by himself. She and her husband were a team. Blaming him for his miscalculated debt was not going to solve their problems.

A porter at the hotel's entrance showed her the way to the hotel lounge, but the only person there was a tired-looking barman, who suggested she try the restaurant.

Edward Serame was sitting at a table in the far corner. He was dressed in a smart shirt and slacks. Moshidi was glad to have trusted her instincts. She would have felt ridiculous in a pants suit.

As she walked towards his table, he stood up and greeted her with a wide smile. He wasn't exactly a tall man, she noted; he barely came up to her shoulder.

'Ah. Moshidi . . . such a pleasure to finally meet you,' he said as he extended his arms for a surprisingly warm hug.

She embraced him awkwardly and took a seat opposite him.

He gazed at her, eyes twinkling. 'I'm really glad you made the time to meet with me,' he said.

'Well . . . I'm happy to meet you too. My husband has told me a lot about you.'

'Yes. Yes. Likewise. Do you want a glass of wine? This is a great Chardonnay. Though Solomzi says you're a champagne lover. Is that what you'd prefer?'

Moshidi was genuinely surprised at how pleasant Mr Serame seemed. She'd expected a nuts-and-bolts businessman and a professional meeting in the lounge. No social niceties.

Maybe this was going to be easier than she'd anticipated.

'A glass of Chardonnay would be just fine, Mr Serame,' she said. 'Thank you.'

He called the waiter over and ordered a glass to be brought for Moshidi.

'Please call me Edward,' he said, smiling. 'No need to be so formal.'

'Edward, then.' Moshidi smiled back.

'So, how's the world of purchasing at the bank?'

'It's good. Great. Very challenging, but I enjoy every minute of it.'

'I'm sure you do. Is the bank progressive in its transformation agenda? Do you give preference to poor black suppliers like us?'

Ah. The penny dropped. No wonder the man was being so courteous. He was hoping to do business with the bank.

'Yes. In fact, I'm one of the people championing our empowerment programme. We've really changed the way we do business with our suppliers, but I tell you, it wasn't easy.'

He nodded.

The waiter arrived with a glass, polishing it with a napkin before placing it gently on the table. At a nod from Serame he took the bottle from the ice-bucket beside his chair and poured a couple of centimetres for Moshidi.

'Have a taste and tell me how you like it,' said Serame.

She sipped the wine and smiled. 'Very nice.' She nodded. 'Almost as good as my favourite champagne.'

He laughed. 'I knew you were a formidable woman. Do you remember the first time we met?'

She was completely baffled. She could not recall meeting the man before. She shook her head. 'Now I'm embarrassed. I'm sorry. I'm usually very good with remembering people . . .'

He laughed at her slight discomfort. 'No, to be fair, you probably wouldn't remember. We were not formally introduced. I only observed you from a distance. But I was absolutely taken by your beauty.'

Ooo-kay. This was a little odd. Serame was a charmer, for sure.

'I hope we can enjoy a starter before we have our main course?'

Good God, Moshidi thought. Dinner.

This was going to be a long night.

'I've actually already eaten,' she said. 'I don't think I'd manage a main course. Maybe I'll just have a starter . . .'

He smiled. 'That's great. I'm so glad to hear that,' he said, seeming to enjoy himself. 'I love that dress. It looks so good on you. You have the perfect body to pull it off. You're really a stunning woman, Moshidi.'

She shook her head. This was really awkward.

'So . . . I'd like us to discuss the loan that you gave to my husband . . . Edward.'

He looked at her and licked his lips. 'What about it?' he asked.

She took another sip of wine, ready to launch into her winning proposal. 'Well, you know, the business has taken a few knocks over the past year or two but we're getting back on track. We have a few projects that need some considerable capital investment on our side so we need a bit of breathing room in terms of the repayment plan . . . I was hoping we could look through some proposals I've drafted . . . ?' Moshidi gingerly felt for her handbag, intending to whisk out her tablet.

'No, no, no,' said Edward, gesturing with his hand.

She stopped in mid-whisk.

'Moshidi,' he said, reaching across the table and taking her hand. 'Really. There's no need for all that. This' – he looked emotional – 'this is enough. Please.'

She shrugged, nonplussed. 'But . . . I think it's important that we talk about this.'

'No, listen,' he said, leaning into her. 'This – is enough for me. You don't know how thrilled I was when you finally said you'd meet with me. I've been dreaming about this day since I first laid eyes on you.'

She shook her head. 'I don't . . . I don't understand.'

He patted her hand gently, then cupped it into his. 'When I said that this would be enough, I meant it. It's the promise I made to your husband, and trust me, I'm very discreet.'

'What is enough?' she asked, feeling more confused than ever.

'I've booked our room . . . I actually took the honeymoon suite. I know you're very private. And I promised Soli it would only be one night . . . and that's it. That's all . . . you know. And you never know – maybe we strike up a connection and we want to develop it into something more . . . who knows? But, baby, that's entirely up to you.'

Suddenly her head started spinning. She thought back to the dream she'd had, the one with her personal trainer replacing her husband. Was this another dream . . . or was this really happening? What was this man saying exactly?

'So . . . you say you . . . what did you agree to with my husband?'

'Exactly what he told you. One night. Then the debt is gone. All of it. Moshidi, I have millions in my bank account. I'm not bragging but honestly, money has taught me to appreciate the real things in life. The things that matter. I first saw you at Inanda. The polo match? You were wearing this little black-and-white dress and these huge sunglasses. You looked like a queen. I wanted you instantly. And I've never stopped wanting you. I can't help it. It's the only reason I befriended Soli. I'm sorry to say that. But the heart wants what it wants. When you called, I was over the moon! And I loved that you took the bull by the horns!' he exclaimed, pumping his fists like a cheerleader.

Moshidi stared at him in confusion.

'You're so exciting. Exactly the woman I imagined you to be! Please . . .' he said softly with that smile again, 'please do me the honour of spending the night with me. Then . . .' He shrugged bashfully. 'Then we'll see where that takes us.'

Moshidi stood up, her body trembling uncontrollably. She took a deep breath, grabbed her wine glass and threw the contents in his face.

'Fuck you! You think I'm for sale? What the hell? Disgusting pig!' She grabbed her bag and bolted out of the place, tears foiling her eyes.

She hated Solomzi. Despised him with every fibre of her being.

Her own husband! The father of her children.

Could she ever face seeing him again, knowing what he'd done? Could she lie in the same bed with him? Wake up next to him every day? Never! This was the ultimate betrayal.

She was shaking with rage. She could barely drive.

This was the last straw. Her husband had literally prostituted her to one of his golf buddies for money. Another one of his gambles, but this time *she* was the pawn in the game. Unbelievable!

When she realised she'd run a red light, she forced herself to calm down. She began to question everything about her and Solomzi's marriage. Had any of it ever been real? She thought back to their first meeting at Thandi's penthouse. Had he scoped her out because of who and what she was at the time? He had been quite intentional about plucking her out of the many women at that party. Had he picked her based on her ambition: ergo, her prospects in life? Was she naive to have thought that he'd just fallen head over heels in love with her at first sight?

At this very moment, nothing about her relationship felt genuine, even though it was ten years and three children later. Not when her husband could offer her body in a sexual bet with another man.

She kept shaking her head.

Her mind was made up. It was over. If there was ever a sign that she needed to end her shallow marriage, then this was it.

As she reached her driveway, she pulled into the garage, ready for war. Solomzi's car was not there. The nerve. Surely he wasn't still at Fridays? She called him on his cell.

'Where are you?' she demanded.

'I'm on my way, *sthandwa sam.*'

She dropped the phone irritably. As she walked out of the garage to go upstairs to change, she kept murmuring under her breath, preparing to unleash her rage.

She checked in on the kids, who were fast asleep. Their nanny had already retired to her quarters. She looked at the time – 10 p.m.

Mxm! Worse – where did he think *she* was?

Having sex with Edward Serame? Really?

She was going to divorce him. That's what she was going to do. This was unforgivable.

She marched to her bedroom, took off the black dress and threw it towards the walk-in closet, hardly believing the experience she had just had.

She kept shaking her head.

Should she call Lerato? No. She was probably sleeping by now, and she had her big presentation tomorrow. Besides, she was too mortified by what she had just experienced. She wondered if she'd ever be able to tell anyone about what her husband had done.

After changing into her sleepwear, she went downstairs to get herself a glass of whisky.

Then she got into bed and waited . . . whisky in hand.

Twenty minutes later, she heard Solomzi's car veer into the driveway.

She heard the garage door opening.

She was poised for a fight.

Solomzi came into the bedroom. He went up to her, stuck his hands into his pockets and stood there, swaying slightly.

'So . . . how did the meeting go?' he asked.

She could tell he was drunk. Heavily drunk.

Moshidi shook her head. 'How do you expect the meeting went, Solomzi? Do you want to hear the details? All of them? Do you think you can take it?'

'What . . . why . . . eh – what do you mean by the details? Hm? What did you do?'

'I did what you agreed I would do. What else did you expect?'

'You . . . you did . . . you did what . . . what wait . . .' He was stammering and staggering.

Now she was violently indignant.

She rose up and looked him square in the face. 'Fuck you, arsehole!' she said, pushing him. 'What the fuck do you take me for? You really thought that I would sleep with that man for *money*? For a debt that you took so I could spread my legs?' she said, her face contorted with rage. She was punching him on the chest with sad, weak and depleted fists.

'Was any of it ever real, Solomzi? Has this . . . has this only ever been about money to you?' she wailed, mascara-stained tears marking her pain, as if challenging him to not look away.

She faced him, wanting to wound him with her words. 'Did you choose me because you thought I'd be the one to make money for you? Is that all you ever saw in me?'

He was shaking his head vigorously. 'No! Never!' he said firmly. 'I love you, baby. I just didn't think things would go this far.' He staggered towards her, reaching out both arms as if to embrace her.

She pushed him away. 'Don't touch me, you bastard! You disgust me! You're not a man. You have no fucking pride!' she said, spitting in his face.

'Hey! Hey! Hey!' he said, pointing a finger at her. He could barely stand up straight. Such was his drunken state.

She pushed him out the door. 'Get out! Get out! I never want to see you again. Tomorrow, I expect you to pack your bags and get out of my life! You hear me!'

She slammed the door shut in her husband's face and turned the key in the lock.

She was shaking with fury.

Monday – Moshidi

Moshidi got up early on Monday morning, showered, got dressed and took the kids to school – she'd done her bit on their overheads by cancelling the morning driver.

She did not check in on Soli, who was asleep in the guest room.

She went to work feeling exhausted and irritable. She hadn't slept a wink the night before.

She gave Lerato a quick call to wish her luck with her presentation, but she still couldn't bring herself to tell her sister about her encounter with Serame. It was just too humiliating.

When she returned from work, she found a quiet and sombre-looking Solomzi sitting in the lounge watching television with the kids.

'Hey, little gang of munchkins. How was school today?' she said, ignoring him completely.

'Mom, it was my friend Thato's birthday today. I want to show you what she had in her party pack!' said an enthusiastic Zozo. She ran to her bedroom to fetch the source of her excitement.

The boys said, 'Hi, Mom,' and went back to watching the cartoon they were deeply absorbed in.

She didn't say anything to Solomzi, who'd looked up to greet her.

She went upstairs to change and within minutes, Solomzi was in the bedroom with her.

'*Sthandwa* . . . I'm so sorry. I can explain everything. It's all a big misunderstanding.'

She shook her head and admonished him with a raised finger. 'You have humiliated me in the worst way possible. The worst way. I will never forgive you for what you've done. You hear me? I could forgive you for getting us into debt – I could honestly live with that. But for you to sell my body for money . . . there's no coming back from that.'

He sat on the bed and looked up at her. 'Baby, I promise, I never thought it would go this far. At the time, things were going really well. We'd just signed that deal with Correctional Services. You know it was supposed to bring millions. When that whole thing with the minister hit the papers, the scandal just left a big hole in the business. When I took the deal with Edward, there was no way I could have anticipated that the Correctional Services deal was going to get canned.'

'What does that have to do with anything?'

'When I asked for the money from Edward, he'd said that I'd better be able to pay the loan or else he'd want to . . . you know, be with you as payment in kind. Honestly, I thought he was joking. And besides, I was confident I was good for it because of our financial position at the time, so I didn't even dwell too much on that.'

She shook her head. 'You don't get it, do you? Are you aware that up till yesterday, when I was standing here with you, talking about that meeting, you had a choice to prevent me from humiliating myself with that man? Up to that point, you knew that if I presented myself at that meeting, his assumption would be that I was there to sleep with him, hmm? Yet you let me leave my house, dressed to the nines, to unknowingly offer myself as a prize for erasing your debt? Do you actually understand what you've done here? To my pride? My self-esteem?'

'I'm so sorry, Moshidi. I tried to stop you . . . don't you remember that? I really tried. I had no idea you'd gone and called him again after you'd snatched my phone that one time. I honestly didn't think it would go this far.'

'Listen, save me the platitudes. This marriage has been at a dead end for a while now. There's just no love or honour in this anymore. When I said yes to you, I wasn't forming a corporation. I could have gone to CIPC for that, you know. I thought I was starting a lifelong union with someone I loved. But you! Selling me to the highest bidder is just proof that you were never in this for the right reasons.'

He buried his head in his hands. 'Please, Moshidi . . . give me a chance to make it up to you. For the sake of our kids. Our properties. Everything we've built together.'

'Ha! He says "our properties". I'd have been surprised if you hadn't mentioned those. *Ntate*, we . . . don't worry about your precious properties, okay? At this point, I just want to save my sanity, find myself . . . my true self, away from all this stuff that has blinded you to what really matters in life. So, don't worry about all the bling we've accumulated. I'm not going to get into an ugly tussle with you about all that. If you can sell me for money, I'd hate to fight you on material stuff cos I don't know what else you're capable of. All I want from you is a quick, painless divorce. Do you think you can help me with that?'

Moshidi brushed past him and walked downstairs, leaving Solomzi staring after her.

'Where are you going?' he called out.

'None of your business,' she snapped back.

'When will you be home? Moshidi?'

Moshidi turned and stared daggers at him.

'Maybe never,' she said.

Monday – Lerato

Lerato was stressed. The presentation to the executive committee had not gone well. The CRM system she and her team had been working so hard on designing for the telecoms merger had had a lukewarm reception at best.

Their solution was deemed 'poor, unsophisticated and below par for a senior team' at Optima Data.

She was crushed. Although the criticism was detailed in highlighting the shortfalls of their solution, she was still gutted that something they had worked on for so long was deemed unsatisfactory. After the brutality of the meeting, she felt light-headed and her heart was racing uncomfortably.

She needed to calm down. She'd taken her hypertension medication in the morning, but she was sure her light-headedness was due to the strain of the meeting.

She texted Lawrence, asking what time he'd be able to knock off. He texted back:

Hey, babe. How did the meeting go?

Awful. It was a bloodbath. I need you. Please tell me you can knock off early.

Let me get a client meeting out of the way. I should be free by 4.

Perfect. Tell me when you get home and I'll come through.

She sat at her desk and drank the bottle of lemon water that she always kept handy for her occasional light-headedness. She did some deep breathing and nibbled at some nuts and dried fruit, wishing the time away, waiting anxiously for Lawrence's text.

She still could not believe how much this man had come to mean to her in such a short space of time. Her body instantly came alive at the sight of him. She had never known such passion in her life. Making love to him was so different to anything she had experienced before. She couldn't wait to see him. She wished she could be with him every single day.

Just then, her husband called.

'Hey, sweetness. How did the meeting go?'

She sighed. 'It was awful. They didn't like our solution at all. Still lots more coding work to do . . . I feel I've let my team down because when they were pointing out our shortfalls, I could see exactly where we went wrong. I don't know . . . I think I'm losing my edge.'

'Aww. Come home. I'll give you a massage.'

'I have to put in a few more hours. I'll probably be home a bit late tonight.'

'Are you sure? Please take it easy,' said Mzwandile.

'I will. Thank you.'

After she dropped the call, she hung her head in shame and frustration. Was this really her life? She was practically having two conversations with two men about the same thing almost every day.

Last week, she'd surprised Lawrence with dinner at his apartment. He'd cut her a key to his place so she could work there anytime the strain at the office became too much for her.

She'd decided to cook for him for the first time; but then she'd had to go home because Bongani called to say he'd lost his house key so he couldn't gain access to the house and Mzwandile was working late.

When she got home, she found her son tired and moody because of a bad day at school. She decided to cook him his favourite dinner, which meant that she'd cooked two dinners for two separate households in one day.

She wondered how polygamists coped with running multiple households. But of course, they were mostly men, so you could be sure they never needed to cook for both *small house* and *big house*.

Her life was a soap opera.

At around ten past four, she called Lawrence.

'Babe, I need to get out of this office . . . Can I come over yet?'

'You've got a key, Lerato. I don't know why you still ask for permission to come through. But I've just walked in the door – so come home, babe. I'm here.'

At four thirty, she drew up at the entrance to Lawrence's complex. She smiled at Jabu, the security guard on duty, signed the visitor logbook he handed to her and parked in her usual visitors' bay.

She took her handbag and stepped out of the car. She really wasn't feeling good. She felt dizzy. Like she was about to have an anxiety attack. Her heart was beating fast. She really needed to take it easy, she thought, stopping for a moment to allow the dizziness to clear, taking a few deep breaths.

When she got to the apartment, Lawrence was standing at the door, looking at her with such concern in his eyes that her heart just melted.

'Geez, look at you. No one died. I'm okay, I promise,' she said as she went in for a much-needed hug.

Lawrence closed the door behind her and held her to his chest. 'Are you sure you're okay, babe?' he asked.

She nodded.

He took her by the hand and led her to the lounger. He took off her shoes and started rubbing her feet.

'I'm sorry it didn't go as you expected. What did they say?'

She sighed. 'Look . . . it's not a complete disaster. But it means we're going to have to pull in extra hours for about another week and a half to get it to where it needs to be. I'm so exhausted I feel like . . . I don't know how I'm going to get the energy to do all that extra work in such a short space of time.'

He kept rubbing her feet. 'Have you eaten today?'

She shook her head. 'Not really. Just some nuts and dried fruit after the presentation.'

Lawrence went to the kitchen and washed his hands. In a few minutes, he was back with two glasses of red wine and a warm meal. He'd ordered takeaway before Lerato arrived.

'Here – I got you Nando's . . . and some wine. Calm down and relax,' he said as he went to sit on the lounger, propping himself behind her and hugging her.

She absentmindedly chewed on the food, then took the wine glass and had a few sips. It was very relaxing. She couldn't believe she was now a wine drinker of sorts. She only ever drank with Lawrence, but it still shocked her how much this relationship had changed her.

They both emptied their wine glasses, not talking, just enjoying being together.

Then, when he felt her body starting to ease down, Lawrence took Lerato by the hand and led her to the bedroom.

He slowly undressed her, drinking her body in, kissing her on her neck, nibbling her ears, sucking her nipples till her body felt warm and fluid, like melted chocolate.

By the time he entered her, she was completely lost in the moment. All thoughts of the project, the stress of work, simply dissipated into the merging of their bodies. He took her in different positions, each time leading her to powerful climaxes that felt like waves crashing into each other.

When they were both spent from the passion and ecstasy of their union, they moulded into each other's arms and drifted off into contented sleep.

Tuesday

His body felt electrified from within. Sparks of anxiety charged through him as he held the phone and dialled the local police station for the umpteenth time.

He paced the kitchen, worried sick about his wife.

Where was she?

She had not come home last night.

This was a completely foreign occurrence in all their years of marriage.

She had been acting strangely lately, yes, but he'd put it down to . . . all of their . . . stresses, complications. And last night – well . . .

But no. This was not her.

Something was wrong.

He had already been to the police station to file a missing person's report, but the police didn't seem inclined to take the matter seriously. They said that for an adult to be considered missing a forty-eight-hour period was required.

Wives went 'missing' all the time, the desk sergeant told him.

He'd filed the affidavit regardless.

They didn't know his wife.

The Car

Jabulani Khambule settled on the couch in his bachelor pad – a one-roomed cottage that had been built at the back of his mother's house in Thokoza, Soweto. He liked to call it a cottage because that's what people in the suburbs called back rooms, even if his friends laughed at him whenever he used the word.

'This is the hood, bro. A back room is a back room. There are no cottages here,' they'd mock him.

But he always hoped for better days ahead. Working in the suburbs every day did that to you. It made you long for things that maybe you had no business longing for. Seeing your fellow black folk driving around in fancy cars, ordering pizza every day, drinking nice drinks. Why them and not him? Just a few years ago they were living in the same type of four-roomed house as his. Was the struggle against apartheid only for the benefit of a few chosen bastards?

He went to the mini-bar fridge by the main door of his cottage, opened it and grabbed a bottle of beer. He was through feeling guilty about drinking on a weekday and cared not that it was only ten in the morning. Not when he had to wake up in this dingy room every day. No girlfriend, lousy pay, and stuck at that job for God knows how long.

He'd worked the day shift yesterday at the townhouse complex he called his workplace and was bracing himself for the night shift that awaited him. It started at 6 p.m. so he reckoned he could enjoy his drink, watch TV, then sleep it off before waking in the afternoon to get ready. The night was only his companion when it involved drinking and tavern-hopping with his friends. That was what nights were for; not guarding the homes of the privileged.

He looked for the TV remote. The place was a mess. The two-seater couch took up most of the space he referred to as his living room. The bed was just a metre away from the couch. He had arrived home after his shift and strewn his clothes on the floor. His mother usually did his laundry on Friday, so he only needed to pack everything into the laundry basket on Thursday.

He finally located the remote wedged between the couch cushions and channel-surfed until he settled on the news. He was glad his mother had installed cable TV; he only enjoyed watching the news and sports.

He sipped his beer lazily but stopped and sat up straight when he saw a black Mercedes-Benz beaming out of the screen and what looked like a crime scene, sealed off with that yellow police tape, and a news reporter standing in front of it.

He turned up the volume.

'. . . on Rivonia Road in the early hours of this morning. The woman's body was found in the driver's seat. The name of the deceased, a police spokesperson said, has not been released pending investigation into the cause of death. They declined to say whether foul play was suspected but are calling on anyone who has any information to come forward.'

He banna!

He knew that car – and that registration number!

Not only that, but he had seen it as recently as yesterday, an hour or so before he'd knocked off at 6 p.m. when his colleague Sam came on duty.

It belonged to that fancy woman who came to visit the Zimbabwean guy in his complex. Like all visitors had to do, she signed in at the gate. He had always been curious about her. She came at odd hours but didn't usually stay longer than an hour or two. She never stayed the night, which made him wonder if she might be married. She was quite a bit older than the Zimbabwean guy, although he could see why he would be attracted to her. She had a beautiful engaging face, and always a smile for him and a wave when she left again.

He hadn't looked to see whether she wore a wedding ring, but he harboured some resentment. He hated how foreigners felt they could sleep around with women in South Africa. Was it not enough that a South African like him was working security while foreigners like that Zim guy carried on as though they owned the land? Now he had to watch helplessly while they slept with married women too?

Ja-ne. Everything was wrong with this country these days.

He thought about what he'd just witnessed on the news. He hoped they'd repeat the story during the ten-thirty news slot. There had been a number to call on the bottom of the screen but it was gone before he could write it down. That foreigner probably had something to do with her death.

But first he should phone Sam. He dialled his colleague's number but the call went unanswered. Damn!

He gulped down his beer and went to the fridge to get another. He could feel the adrenalin kicking in. What he wouldn't give for that *kwerekwere* to have something to do with this woman's death! He-he! Payback time. The underdog also deserved some triumphs in life.

And this was a big one. He could already imagine himself regaling his friends with the story at the tavern on Saturday.

After the second bottle of beer, he tried Sam again. He picked up the call but within seconds, he heard the dreaded voice of the white woman from the phone company.

'You have insufficient airtime to make a call.'

Voetsek!

Insufficient airtime. Insufficient airtime. *Nywe nywe nywe.*

Now he had to go to the *spaza* shop to buy airtime. *Eish!* He was feeling so lazy today. Was it worth it?

To put a smug *kwerekwere* behind bars? Of course, it was worth it!

He checked his wallet to see if he had any money left. Payday was two days away.

He'd learned to ask his mother to keep his transport money for the month because he knew he could end up spending it all on beer. He had thirty-five rand left.

His mother also made him lunch and takeaway dinner and his transport for the next two days was sorted.

Okay. He would buy twelve rands of airtime, but would it be enough to call Sam *and* the number on the bottom of the screen? *Eish.* Knowing the police, they'd probably put him on hold forever. *Yho!*

No. He had to use his mother's phone.

He brushed his teeth so she wouldn't be able to tell he'd been drinking and went to the main house to talk to her.

Immediately when he walked into the house, she glared at him with an unnecessarily cross expression on her face.

'*Ufunani?* What do you want, *wena?*'

'*Hawu*, Ma. Since when do mothers greet their sons like that?'

'You're a handful, *wena*. I don't have money to lend you. Just know that,' she said irritably.

'I'm not here to ask for money, Ma. A woman has been killed at my complex . . . where I work, Ma. I want to call Sam. Because I think they killed her at the complex.'

'*Yho!* Are you serious? Do these rich people do such barbaric things?'

Jabulani shook his head solemnly. 'My work is tough, Ma. Don't be fooled by their fancy cars and clothes. Those people are savages. Give me your phone. It's urgent. I need to make sure there are no more deaths at the complex.'

'Oh, shame, *mntwanam*. Your job is so dangerous!'

He shrugged. 'I'm just a simple man saving lives. What can I do?'

'*Thatha*. Take the phone. Do your job, my son, but please be careful,' she said as she grabbed her bag from the chair on the table and handed her phone to Jabulani. She slumped on the dining chair, made the sign of the cross and watched him with pride.

Jabulani dialled Sam's number and waited for the voice on the other end.

'Sam. *Unjani?*'

'Hey, I'm trying to sleep, Jabu. Why do you keep calling me?'

'No, man, listen. This is important. You know that woman with the black Merc? The one who visits that Zimbabwean in unit number 89?'

'Hey, bro. I know her. Why?'

'Sam, they found that woman's dead body this morning, *bafo*. On Rivonia Road. What time did she leave yesterday? She came in before I knocked off, but I didn't see her leave.'

'*Bafo*, hey, hey, hey. You know, a strange thing happened last night. In fact, it was early this morning. Around one a.m., I saw that Merc driving out, but it was two guys. I didn't see a woman in the car.'

Running Late

Despite the great show she'd put on for Solomzi last night, after slamming out of the house, Moshidi had spent a miserable hour driving around the suburbs aimlessly. Where did women go after they made a dramatic exit?

She filled the car up at a petrol station on Rivonia Road and got a take-out coffee and a burger from Nando's, which she didn't eat. Then she'd driven home, expecting Soli to be waiting up anxiously for her. When the only sign of him was a gentle snoring from the guest room, she took the remains of the whisky bottle to bed with her and went to sleep in her clothes.

Now she was dressing for work, running late, worrying about the traffic to school – she had an all-day seminar at the office – and she had a very bad headache.

Her phone rang. It was Mzwandile.

'Morning, Moshidi. How are you?'

'Hi, *sbali*. I'm fine. How are you?' she asked, putting on her high heels, phone tucked into her neck.

'Moshidi, have you heard from Lerato?'

'No,' she said absentmindedly. The strap of her heel came off as she was trying to lock the clasp. Good God. This was all she needed. These were one of her favourite pairs. 'Why?' she asked.

'She didn't come home last night.'

'What? That doesn't sound like Lerato,' she said, lines of worry furrowing her forehead. She hoped Lerato hadn't spent the night at Lawrence's. That would be stupid and irresponsible.

Ever since her sister had told her she had feelings for the man, he was all she ever wanted to talk about. She was obsessed with him.

'I'm worried sick, Moshidi. She's not answering my calls. She's been working late most of the past two weeks on her project, but she's never stayed out all night. I don't know . . . I feel like something's seriously wrong.'

Moshidi sat down on the bed and scratched her forehead. She heard his anxiety and now she felt it too. 'Listen, *sbali*. Let me call her quickly. I'll get back to you,' she said.

She dropped the call and immediately rang her sister.

Lerato's phone went straight to voicemail.

What on earth?

Suddenly, she too had a very bad feeling.

She prayed that Lerato hadn't done something stupid. Could she have spent the night with Lawrence without so much as calling Mzwandile to make up an excuse? Or calling her to make one up for her?

This affair – if that was even what it was – was getting out of control. She had known instinctively her sister would get sucked into this relationship.

As soon as she got to the bank she called Lerato at work but was told she hadn't come in yet. Throughout the day-long seminar, whenever she got a quick break she kept trying her sister's phone and got voicemail every time. She tried calling Mzwandile but got voicemail on his phone too.

When she returned from work, she stepped into the house to find an ashen-faced Solomzi staring at her.

'What?' she said.

'Moshidi . . . I'm sorry. It's about Lerato.'

Her hands started shaking uncontrollably. Tears welled in her eyes.

'What? What Solomzi?'

'We've lost her, Moshidi. We've lost Lerato.'

She dropped her handbag on the floor, her whole body crumbling.

'No! Not my sister. Not Lerato!' she wailed as Solomzi held her tight, trying to comfort her.

Bare Facts

How Lawrence had managed to show up for work after what happened last night, he simply didn't know.

He'd had a shower, eaten some fruit, pulled on clean clothes – avoiding looking at the bed – and even said good morning to the security guard on his way out of the complex.

He'd been sitting at his desk for the past hour, staring blankly at his screen. He wished the Perspex panels on either side of him were more opaque so they could block him from his talkative colleague, who was now finally, mercifully, engrossed in his PC, his ears safely snuggled behind earphones.

The phone on his desk rang, jolting him from his dark thoughts.

'Good morning. Please come down to reception. There are some gentlemen looking for you.'

'Ah . . . gentlemen? I don't have a meeting scheduled.'

'It's the police, sir.'

Fear gripped him as he processed what he'd just been told.

So soon? What had happened?

He tried to stand up but felt his legs buckle underneath him.

Frans looked up at him, taking off his headphones.

'Are you okay?'

He just looked at him and nodded, then ambled his way down to reception, taking the stairs. When he reached the foyer, he saw two men seated on the chairs. They were not in uniform, but he could tell they were cops.

They stood up by way of greeting.

'Mr Moyo?' said the taller one.

He nodded, not trusting his voice.

'Can you come with us to the station, sir?' the second cop asked. 'We have some questions relating to your whereabouts in the early hours of this morning.'

'Um . . . can I ask what it's in connection with?'

The policemen exchanged a look.

'It's a delicate issue. I'm sure you wouldn't like us to discuss it here,' the first cop said, eyeing the receptionist. 'I'm Detective Kgomo, by the way.'

The receptionist was surveying the scene with the practised glint of an office gossip.

Was this the moment that up-ended his entire life as he knew it? Were they going to handcuff him? Right here, right now? Was he going to be locked up?

'Eh . . . okay. Is it all right if I follow you in my car?'

Detective Kgomo nodded. 'Sure. You'll find us waiting outside. We're driving a white Toyota Corolla.'

He nodded and took the lift back to his office. He was sweating buckets.

When he got to his desk, he told Frans he'd been called to an emergency. He scooped up his keys, his wallet and his phone. In the corridor as he walked towards the lift he made a call. The phone went unanswered.

Damn!

Who else could he call?

No one. He didn't know anyone else who had legal connections.

He sighed.

Tried a second time while waiting for the lift.

'*Sha*. You okay? I didn't sleep all night—'

'Shit's hit the fan,' he said. 'Police are here. They want me to go with them to the station.'

'Shit. Shit. Shit. Let me call Munyaradzi – he's a good lawyer. I'll call you back. Don't say anything till I can get him to come to the station. Call or text when you get there and tell me which one.'

'Okay . . . I really need you to come through for me, my friend.'

'Trust me. I got you.'

He dropped the line, feeling somewhat relieved. There had to be a way out of this.

In the lift he pressed the button for the basement, got out and walked to his car, feeling his legs trembling. The officers' white Toyota Corolla was idling in the parking lot.

He followed them as they drove out of the office complex towards the Morningside police station.

His phone rang. It wasn't good news.

'Munyaradzi isn't picking up, but I'll keep trying.'

'Shit.' He could see the cop looking at him in his rear-view mirror.

'Admit to nothing. Nothing but the bare facts.'

He found it hard to imagine how he could admit to the facts without incriminating himself but took heart from the fact that they had not charged him with anything. What was it they said in movies? Routine questioning . . . or so he hoped.

When they got to the police station, the two officers walked him to a room which he assumed must be used for police interrogation. He would feel better if he had a lawyer in the room. But . . . asking for a lawyer . . . wouldn't that make him look more suspicious? And anyway, Munyaradzi was so far none the wiser, so stressing about lawyers was irrelevant.

He would use his own wits to traverse the situation . . . for now.

Detective Kgomo started the round of questioning by proffering a photocopy of an ID card and asking: 'Are you familiar with this woman?'

He made a show of examining the photo on the ID, trying not to let his face betray the emotion it evoked in him.

He nodded.

He couldn't believe this was happening.

She looked so young and innocent in that picture. His heart felt like it was collapsing in his chest.

'Mr Moyo? How do you know the lady in this photo?'

He shifted on his weight, fingers interlaced. 'She's my girlfriend,' he said.

The two detectives looked at each other.

The second asked him, 'When did you last see your *girlfriend*?'

He said the word sardonically. Like a swear word.

'Um . . . I saw her yesterday. After she knocked off from work.'

'So, did you pick her up from work, or how did the two of you meet?'

'She called me. Told me she was knocking off early. I asked her to come by.'

'To your place?'

'Yes.'

'Was this the first time she came to your place?'

'No . . . um . . . It's a new relationship, but she's been there a few times.'

The men nodded their heads, jotting down notes on their pads.

'How long have you been in this relationship?' Detective Kgomo asked.

He looked up and to one side, as if trying to recall. In truth, he'd been obsessively analysing everything about their relationship over the past few hours.

'I think it's about two, three months.'

'Is it two months or three months?'

'Um . . . I travel a lot so it's sometimes hard to keep track of time. I'd say it's about three months. Yes. It would be three months now. Or two. Two months.'

Detective Kgomo asked, 'At what time did she come to your apartment, did you say?'

'Yesterday?'

'Yesterday.'

Here we go, he thought miserably. The slippery slope begins.

Should he ask to speak to his lawyer now?

He decided to stall, answer the question with a few questions of his own. That's what they did in the movies.

'Excuse me, why are you asking me all these questions? Is there something wrong . . . if I may ask?'

The other officer shrugged. 'You tell me. *Is* there something wrong? Do *you* know if there's something wrong?'

Now it was his turn to shrug. He wasn't sure whether he quite pulled it off, his shoulders were shaking so much already.

Would I be incriminating myself if I say I'd tried to call her? Damn! I should have tried to call her! But they can check cell phone records, can't they? And they would see I haven't . . . No. Damn! His head was all over the place. *Rather . . . No, I never call her. Not during the daytime. Or I only ever call when she calls first. Which makes sense given her marital status. Yes! That will work.*

'Well . . . you're getting me worried. I mean . . . I don't know what this is about but . . . I probably have to confess that . . . we . . . she's . . . um . . . my girlfriend is a married woman. So I was shocked when you showed me her photo because I was with her yesterday . . . but, you know. I . . . we don't call or text after being together. I don't know if you understand what I'm saying . . . I don't know if I'm in trouble because of her . . . you know. Her marital status.'

'No one said you're in trouble,' Detective Kgomo responded. 'Why would you think you're in trouble?'

He shrugged. 'I don't know. I mean, eh . . . she's a married woman . . . Did something happen to her? With her husband?'

The two detectives looked at each other then, glanced at him.

'Mr Moyo, we are just here to gather facts. Unless of course you know something that will make our job easier. Something you wish to share with us?'

He shook his head.

'So, you say the lady came to visit you yesterday after work? Around what time was that?'

'Around four thirty, four forty-five p.m.'

'And then? Please take us through what happened.'

'She came through and, eh . . . we had a meal . . .'

'Who prepared the meal?'

'Um . . . I did.'

'So how long did that take?'

He shrugged. 'About an hour, give or take.'

'What was she doing while you were preparing the meal?'

'She had a laptop on. She was doing some work.'

The officers scribbled on their notepads.

'Then what happened, Mr Moyo?'

'I finished preparing the meal. We enjoyed it . . . with some wine. Then we, well . . . you know . . .'

'What happened, Mr Moyo?'

'Um . . . we . . . had intercourse.'

'Did she consent to the intercourse?'

'Yes, of course. We are, and have been, in a relationship.'

'Then what happened?' asked Kgomo, jotting on his notepad.

'We chatted, then cuddled. Then we had a nap.'

'Was there any altercation? Disagreement?'

'No. No. We never had any fights.'

'Had? Any reason why you're using the past tense?'

He tried to shrug again, feeling alarmingly exposed. 'Well, I don't know why I'm being questioned. I don't know if this has something to do with her husband maybe . . . finding out about us.'

'Continue. What happened next?'

Had he just fallen into a trap? He tried sounding nonchalant.

'She got up. She usually gets up first . . . So, she took a shower and . . . got dressed, then . . .'

Cameras. Security cameras at the gates. The cameras would have registered the time the car pulled out of the complex. Shit. Shit. Shit.

He wanted to gasp for air but that would be a dead giveaway.

How the fuck did he get into this mess?

'Um . . . then I got up. I was feeling . . . I wanted to spend more time with her. I was being a bit selfish because she always worries about going home on time. To her house, I mean. But for some reason . . . I really needed her last night. I'm deeply in love with her.'

The officers' faces turned cold. They seemed put off.

Maybe he was giving too many details about their love life.

Bare facts. Nothing but the bare facts.

'I mean . . . I obviously never have enough time with her . . . because of her marital status. So yesterday, I insisted . . . I mean, I *asked* . . . her to stay longer.'

'How much longer? What time did she leave your apartment?'

'Very late.'

'What time, Mr Moyo?'

'Um . . . I think it was around one o'clock in the morning . . . yes . . . around one a.m.'

'Did she drive herself out of the complex?'

He started shifting on his weight again. 'No. No, she didn't drive herself. She . . .'

'Yes?' asked Detective Kgomo.

'We'd had a few glasses of wine. She's a light drinker, but she . . . she'd had more than usual. So I asked my friend to come over. Then we drove her out.'

'Your friend came over?'

'Yes. In an Uber.'

'What is the name of your friend?'

Shit. Shit. Shit.

Now it's not only myself I'm incriminating.

But actually. This could work. It could make sense . . .

'His name is Kudzayi Makwembere,' he said. 'He came over. We had one or two more drinks, then we drove her out of the complex, in her car.'

'Who was driving?'

'Me.'

'And where were your friend and the woman?'

'My friend was beside me, in the front passenger seat. She wanted to lie down a bit. She was really out of it. So she was lying on the back seat of the car. So my friend – Kudzayi – suggested we pass by his house. Give her some coffee so she could sober up before she drove herself home.'

'Why didn't she have coffee at your house?'

'Um . . . I don't keep coffee at my place.'

'So, you drove out of your place at what time?'

'One o'clock, one a.m. . . . . Around that time. In the morning.'

'Just to get coffee at your friend's place?'

'No. But my friend was worried . . . about how drunk she was, so then he suggested we stop by his place. In Sandhurst. It's not far from my home.'

'O-kay. And then what happened?'

'We pulled into my friend's place in Sandhurst. Had some coffee. But then she still wanted us to drive her out. She's not much of a drinker and she's not used to driving at that time of day . . . night . . . day . . . '

'And then what happened?'

'We drove her halfway, then took an Uber back home.'

'Hmph. Such gentlemen. Halfway where?'

Shit.

Cameras. Johannesburg cameras.

'By the gas station on Rivonia Road. Then we took an Uber back home.'

'So, you had quite a night, *neh*?'

He folded his arms. Was it over?

'Is she okay? I hope she didn't get in trouble with her husband?'

'Mr Moyo, your girlfriend is dead,' said Detective Kgomo, leaning closer to enjoy studying his face for a reaction.

'Oh my God! What?'

And then Lawrence Moyo broke down and cried, burying his head in his hands.

'Okay, Mr Moyo, okay,' said Detective Kgomo, turning over to a clean page in his notebook. 'Now tell us what really happened.'

Kudzayi

Kudzayi. He will call Kudzayi. He always knows what to do in a crisis.

Thirty minutes later he hears a knock on his apartment door. His heart leaps in fright. He peeps through the keyhole and then opens the door hurriedly.

'What's wrong, man? You sounded agitated on the phone,' says Kudzayi, striding into the lounge. 'You don't look good. Here, have a cigarette.'

He takes the cigarette gratefully and places it between his lips for Kudzayi to light it. He hasn't smoked in two years.

He starts pacing, the walls closing in on him like prison bars.

'So, what's going on?' Kudzayi asks, settling down on the couch and lacing his fingers together.

'It's bad, man. Really bad. Shit, I'm in so much trouble.'

'What happened?'

He gazes at the floor and notices a red wine stain on the carpet, only now it looks more ominous, like blood oozing out of the carpet.

'It's my girlfriend, man. She's . . . she's gone.'

'Hey, I'm sorry, man. You said you were really into her. I'm sorry she's gone.'

'Not that kind of gone, Kudzayi,' he says, still pacing. 'The other kind of gone.'

Kudzayi stares at him. 'Wait. What? Your girlfriend – she's dead?'

He nods. Points towards the bedroom with his chin. 'In there.'

Kudzayi jumps to his feet. 'Oh fuck! Oh fuck! Didn't you say she's married?'

He stops pacing for a moment and stands looking at his friend, glass-eyed. 'I have a big problem, man,' he says.

'Shit. What happened? You guys have an argument? What the hell . . . ?'

'It wasn't like that—'

'You do realise you're a foreign national, right? What do you think is going to happen to you if you kill a South African woman – a married *South African woman* – that you just happen to be shagging? You're going to jail, my friend. If the husband doesn't kill you first!'

Kudzayi is panicking more than he is. He smacks Kudzayi on the head.

'You think I don't know I'm in trouble?' he says. 'That's why I called you – to help me figure out what to do. And stop being an idiot. I loved that woman. I wanted to marry that woman.'

Tears fall mercilessly down his face and his body folds on to the couch. He is overcome with fatigue and despair.

Kudzayi shakes his head, hands on his hips. After a while, he sits down next to his friend and pats him on the leg.

'Sorry, man, if I was insensitive. I know you told me how you feel about her, but you shouldn't have let this thing come this far. Married people are a different breed, man. You don't wanna be mixed up with them. So . . . what exactly happened?' He drags on his cigarette, giving a nervous look in the direction of the bedroom.

'She called around four p.m. today saying she was knocking off early at work. I told her to come over, so she pulled in here around like . . . four forty-five, five p.m. She's usually tense when she's here at the apartment. She's a good girl, you know. She's never been comfortable with the fact that she's cheating on her husband. I offered her a massage and gave her a glass of wine. We chatted, had more wine and then we . . . you know . . .'

'Had sex.'

'Yes.'

'And then?' asks Kudzayi.

'Then we sort of cuddled for a while. I drifted off to sleep. I assumed she also did. When I woke up, I tried to wake her . . . And that was it.'

'That was what?'

'She was gone, Kudzayi. Gone.'

Kudzayi puts out his cigarette and stands up straight.

'You're sure that's it?'

'What do you mean by that?' asks Lawrence with a tinge of anger in his voice.

'I mean . . . you guys didn't get into a fight or anything like that? Accidents happen . . .'

Lawrence raises his hands in exasperation. 'I didn't do anything to harm her! What the hell do you take me for?'

'Okay, okay. I just wanted to be sure, all right? Come on,' he says, standing up decisively. 'We are going to have to move the body.'

'Move the body?'

'Lucky I came in an Uber,' says Kudzayi. 'Is that her car in the visitors' bay?'

Thursday

'Mr Msibi. It's Detective Karabo Kgomo at the Morningside police station. How are you, sir?'

How was he? Mzwandile was inconsolable with grief.

His wife had been found on Tuesday morning, her body in the driver's seat of her Mercedes, slumped over the steering wheel, dead of a heart attack just a couple of months shy of her forty-first birthday.

How did the detective think he was doing?

'We're trying, Detective,' he said. 'We're trying. How can I help you?'

'The pathologist's report has been sent to us. We know how anxious you were to get confirmation on the cause of your wife's death. Would you be able to come to the station for the full report?' said Detective Kgomo.

'Erm . . .' Mzwandile said, looking to see if his sons were within earshot. They had taken the news of their mother's death very badly. He wanted to save them from as much grief as possible. 'Ah . . . yes. I think I can drop in . . . maybe this afternoon?'

'Yes. Can you come through at two o'clock?'

'Okay. I'll be there. Goodbye, Detective.'

Mzwandile called his friend Kgothatso, one of the Amadodana from his church group, and asked him if he would accompany him to the station. His church group had been his source of support since the nightmare of Lerato's passing. They came as soon as they heard the news on Tuesday and since then the house had not been empty, what with the church, Moshidi and Solomzi, and Lerato's family and her friends. There was much to be done, the funeral to be planned, the funeral policy to be accessed. He didn't know why he had to come to the police station.

At the front desk he asked for Detective Kgomo. A call was placed by one of the officers to let the detective know of Mzwandile's arrival.

After about thirty minutes of anxious waiting, Kgomo emerged.

'*Dumela, Ntate* Msibi. How are you?'

'I'm okay, Detective. This is Kgothatso Moabelo. A brother and friend.'

Detective Kgomo nodded in acknowledgement. 'Er . . . I think it would be better if I spoke to you alone, sir, if you don't mind. There's some sensitive information I need to share with you.'

'Oh,' said Mzwandile in surprise.

Lerato's body had shown no signs of foul play or brute force. Mzwandile had informed the police about her high blood pressure. The assumption was that she had died from cardiac arrest, so he was surprised at the detective's tone of voice.

He had a quiet talk with Kgothatso, then followed the detective to his office.

'This is the pathologist's report,' the detective told Mzwandile, pulling out some notes from a brown file on his desk and placing a piece of paper with a diagram of a body on it before him. 'As you can see, there are some marks – some bruising – on the deceased's body. These show that your wife's body was either moved or was bumped against some surfaces. The bruising does not look like it's from forceful impact.'

'I see,' said Mzwandile, still puzzled.

'I would also like to draw your attention to the estimated time of death. Here you can see that the pathologist estimates the deceased to have suffered from a heart attack at around six p.m. on Monday evening.'

'I see,' Mzwandile said again, although he didn't.

'About twelve hours before she was found in her vehicle parked on Rivonia Road,' the detective said. When Mzwandile didn't say anything, he went on. 'The official cause of death is cardiac arrhythmia. She had an irregular heartbeat. Which is consistent with what you told us about her issues with high blood pressure.'

Mzwandile was still baffled. 'This doesn't make any sense,' he said, as if talking to himself.

He read the full report, but the more he tried decoding it, the more he felt like he was going down a rabbit hole.

Finally, he shook his head. 'This doesn't make sense,' he repeated, still half talking to himself. 'So you are saying she was dead before she got into her car? I don't understand. How's that even possible?'

'Mr Msibi, are you familiar with a man named Lawrence Moyo?'

Perplexed at this odd question, Mzwandile shook his head.

The detective took a deep breath. '*Shoo*, okay. Erm . . . Mr Msibi, your wife . . . er . . . had visited Mr Moyo on the day of her death.'

'Wh-what? Why?'

'Apparently, she had been frequenting this man's apartment over a period of time.'

'What are you implying?'

The detective just looked at him.

Mzwandile gasped. 'No. Not Lerato. There must be a mistake. Detective, I don't know if you understand the type of person my wife is. Unless Mr Moyo is a colleague or a client, there is no way that she would be going to a man's house.'

Detective Kgomo regarded Mzwandile with an expression that looked like pity. 'I'm sorry, Mr Msibi, but we got a tip-off from the security guard at the complex where Lawrence Moyo stays. Your wife had been to that apartment more than twenty times in the past six weeks. We checked the visitors' logbook to confirm. On the day in question – Monday, that is – your wife arrived at the complex at four thirty. We have CCTV footage that shows her Mercedes pulling in. We also have her signature.'

Mzwandile emitted a lone cry. It sounded hollow, like a man sinking into a bottomless well.

'Mr Msibi, are you okay?' the detective asked. 'Do you need a glass of water?'

Mzwandile nodded.

The detective left Mzwandile to digest the news. When he returned, he gave him the glass and looked at him as Mzwandile allowed the cool liquid to cascade down his throat. He felt sorry for the man. Clearly, he was the strict and disciplinarian type and he seemed to be under the impression that his late wife was the same.

Poor bugger. He'd seen a few of these types of cases.

But how this one had unfolded was another matter. That was definitely a first for him.

'We have been investigating Mr Moyo's involvement in your wife's death,' Detective Kgomo continued. 'We have interviewed him at the station here. He has confirmed that he had an, um . . . intimate relationship with your wife.' The words fell rapidly, like drops of rain on a tin roof, with no reaction from the man sitting in front of him. 'Although Mrs Msibi died from natural causes, we believe we have a strong case to prove that he was complicit in covering up the nature and cause of her death. And moving her body, of course. I can't tell you precisely what the charges will be, maybe obstruction of justice, but a case has been opened against him. I thought you would want to be apprised of these developments.'

Mzwandile seemed lost in a fog. The detective wondered if he had registered anything he had just told him, whether he should repeat it.

'Mr Msibi? Are you okay?'

Mzwandile looked up at him. He was silent for an uncomfortable while.

Eventually, he blinked and said, 'Thank you, Detective. Will that be all?'

The detective nodded, gathering the notes back into the file.

'We will keep you updated on—'

But the chair was empty. Mzwandile was already gone.

Preparations

Around 4 p.m. Moshidi was in her car, having gone to buy more groceries for the Msibi household. She called Mzwandile.

'Hello,' said Mzwandile.

'Hi, *sbali*. I'm on my way to the house. Are you at home?'

'Yes. Your parents are also here. I will see you.'

Moshidi was too distracted to notice his icy tone.

As per custom, various relatives from both sides of the family had been gathering at the Msibi household since Tuesday, when news of Lerato's death had first been conveyed.

Neighbours, friends, colleagues and church members kept dropping in; some in groups, others individually. This ritual would continue until the day of the burial. It was customary for those who knew the deceased to visit the family in order to be present with them during this time of mourning. Moshidi had taken it upon herself to make sure they did not run out of necessary items. The church group, who came at 6 p.m. to offer the evening prayer, seemed to drink a lot of tea. Tea-totallers, she thought to herself, then burst into tears. Lerato would have laughed at her stupid joke.

When she got to the house she found Mzwandile in a foul mood. He greeted her, then went upstairs, leaving it to her nephews to assist her with carrying the groceries to the kitchen. Here Mzwandile's aunts and some women from Lerato's church cell group had been busying themselves over the past two days with baking and cooking and preparing teas and coffees for the many guests. Zozo and the twins were on hand to offer scones and cakes to the visitors. The flurry of activity somehow diluted the sombre atmosphere in the Msibi home, with the sense of community created by all the toing and froing making the grieving process a tad more bearable.

Moshidi went into the lounge to see how her parents were doing. She found some elderly members from Mzwandile's church seated with them. Like Lerato, her mother had high blood pressure and she was concerned about her, but they seemed okay for the moment. She went upstairs to find Mzwandile. Her brother-in-law was sitting on the bed he and Lerato had shared, his face both sad and angry.

She closed the door and went to sit with him.

'How are you, *Ndlondlo*?' she said, addressing Mzwandile by his clan name.

He was quiet, staring at his hands. 'You knew. Didn't you?' he said.

'Knew what, Mzi?'

'About Lerato's affair. Tell me the truth, Moshidi.'

Moshidi steepled her fingers and pursed her lips.

Well. That was unexpected.

He gazed at her, but this time Moshidi was unable to read his expression. If she had to describe it, she would say he looked lost. Like he was outside of himself. His eyes looked haunted. The boys had told her he had been to the police station earlier this afternoon, while she was out shopping for food, but only to pick up the pathologist's report.

'Wha—what makes you think . . . ?' she stammered.

'They told me at the police station,' Mzwandile said, and now his voice was trembling with something else, something like anger.

202

'Oh. . . what did they tell you?' she asked.

'No. I would like to know what you knew. You and your sister talked about everything. Were you in support of this affair? Hmm? Did you encourage it?'

The look in his eyes. He'd never looked at her like that before. It was almost menacing.

'Look, *sbali*, I didn't really know much about what was happening with Lerato over the past few . . . days, you know. The main thing she complained about was work. She just seemed overwhelmed.'

'And the affair . . .'

She shrugged. 'Maybe it came about as a result of the stress at work . . . I don't know.'

'But I supported her. Always. You know that. Even on her last . . .' He sighed. 'Even on *that* last day, on Monday. I called her. I checked up on her. I even asked her to come home so I could take care of her. But the joke's on me. Ha! She chose to go to him instead. That's what kills me. She was stressed, I offered to be there for her, but they say the camera doesn't lie. And in this case I mean the CCTV camera. The tapes show her voluntarily going to this man's house.'

An uncomfortable silence.

'I'm so sorry.'

'Look, after what I heard today, I don't know what's going to happen here.'

'What do you mean?'

'Moshidi, when everyone leaves today after the daily prayer, I am going to need to talk to your family. I don't think I can bury your sister.'

'What?! Isn't that a bit extreme? I think maybe you need time to process everything. There's no need to make rash decisions, *sbali*!'

'Shhh . . . you're being loud. There are people here. When everyone leaves, I want a meeting with your family to discuss what I've discovered.'

'But . . . don't you think you need to talk to the boys first? This . . . I don't exactly know what you're thinking, but are you aware that this could destroy them?'

'If your sister had cared about them, she wouldn't have gone and died in the arms of another man.'

'What are you saying, *sbali*? Lerato had a heart attack in her car on her way home from work.'

'A heart attack, yes. But the pathologist's report says she died twelve hours earlier than when they found her in the car. She died at that man's place. He put her in the car and then he left her.'

Moshidi could hardly wrap her mind around what Mzwandile was saying, but he wasn't finished.

'I'm not going to bury a whore in my house,' he added.

'Don't call my sister that! You know she was much better than that!'

'Was she?'

She stood up and slapped him. '*Mxm*. Maybe if you'd been more honest, she wouldn't have had to run into the arms of another man!'

Moshidi stormed out of the bedroom in angry tears.

Friday

Mzwandile started the day by calling a meeting with his sons. He had decided to wait till the next morning before he made his announcement, as Moshidi had advised. Not that he held any brief for her. She was the person he despised the most from this entire nightmare. If anyone was to blame for wrongly influencing Lerato, it was her sister.

It was a warm morning. Spring was in full bloom with its hopeful blossoms, fertile lawns and blue skies. He sat outside on the patio with Lwazi and Bongani, all of them making a pretence of enjoying their breakfast oats. This was the first time they had attempted to sit together for a meal. They had all lost their appetites since the news of Lerato's passing.

'Lwazi, Bongani, I am going to need to talk to you as men today. You know that I love you . . . you're my sons, and I'm very proud of the young men you are becoming. Your mother and I have raised you to be God-fearing and to live by Christian principles.'

He bowed his head, struggling to contain the tears from escaping.

'When I went to the police station yesterday to get the pathologist's report . . . I discovered things about your mother that reveal . . . that show . . . that the devil had got hold of her in the last days of her life.'

'Dad, you can't say that about Mom!' said Bongani.

'Bongani, I know how you feel. Trust me. I couldn't believe it myself, but it's there for either of you to see. Your mother committed one of the most unforgivable sins. She was in an adulterous relationship with another man.'

Lwazi stood up and pushed his breakfast plate over the table. 'I will not allow you to speak ill of my mother when her body is still lying cold in the mortuary!'

Mzwandile grabbed Lwazi by the arm. 'You think this is easy for me, Lwazi? Hmm? Try sitting in a policeman's office listening to him tell you that your wife frequented another man's house more than twenty times in a matter of weeks! Sit down, *mfana*, and listen. Because I am only going to say this once. I am going through a lot and I need you boys to understand my decision.'

Bongani was scowling, the veins on his neck standing out. 'What decision?' he asked sulkily.

'I am not going to bury your mother,' Mzwandile said.

'What?' Lwazi and Bongani said in horrified unison.

'I have prayed about this—'

'For how long?' Lwazi interrupted his father. 'You only went to the police station yesterday.'

'Look, Lwazi, I am a man of principle. If you never know or understand anything else about me, you need to understand this: my yes is a yes, and my no is no. I will not be disgraced in my own house. I will not bury a woman who has been unfaithful to me, my home, my Christian discipline, and the very foundation of my family life. Your mother committed a cardinal sin . . . she committed infidelity in our marriage. She died in the arms of her lover—'

'What?' both boys said again.

'Mom had a heart attack,' said Lwazi.

'Yes, she did,' said Mzwandile, 'while in the arms of another man.'

They stared at him.

'You have never, and will never, hear anyone on the streets saying that I, Mzwandile Msibi, was unfaithful to *my* wife!' Mzwandile continued. 'I cannot find anything in my heart that compels me to bury her as my wife or partner. As I said, I have prayed about this.'

'And does the Bible not say: "Let he who is without sin cast the first stone"?' said Bongani, on the verge of tears. 'So you are going to humiliate her for one thing that she did . . . which you don't even have concrete proof of, except for one visit to the police station . . .'

Lwazi shook his head over and over. 'There is no way I will ever believe that Mom was unfaithful to you,' he said.

Bongani looked at his dad and scowled at him again. 'There is no way *I* will ever believe that your heart would be so cold as to disown her on her passing. If you do that, Dad, you might as well disown me too,' he said.

He stood up and walked off, his head high. After a minute Lwazi followed him.

Blood Pressure

'What did he do?' Moshidi's mother asked.

'Mama, take it easy, please,' said Moshidi, anxious about her mother's blood pressure. 'Papa, we're going to get through this, right? As a family. We are going to bury our own. Regardless of what Mzwandile Msibi is trying to do to tarnish Lerato's legacy.'

An assortment of Moshidi's relatives were sitting in her spacious living room having morning coffee and scones, waiting for Rakgadi Mary to update them on what she had been told by a member of Mzwandile's church.

'What did he do?' her mother repeated.

'He sent a notice to the church to say that the Msibi home was closed for visits and condolences. He also stated on the email to the church that he would not be available for any enquiries regarding Lerato's funeral. He put down Moshidi's and my name for additional enquiries,' said her aunt.

Everyone gasped in shock.

'That bastard!' said her father. 'He's the devil himself.'

Lerato's mom started fanning herself. She rocked her body back and forth, moaning softly and repeating the words, '*Bathong, ngwana ke.*' My poor child.

Solomzi, who had temporarily survived the divorce threats of only a few days ago, keenly aware of the thin thread by which he was hanging, was trying his best to be the model son-in-law.

'Maybe I can call *sbali* and convince him to think more clearly?' he volunteered.

'No, no! You want us to beg him to bury our daughter as if he's doing us a favour? No. We are Bafokeng . . . the people of the golden sun, who triumph over insurmountable odds,' Moshidi's father said theatrically.

'And have been doing so for centuries! We are not going to beg a Zulu boy to bury our child. How can we do that? How can *I* do that while I, her father, am still alive and kicking. Hmm? What nonsense is that? If he wants to disown my daughter, let him go! Even you, Solomzi. If you try and pull these kinds of stunts with my Moshidi here, you must know that I, Akanyang, *wa* Bafokeng can bury my own children!'

'*Papa-we* . . . calm down,' said his wife. 'Don't get you yourself so upset, please.'

Her husband took out his handkerchief and wiped his brow. 'Jesus, man! Moshidi, come here, my child,' he said, rising. He took her by the arm and led her to the kitchen. 'I want us to talk privately. Me and you. Your mother's heart is like your sister's; she can't take all this drama. I want to understand this situation *ya* Lerato properly. But we can't air her dirty laundry among all these people,' he said conspiratorially.

Moshidi nodded. 'Go upstairs to the twins' room. I'll come and tell you everything I know,' she said.

As her father went up the stairs, Solomzi came into the kitchen.

'Babe, is everything okay?' he whispered.

Moshidi rolled her eyes involuntarily. She was still annoyed with him, but the current situation forced her to suspend her anger in order to retain what was left of her sanity.

'Listen, do me a favour,' she said. 'Make sure that Rakgadi Mary and the girls keep everyone fed and happy. And keep an eye on my mom for me. She took her medication this morning but just keep her calm. I'm going to have a word with my dad upstairs, okay?'

He nodded. 'Sure. I'm here for you, babe.'

Oh gosh. Talk about milking the situation for all it was worth.

Mxm. I'm still divorcing your ass, she thought, staring daggers at his retreating figure.

She made two cups of tea, placed them on a tray and took them to the twins' room where she found her father waiting.

He lifted the cup and took a sip, then placed the tea back on the tray. He folded his arms and said, 'So, tell me everything. What's really happening here, Moshidi?'

'*Yoh*, Papa. It's not a good situation, I must say. I don't even know where to start.'

'Is it true what that man said? Was Lerato being unfaithful?'

Moshidi drank her tea, not knowing how to look her dad in the eye. Where to start? Her dad was not very conservative, but he had tried his best to raise them with good values. He was more of an African spiritualist than a Christian, but he believed in a strong moral code and wished to see his daughters embody those values.

'Well . . . I mean . . . my sister, you know. She wasn't that happy towards the last . . . I'd say about the last couple of years of her marriage.'

He shrugged. 'You young people. Whoever promised you that you would be happy every year of your lives? The obsession with this elusive happiness just baffles me.'

'No, Papa. Lerato wasn't like that. She wasn't fickle about such things. You know what a goody-two-shoes she was. It's not as if she was demanding heaven and earth from the man.'

'So, what was the problem?'

'Well . . .' she said, blushing. 'Mzwandile had stopped being intimate with her. I mean, completely. For more than three years.

210

She talked to me about it. She tried prayer, she fasted . . . you know. All the typical Lerato things that she'd do when she had a problem.'

'*Eish*. Shame, my poor child.'

'Eventually, she confronted him somehow, and he confessed that he was . . . asexual.'

'Hmph,' said her dad distastefully. 'What's that now? *Hayi!* Zulus! Every year, every single year, they come with something new in these bedroom matters!' He shook his head. 'You know, I've always suspected there was something strange about that boy. I was telling your mother the other day . . .'

Moshidi laughed, thinking back to her own reaction when Lerato had told her. She and her dad were so similar.

'Hey, Papa, *ema*. Wait,' she said, enjoying the unexpected comic relief. 'So according to Mzwandile, this thing of his – this asexuality – made him lack sexual feelings. He said that he wasn't attracted to anything. He lacked desire – for anything. But he maintained that he loved her.'

Her father sipped his tea, looked at his daughter and laughed. 'You're joking.'

'No. That's what he told her.'

He kept shaking his head. 'You modern people. You like telling each other lies. I've been around for seventy-five years. I've seen it all. Men who like men, women who like women, old women with young boys, young girls with old men – everything! Rustenburg is a mining town! Everything happens there. But *taba e, ya* Mzwandile. No, man. It's impossible. The boy is lying. Maybe he was having an affair. Or maybe he likes boys. This asexual business? No.'

'*Hayi*, Papa. I don't know. Apparently, there *is* such a thing, but the big issue we need to focus on is what we are going to do now that Mzwandile has decided to disown Lerato.'

'Okay,' said her dad, interlacing his fingers. 'So, we'll take over the funeral arrangements. We'll bury her at home, *ko* Phokeng.

Which is the best because even your grandmother and your great-grandmother's graves lie there. She will be in the company of her ancestors.

'You need to communicate with her boys. Those are good kids. They deserve to bury their mother. She adored those boys, and it's important to involve them in the arrangements.'

Moshidi nodded. 'I'll check if she has a funeral policy, but I have some savings that I can access from the bank. It will take about twenty-four hours for the bank to release the funds.'

'Okay. Your mother and I also have some money put away. Just emergency funds. And I'm sure the family will help us here and there.'

'Very good. You're such a champ, Papa. I'm proud to have a parent like you. I really can't believe that Mzwandile would bail out at the last minute knowing how elaborate and costly funerals are!'

He nodded. 'Don't dwell on it too much, my child. He obviously knows exactly what he's doing, but we won't let him tarnish Lerato's name nor our family name. One more thing . . . what exactly did Msibi find out from the pathologist's report?'

Moshidi sighed. She had hoped not to have to go into these particular details. But then again, this was her father. He had been a local hospital inspector, so he was accustomed to these kinds of matters.

'So . . . Mzwandile gave me the name of the investigating officer . . . Detective Kgomo – that's his name. I contacted him this morning and he sent me the report. What we can make from the report is that, apparently, Lerato died about twelve hours before she was found in her car. So she died at this man's place . . . Lawrence. He lives not far from here in Bryanston. She went to his house late afternoon Monday. And that is where she died. In his . . . in his bed. It's conclusive on that report. Her official cause of death is cardiac arrhythmia. She had been seeing him for a few months . . . she told me about him. She was happy, Papa. I know you might not want to hear that but . . . she was happy in her last days. Happier than I'd ever seen her.'

'So they are sure he didn't do anything to her?'

She nodded. 'But you also viewed her body,' she said. 'She doesn't look like she was harmed. What they did discover is that her . . . the man . . . Lawrence . . . moved her body. He put her in her car and drove her to where she was found. I don't know why he would do that . . .'

'We need to talk to this man. Moshidi, find out how we can contact him. According to our culture, we will need to fetch my daughter's spirit at the place where she took her last breath.'

'What?'

'It's an important traditional ritual. And given the turmoil around my little girl's death, it's even more important that we fetch her spirit so that we can release her.'

Moshidi shook her head. 'I don't understand.'

'What kind of a Motswana are you, my girl? When someone dies, especially under tragic circumstances like this, we go, as her family, to perform final rites of passage into the otherworld. It's not witchcraft or something funny like that – I know how Westernised you girls are. It's just a way for her ancestors to release her from where she is and take her back home. Given how your brother-in-law has abandoned her, you don't want her to be a wandering spirit, now, do you?'

His words chilled her to the bone.

'But . . . given her Christian principles, don't you think she'd be uncomfortable with that?'

'Well, what has her Christian husband done for her during her hour of need? Besides, this is not something sinister. We will bury her in the Christian way, my child. But we also need to honour our ancestral traditions. That is who we are. There is a lot of unhappiness around the way that she died. If we don't do this, her soul may never know eternal peace.'

Umgosi: The Rumour Mill

Noma had an appointment at the spa with Mrs Gumede. News of Lerato's death had shaken the entire social club, especially now that the tawdry details surrounding her death were slowly trickling in.

She felt bad for Lerato, dying under such compromising circumstances. She'd spoken to Moshidi several times after her sister's demise and she worried how it must all be affecting her.

In fact, the social club was supposed to attend *matshidiso* at the Msibis' home but apparently there had been a drastic change of plan. Honouring *matshidiso* was an important aspect of Khula's ethics, especially because it was such a cornerstone of burial rituals in African culture. It was all about being there for the grieving family and making them feel that they were not alone during their time of loss.

Young, demure, virginal Lerato was gone, and under such bizarre circumstances!

It was all so shocking!

September was supposed to have been the Msibis' turn to host the social club event, but with the long weekend for Heritage Day, they had postponed it to the next month. No doubt that wasn't going to happen now.

The image of the last time she had seen Lerato – stepping out of a car at the Red Marketing building – kept coming back to her.

And with these mysterious revelations about her death that were filtering through, her suspicions were taking firmer shape. She was putting two and two together. She was bursting to discuss her suspicions with someone and who better than Mrs Gumede, a gossip of note. She would lap up the news Noma had for her.

But there was another reason she needed to sweeten up the old woman. It was to do with The Young Man and his intriguing proposition last weekend. 'You will love it!' Tafadzwa had said, and he had been right. She did love it.

Since the very first time she and Tafadzwa had met at the mining *indaba*, she had known their relationship would bear fruit. Now that fruit was ripe and juicy and ready for the plucking. All their subsequent discussions, their animated sharing of visions, had led to this place. They had a plan – which was proceeding apace – and a strategy.

Noma had always been academically gifted but having grown up as the daughter of a gangster, then marrying a heist kingpin, the worry was always at the back of her mind that she would never be able to shake off her dubious past. She loved money and all that it offered her in life, but her intellect demanded that the money should elevate her standing as one of the most illustrious figures in the South African business world. After all, she had the beauty and the brains so why shouldn't she also command respect and gravitas in the world of business?

When she became the COO of Zebula Mining, she thought she had reached the zenith of her career. But since meeting Tafadzwa, the scales had fallen from her eyes – in so many ways. She began to see her prior ambitions as pedestrian. Fate had so much more in store for her and it was Tafadzwa who helped her believe she had more to offer than she'd ever allowed herself to dream.

The fruit was a gold mine. Literally.

Tafadzwa had convinced her to purchase Kuenda Mberi gold mine in Zimbabwe. The plan was that he would retain ten per cent of the mine and assist with the operations. The difference between this deal and the many others that she had clinched for Zebula Mining was that Tafadzwa wanted her to own the mine in her personal capacity. Imagine that?

The restraint of trade clause in her contract with Zebula prevented her from dealing in chrome but Kuenda Mberi was a gold mine, which meant that she could potentially purchase the mine under her own name. She had moved swiftly, bought a shell company to set the wheels in motion for this bold, exciting move. She had also submitted her resignation at Zebula, which required her to serve a twelve-month notice period.

Tafadzwa was everything she had ever wanted in a business partner. Visionary, astute and a true epicurean, just like her. She was certain he was her twin spirit. And they shared a fine taste in clothing too. Conversations with him were always thrilling. In the beginning, as she fell under his spell, she'd almost convinced herself that there was a romantic spark between them but after their last meeting, it had finally dawned on her that his interest in her was purely of a collegial and friendly nature. She suspected he could be gay, but she had found some of her business associates on the continent quite coy about such matters so she wasn't going to broach the subject – unless he raised it himself, which so far he hadn't.

She'd invited him to be a VIP guest at the annual golf charity event organised by Zebula, which was coming up quite soon. Frans at Red Marketing was putting the final pieces in place now. She and Tafadzwa were planning to use the event to start wooing potential partners for their gold mine. Which was where Mrs Gumede came in. Noma scanned the entrance to the spa, hoping the old lady hadn't forgotten their date.

Normally, she would have discussed all of this with Julius, but for some reason, she had held it to herself. That man had so many secrets already. And these past couple of months he'd been more secretive than ever – meetings at all hours, phone calls he took outside in the garden, evasive answers to her questions – he scarcely noticed anything she did or said.

As she got undressed, she sighed with pleasure, thinking of all the exciting new avenues on the horizon, keeping an eye out for Mrs Gumede. She needed to solidify her relationship with the Gumedes. Mr Gumede had a gold beneficiation company and a partnership with him would be advantageous. But she knew the old lady was very territorial; Noma needed her on board before she could engage seriously with her husband.

Mrs Gumede arrived ten minutes later, Noma already relaxing on a lounger by the pool in the spa's recreation area. The older woman waved and smiled by way of greeting. Before long she appeared from the changerooms in her gown and slippers. As she sat next to Noma, a frown drawing fine lines on her forehead, she said, 'Such awful news about Lerato. Can you believe it?'

Noma shook her head. 'It's all so sad and confusing. I mean, it's bad enough dying of a heart attack, but all the strange rumours about a secret lover and her husband refusing to bury her? Unbelievable!'

'What?' said MaGumede, craning her neck to hear more.

'Well, I probably shouldn't be telling you this, but—'

Just then their two masseurs appeared, ready to take them to the treatment rooms. The disappointment on MaGumede's face was undisguised. Juicy gossip would have provided her with more relief than the hour-long massage, but the wait would make her even more receptive.

When they returned feeling restored, they went into the sauna to relax some more.

It didn't take long for MaGumede to pick up the thread Noma had left dangling.

'You were telling me about Lerato? So it's true? The sordid affair?'

Noma cringed. Was it really all that sordid? It hadn't been that long ago when she'd thought that Tafadzwa's interest in her wasn't platonic. In all honesty, she herself had entertained the idea of having an affair, had been on the brink of embarking on one. She felt strangely protective of Lerato, given the circumstances around her demise. But she needed the Gumedes on board for her mining project. She decided to throw the old dog a bone.

'I actually think I know who she was having an affair with,' she said casually.

MaGumede rose from the sauna bench and looked down at Noma, who was lying on the bench below enjoy the relaxing steam.

'Really! Do tell!'

'So, I'd had a meeting with my CSI team at Red Marketing. Turns out they're based in the same building as the company Lerato worked for. I first bumped into her in the parking lot, and she was looking a bit jittery. Then the next time I went there for a meeting, I saw her coming out of a car . . . and giving a kiss to the guy who was driving . . .'

'What? No! In public like that?'

'Yes. And I thought then he looked familiar. I'd seen him before that day. Turns out he works at Red Marketing.'

'No!'

'Yes! My account manager there, Frans, confirmed it. His name is Lawrence. Apparently, he's a Zimbabwean and he's been working at Red for some time now.'

'*Shoo!*' exclaimed MaGumede. 'A whole Zimbabwean! So, you think he's the one she was having an affair with?'

Noma sighed, ignoring the jibe about Lawrence's nationality. 'Do I think so? I know so. Frans dished up all the dirt. He says they used to have lunch at the cafeteria together every day! And recently, he said, they had become scarce at the cafeteria, but that Lawrence had taken to "long lunches" outside the office.'

'Ha! Wasn't Lerato supposed to be a born-again Christian?'

'*Hey wena. Uyabazi abazalwane kodwa?* These so-called devout Christians are the worst.'

MaGumede shook her head in disbelief. 'I thought she was this stuck-up goody-two-shoes, but it seems she was busy, young Lerato, hey?'

'Very busy,' said Noma, satisfied that she had sated MaGumede's appetite for salacious gossip.

'*Shoo!*' said MaGumede, smacking her hands in delicious shock.

'I still feel bad for her. Dying the way, she did,' said Noma.

'Yes . . . and she was still so young. Poor thing. I sort of liked her, even though I found her a bit strange.'

'Who knows what led her to having that affair?' said Noma, once again thinking about her own situation. How distant The Duke had become lately. It was as though he was consumed by something big and threatening. Something outside their marriage. As if his mind was occupied elsewhere. She shook the thought away impatiently. It was another woman for sure.

'I just wish couples these days would still believe in monogamy, like we did in the olden days,' said MaGumede piously.

Noma felt ripples of irritation slide down her spine. 'Well, for a relationship to be monogamous, both parties must be faithful,' she said.

MaGumede laughed. 'As if men are capable of fidelity.'

'Then those were not monogamous relationships that you were in, in the olden days, MaGumede,' she said. Then, realising that being tetchy with the older woman wasn't going to help her cause – she still needed her – she added, 'Anyway, let's not spoil this beautiful treat. I feel so relaxed.'

MaGumede sighed pleasurably. 'So do I,' she said.

They were both silent for a while. Lost in their own thoughts.

'By the way,' Noma said, after a suitable pause, 'you and Mr Gumede must come to our golf day.'

'But of course. When is it?' asked MaGumede.

'In three weeks' time. I'll get my PA to send you the formal invite.'

'Sounds wonderful. Something to take our minds off this horrible tragedy,' said MaGumede.

Noma was relieved. All the pieces were falling into place without her even breaking a sweat.

The Call

When Mzwandile had extricated himself from Lerato's funeral arrangements, he'd handed all of her personal effects – the items the police had recovered from Lerato's car and subsequently released to him when he went to identify her body – to Moshidi. Among these were her handbag and her mobile phone.

Moshidi had been wondering how she was going to get Lawrence's number.

Could she ask the police to give it to her?

Mzwandile had said that they would be instituting criminal charges against him for moving Lerato's body. She was still not sure how she felt about that. Did she want to see him serve time in jail for this act?

Time.

Time was running out.

For all she knew, Lawrence might be in a prison cell already.

She went to her bedroom and removed Lerato's bag from her walk-in closet. She took out her sister's phone and set it to charge, then busied herself tidying up her room while she ran through all the arrangements that needed to be concluded before Lerato's funeral.

They had moved the funeral date to the upcoming Wednesday because they had needed to take over the funeral arrangements from Mzwandile who, before he abandoned her altogether, had planned to bury Lerato on Saturday.

She still could not believe the stunt he had pulled.

Changing funeral dates was virtually unheard of in the black community. The rumour mill was probably in overdrive.

Members of the social club had wanted to come and *tshidisa* her family that evening, but she had instructed Solomzi to request that they come through the next day.

Noma and Paul had both called in to check on her a number of times.

As she waited for the phone to charge, she reflected on how Lerato's affair had completely altered the neat course that her sister had mapped out for her life. If she had not been with Lawrence, she would have died a more peaceful and far less dramatic death. She sighed, feeling guilty about not discouraging her sister from giving in to the affair.

It had been fairly easy for her to shrug off her personal trainer's advances in the end. The last time she had seen him was on that almost fateful Friday of the Women's Day long weekend. After they'd had their meal, he'd walked her to her car and attempted to kiss her. That was when she realised that she had no feelings for the man whatsoever. She knew that she and Solomzi had hit a major bump in their marriage – she didn't know quite how big a bump yet; the Serame set-up was still ahead – but she did not need yet another man to complicate her life further. If only it had been that easy for her sister, she mused.

After about thirty minutes of charging time, she went to get Lerato's phone. Her hopes of accessing information from it dwindled at the prospect of trying to guess her sister's password. Being a fancy data scientist, Lerato no doubt had a complex code to unlock her mobile phone. She made two failed attempts at cracking the passcode before, surprisingly, getting it right using a combination of Lwazi's and Bongani's birth dates.

Phew! She laughed, scarcely believing it was so easy.

Moshidi started scrolling through Lerato's contacts. She came across two Lawrences.

The first one was Lawrence Fishburne . . . like the Hollywood actor? What on earth?

This was probably some cute code Lerato had used for her Lawrence. Maybe he looked like the actor?

The second one was a Lawrence Moyo. Probably a business contact.

Mindful not to spook him by calling from his dead lover's phone, she took out her own phone and rang the first Lawrence.

'Hello. Fishburne speaking.'

What the heck?

The man had a strong European accent. Surely Lerato would have mentioned that he was from Europe?

'Uhm . . . sorry. This is Lerato Msibi's sister . . .'

'Oh. Sincere condolences for your loss. Such a brilliant woman.'

'So . . . how did you know my sister?'

'She worked on a number of projects for us. How can I help you, ma'am?'

'Oh . . . sorry. Never mind. Sorry to have bothered you,' she said as she ended the call.

Not Lerato's Lawrence then.

She had a sudden brainwave. She went to the WhatsApp icon on Lerato's phone and scrolled through her messages. She saw Lawrence's name and clicked on the chat.

She quickly scanned their many exchanges. There were more heart emojis than in a teen romance thread.

She read their last messages to each other.

From Lerato:

On my way. Can't wait to see you!

From Lawrence:

Hmmph. Dr Feelgood, huh? Where were his medical skills when her sister needed them the most?

Oddly irritated at the exchange, she finally dialled Lawrence's number on her own phone.

The phone rang unanswered. When Moshidi was about to give up, she heard a deep baritone on the other end.

'Hello.'

'Hi . . . um . . . is that Lawrence Moyo?'

'Speaking.'

'This is Moshidi. Lerato Msibi's sister.'

Silence.

'Lawrence, are you still there?'

'Yes . . . yes, I'm still here.'

'You're probably wondering why I'm calling you. I need to talk to you . . . preferably meet with you . . . if you don't mind.'

'Um . . . look . . . I don't know what you know or think about me and Lerato . . . but I just need you to understand that I loved her.' A pause. 'I loved her deeply.'

His voice was breaking. Was he crying?

Tears stung Moshidi's eyes.

She blinked them back and said, 'Lawrence . . . I know. We were very close. She told me about you. I just need to know how she was . . . towards the end. Could you meet me? Preferably today?'

Another long pause on the other end of the line. Then, 'Um . . . okay. I'm at work. How does six this evening sound?'

'Yes,' she said gratefully. 'Six is perfect.'

She recommended they meet at a quiet diner close to both their current locations. She knew he worked in the same building as Lerato, so she made sure not to inconvenience him.

Two hours later, she was at their meeting place, feeling nervous and chilly, both from the weather – autumn chills and a grey sky – and the circumstances of the meeting.

She hadn't consumed any alcohol since news of Lerato's passing because it was prohibited at the home of the deceased or where guests were received, but she needed Dutch courage to handle this encounter. How was she going to broach the subject of her father's unusual request? Based on his surname, Lawrence must be Zimbabwean or Zambian; it hadn't come up when Lerato talked about him. Did he even know of this cultural practice?

When the waiter approached her table, she ordered a single shot of whisky on the rocks.

Lawrence arrived fifteen minutes later. When he walked in, she was instantly drawn to his presence.

He was tall and athletic-looking and walked with a confident stride. He was wearing a zipped up black K-Way down jacket, blue jeans and boots. He looked like he was about to go on a hike. What was it he did for a living again? She couldn't remember, but his workplace obviously had a casual look going.

As he approached her table, she noticed that he had a gentle face with unusual but striking features.

Lerato definitely had a type. He was a younger, less nerdy version of Mzwandile.

'Moshidi,' he said in a sonorous voice.

She stood up to shake his hand. 'Hi, Lawrence. Thanks for making the time to meet me at such short notice.'

He nodded as he took a seat and interlaced his fingers. He looked nervous.

'Um . . . would you like to order a drink?'

He nodded and she called the waiter over. He ordered whisky. A double.

As they waited for the waiter to take down the order, they kept stealing awkward glances at each other. When the waiter left, Moshidi finally said, 'So . . . this is a rather unusual meeting. I haven't really figured out what I'm going to say to you.'

Lawrence raised his eyes and said, 'Yes. Well. I wasn't aware you two looked so much alike.'

She smiled. 'I'll take that as a compliment. My sister's always been quite the head-turner. I guess that's why you fell for her.'

He grinned, for the first time looking less mournful. 'She was. I couldn't believe how lucky I was when she finally started talking to me.'

Moshidi nodded.

The waiter arrived with Lawrence's drink and they fell silent again until he'd gone.

'So . . . the reason I called you here . . . I guess, firstly, I . . . well, my family has so many unanswered questions.' She stopped, wishing she'd also ordered a double. Then, pain etched on her face like a haunting question mark, she asked, 'What really happened that Monday, Lawrence?'

Lawrence took a sip of his drink, then put the glass down carefully. He interlaced his fingers again, staring at them as he readied himself for the difficult task.

'You know . . . Lerato and I had been spending a lot of time together. We'd developed something of a ritual. She'd either come to my place at lunch or after work. We'd have such fun; we'd just discovered each other, and I think we both felt like teenagers. We were lovestruck . . . and . . . it was just . . . it was perfect,' he said, pausing to take a breath and another sip of his whisky. 'She'd had an awful day at work,' he continued, 'so she came to my place, we relaxed a bit . . . had a bit of wine—'

'My sister doesn't drink wine.'

He laughed uncomfortably. 'I know she doesn't. But . . . she'd get really nervous sometimes. A glass of red wine relaxed her. She

226

always felt guilty about . . . you know . . . us. I know she loved me, but our relationship ate away at her conscience. It was one of those things that you want so badly . . . yet . . .' He stopped.

Moshidi nodded. 'I know. I understand. Still can't believe you got her to drink. I've been trying for more than twenty years,' she said, laughing softly. She almost added, 'You must have a magic penis,' but thought better of it.

'So anyway, we chilled, had some fun, then she drifted off to sleep. When I tried to wake her, she was unresponsive. I started panicking. I tried to find a pulse. There wasn't one. She was— I was so foolish . . . if I could turn back time, I would have probably done everything differently. I would have just called an ambulance and allowed fate to take its course. It's just that the situation looked so bad at the time I thought I had no other choice but to move Lerato from my house so that there'd be no trace of our connection.'

Moshidi sighed. Then she looked him in the eye. 'But . . . why?'

He furrowed his brow and rubbed his eyes. 'It was stupid, I know that now. I was so stupid! I just thought of so many things. Maybe the police would think I'd harmed her . . . Then the fact that she's married – what would her husband think? The authorities? And the fact that I'm foreign . . . I just let my imagination run off with me. I called a friend, who just made me more paranoid. The friend came over . . . we carried her . . . it's the worst thing I've ever done . . .' he said, breaking down in tears.

She watched him, partly feeling sorry for him, partly angry at him. Yet somehow, she couldn't find a reason to distrust him. There was something fragile about him. Besides, the pathologist's report did confirm everything he said. His greatest crime was trying to pretend that he had not been with her sister that evening. Whether he had done it to protect her or for his own ends was for him, the law and his conscience to deal with.

'Lawrence, I have seen the pathologist's report. Hearing your version of events just corroborates what we already know. I can't judge you on the decisions you took because I don't know what I would have done in your position. I'm very angry that my sister had to die in such an ungraceful way, but I know her circumstances. I know what was happening in her life and I know what pushed her to make some of the decisions that she did. I just pray that her soul is at peace, you know. That's all I can hope for.'

Lawrence gave her a relieved half-smile.

'Which is why I'm actually here,' said Moshidi.

The smile changed to a frown of concern. Lawrence took a sip from his glass. He nodded as a sign for her to continue speaking.

'Look, my family is very traditional. We believe that for some-one who died under these kinds of tragic circumstances to rest easy, we need to perform certain rituals at the place where that person took their last breath.'

Lawrence's eyes widened. 'I'm sorry . . . I don't understand.'

Moshidi sighed. 'I knew this would be the tough part of this conversation. To be honest, I've been sent by the elder members of my family. According to our tradition, we have to perform certain prayerful rituals to "fetch" the soul of a loved one to take her to her burial place. Basically, we need permission to come to your home in order to do this.'

To say Lawrence was caught off guard would be an understatement.

'Um . . . wasn't Lerato a devout Christian?'

Moshidi nodded. 'She was. But my family . . . especially on my dad's side, still believe in acknowledging our ancestors in everything we do. My sister's husband has declared that he will not be burying her. So this is just a dark mark on Lerato's legacy. You can imagine the scandal of a married woman who will not be buried by her own husband. It's not something Lerato could have possibly imagined for her legacy. That is why it's so important that we carry out this ritual.'

Lawrence couldn't believe what he was hearing. Their relationship was a hurricane that had wreaked havoc on so many different facets of their lives. Before this meeting with Moshidi, all he was worrying about was his own future and personal reputation. It was only now that he realised that Lerato had been disgraced in her death. What must her children think of her? Her church, her entire community?

Her rubbed at his forehead. 'Wow. I hadn't realised how serious this situation was. I'm so sorry. The last thing I would have wanted was to shame her. She doesn't deserve that . . .' he said, now breaking down and openly crying.

Moshidi bit her bottom lip and said, 'Please consider doing this for my family. We love Lerato and won't let the world dictate how we choose to remember her. All that we ask is that you allow us to do what we need to do in order for her soul to rest well.'

He nodded, trying to get his tears under control.

'Do you mind if I take a day or so to think about this?' he asked. 'I want to do the right thing, but this is something unexpected . . . and . . . wow. I just need to be sure that I'm making the right decision. If you don't mind?'

Moshidi considered his request, then nodded. 'I guess I can understand that,' she said. 'But please . . . we don't have much time. Her funeral is on Wednesday.'

'Where?'

'At our family home in Phokeng in the North West Province.'

'Do you think I would be allowed to attend the funeral? Just to say my last goodbyes?'

Moshidi nodded again. 'I think she would appreciate that,' she said.

Lawrence gave her a sad smile. 'Thank you.'

As Moshidi walked to her car she felt completely and utterly drained.

If she and Solomzi were in a better space, she'd have asked him to carry out this particular task, but at least it was done now.

Matshidiso

The Duke waited in the Maserati, counting down the minutes before his wife would finally be ready so they could get to their appointment and not, as usual, be the last ones to arrive.

Was she taking longer than usual to get ready these days or was he getting more annoyed as the years piled up?

He shook his head. Nomathando Manamela.

She wasn't really so bad . . . but this waiting had been more palatable when he had someone on the side to make up for the tedious aspects of marriage. Unfortunately, there was no time for that, not at the moment anyway.

While he waited, he went over the plan one more time as he and the boys had rehearsed it.

He smiled in satisfaction. It was watertight. Simple. Clean.

By 6.50 a.m., on Wednesday next week, The Duke and his team would be at Danie Wiese's office building. They had only fifteen minutes max to carry out the heist – or at least the important part of it, which was to overpower the security guards, disarm all alarm systems and, most importantly, be there when the night-shift guys opened the vaults for inventory tracking before the day-shift changeover.

Security protocol required the night-shift guys to place the jewellery in the vaults in the evening after the day staff knocked off. The operations manager arrived at six thirty in the morning, along with the day security manager and two other security personnel. She was in charge of doing inventory to track stock during the shift changeover.

They would typically take about an hour to do the inventory and record it on to the operations system to confirm the amount and value of the stock at the beginning of the new business day.

This was the window in which The Duke and his team had the chance to make hay while the sun shone. Once they'd disarmed security, they'd be free to clean up the place, get their bounty and get out of there.

He thought about giving a gentle toot on the Maserati's horn, but he'd tried that once with Noma and she'd gone back inside and deliberately changed her outfit three times. He'd learned that lesson. He looked at his watch and did a quick calculation.

In the time it took his wife to get dressed for an appointment, he could have executed not one, not two, not even three heists. More.

Finally, Noma stepped out of the house in a cream-white fig-ure-hugging Cavalli dress and stilettoes.

They were going to offer condolences to a grieving family. She looked like she was going to one of her upscale fashion shows.

'Sweetheart . . . don't you think that is too dressy for *matshidiso*?'

She twirled. 'You think?'

He looked at her quizzically. 'Baby . . . man. Really?'

'Okay. Okay. I'll be back,' she said, sauntering back to the house.

Twenty minutes (or another heist) later, she returned, this time wearing something slightly more demure. Sometimes, he honestly could not believe this was his life.

In the car at last, Noma turned to him and said, 'Have we depos-ited the social club's contribution towards the funeral arrangements?'

He nodded, focused on the road. 'I did it first thing this morn-ing,' he said, when he realised she was waiting for him to answer.

They drove on in silence.

'It's so sad what happened to Lerato,' Noma said after a while. 'It's the kind of thing that could happen to any of us.'

'What do you mean?' he said, frowning into the rear-view mirror.

She shrugged. 'Well, we're not exactly spring chickens. I also have high blood pressure. And you and your cholesterol . . . We could both drop dead. Tomorrow.'

'No. Not me. And no wife of mine would drop dead in some dodgy apartment, fucking another guy. Never! I feel bad for the husband. Mzwandile. Such a nice guy . . . to have this happen to him? And with a *kwerekwere nogal*. Imagine!'

Noma looked at her husband with contempt. 'Wow! You're one to talk,' she said.

'What do you mean?'

She was silent.

Then. 'You know what I mean. Lovey. Whom you wanted to turn into a second wife. And then there was that crazy one in Klerksdorp – what was her name? The one with the squinty eyes. *O le wa skielbog*, man. *Kana*, what was her name?'

'*Mxm*. That's ancient history. Let me tell you something, it's a pity that Mzwandile guy is a Christian. If he was one of my bros, I would have sorted him out by now. Do you know that at Sethego hostel alone I know of at least five Zulu guys who'd be more than happy to clean up this mess for him.'

'What are you talking about?'

'I'm telling you, Noma. If Mzwandile wasn't so timid, I would have long ago hooked him up. Ten thousand, even eight thousand rand, and I tell you, that *kwerekwere* would be dead by midnight.'

Noma looked at her husband incredulously.

They drove on in silence.

'*Sies!*' she said finally, spitting on the floor. 'Men! The double standards!'

'Double standards my foot! And just so you know, I'm not burying that bitch. Not after what she did to Mzwandile,' he declared.

He'd started the fight on purpose. He and Noma always attended weddings and funerals together. It was a tacit agreement in their marriage that they'd upheld without fail for all these years.

But Wednesday was D-Day. He had already requested leave at work. Wiese was adamant that the robbery needed to take place that day. It was going to be the quietest and sleepiest day at the office, with most of the staff away on their team-building thing. Everything was set up.

'So you expect me to attend the funeral by myself? You want me to look like an idiot just because . . . what exactly?'

'You think Julius Manamela will bury an unfaithful slut, whose own husband disclaimed her for dying in the arms of a *kwerekwere*? Never! You don't know me, *wena, neh*?'

'So, turn the vehicle around! Why are we even going to *matshidiso* then? Hmm?'

He shrugged. 'This is different. Today I'm showing up for Solomzi. He's a decent guy. Besides, the whole social club will be there. I don't want it to look like I'm snubbing him. But attending the funeral when Mzwandile made it clear that he wants nothing to do with this? No way.'

'Fuck. You men are toxic! That is utter bullshit. So if you had died in the arms of your Lovey, what was going to happen? Hmm? Were you going to be buried by her and her family?'

Hmm. That was a question. He must tread carefully. After all, who knew if he was going to have another affair?

Answer: highly likely.

'Answer me! If you were to die in the arms of one of your lovers, *wena*, Julius, would I need to follow Mzwandile's example?'

She'd called him Julius. Not even Duke. This was bad. Thankfully, they had reached their destination.

'Baby . . . we're here. Let's calm down, please.'

Noma was seething with rage. Right now, she wished she had the phone number of one of her husband's Zulu men. Then *he'd* be the one who'd be dead by midnight. The utter nerve of this man!

Consequences

'Lawrence Moyo!' yelled the prison guard.

Lawrence regarded the dirty grey cell he was sharing with six other men, one of whom was his good friend Kudzayi. Someone had pissed on the floor earlier in the morning. The place reeked with all sorts of pungent smells.

He had been there for more than forty-eight hours. They had arrested him the day after his meeting with Moshidi. What broke his heart was that Kudzayi had been arrested along with him. Guilt ate him up like an ulcer. No matter what had transpired, Kudzayi's intentions had been noble.

When his name was called out, he and Kudzayi walked up to the prison bars together, hoping that their bail had been posted.

The guard unlocked the cell and said, 'It's your lucky day, Moyo. Come.'

Lawrence looked at Kudzayi and then back at the guard. 'What about Kudzayi Makwembere? We have the same lawyer.'

The guard just looked at him and said, 'Nope. Only name I have here is yours, Moyo. Unless you want to trade places with your girlfriend here.' He pointed at Kudzayi and laughed.

Kudzayi looked surprised. Betrayed, even.

'This doesn't make sense,' he said. 'Call Munyaradzi, Lawrence. Get him to clear up this mess. Please?'

Lawrence nodded. 'I'm sorry, *shamwari*. I promise I'll get this sorted soon. This must be some kind of mistake.'

The guard escorted him to the office to sign his release form and to collect his belongings.

Immediately when he got his phone, he called Munyaradzi.

'*Sha* . . . Lawrence here. What happened? How come you didn't post bail for Kudzayi?'

'Hey . . . your guardian angel's been hard at work, my friend. I can't believe what a lucky bastard you are. Do you know who posted the bail money for you?'

He shrugged as if his lawyer could see him. 'Who?'

'I was contacted by your lover's sister. She posted the full amount.'

'What? Wow,' he said quietly, then asked, 'but what's going to happen to Kudzayi?'

'Don't worry, I've managed to secure his bail bond. He'll be out by this afternoon. Just keep your head down till you're both out. I think I have a strategy for your defence. Especially since the family seems to have taken such a shine to you.'

'Listen, Munya, I don't really want to look like I'm taking advantage of the situation. They have their own reasons. I told you about it. I think we should try and separate the two issues.'

Munyaradzi laughed. 'Look, you keep being Prince Charming. My job is to keep you fools out of jail.'

'It's not an act,' said Lawrence defensively.

'Fine, fine. I know. But just be careful what you say. You may want to impress your girlfriend's family with your undying love but, ultimately, you have to try and retain your days as a free man. You understand what I'm saying?'

Lawrence hesitated. 'Sure. Listen, please make sure Kudzayi's out of that jail cell today. The conditions there are messed up, man.'

Munyaradzi laughed. 'Sun City's worse. Trust me. Which is why I'm working so hard for you boys.'

Rest

Tuesday morning. The day before Lerato's funeral. As if in sympa-
thy, the clouds condensed into a thick grey mass in the early hours.

Moshidi, Solomzi, her mother, father, Rakgadi Mary and their
spiritual healer, driving in two separate cars, set off for Lawrence's
apartment.

Lerato's casket would arrive at Moshidi's home later that afternoon. It was important for them to bring her spirit back home by
the time her body was delivered to prepare for its final resting place.

The healer had arrived the evening before from Phokeng. He
had been to their ancestral home to pluck out a twig – *kalana* –
from the old acacia tree that took pride of place in the yard.

The children of the Bafokeng household all had their umbilical
cords buried under this tree once they were delivered from their
mother's womb as a symbolic representation of their rootedness to
their family ground, and as a means of celebrating their mother's
fertility and her ability to expand the family tree.

The healer had also brought snuff and a two-litre bottle of
water as part of the implements they would need to perform the
ritual of transferring Lerato's spirit to its final resting place.

Although Lawrence was still spooked by the entire thing, he had
called his parents in Zimbabwe, not only to tell them what had happened but also to explain the bizarre and somewhat embarrassing

circumstances that had led to this moment in his life. His father had been surprisingly calm about the whole situation. Being a Methodist priest, he had dealt with all sorts of family drama. He told Lawrence to respect the family's wishes but he also suggested he stick around to ensure that there were no dark elements to whatever ritual it was that the family was performing in his home. He had never heard his father sound so superstitious. But then again, these were strange times for everyone involved in the unfolding saga.

When Moshidi knocked on his door with five people in tow, Lawrence welcomed them in and offered them coffee and water. They all declined and sat politely in his lounge while Moshidi made a few courteous comments. She was dressed more conservatively than the last time they had met. A patterned *doek* covered her head, and she wore a jersey, a skirt and a small blanket around her waist.

He had wanted to engage her some more about the bail bond – he felt it was prudent to settle the money back – but it was clear that this was neither the time nor place to discuss such matters.

Moshidi asked if he would let them into his bedroom. The request made Lawrence feel eerie and strange all over again, even though he'd known the request was coming. It wasn't every day that six strangers asked to have time alone in one's bedroom, but needs must.

It struck him that he would probably need to get another apartment after all this. The events of the past week weighed heavily on him. He needed a fresh start, no matter what the future held for him. One thing was for sure, he did not want to entertain the possibility of a jail term.

Moshidi and her family went into the bedroom carrying the *kalana*, the two litres of water and the snuff. They knelt around the bed, hands clasped in a show of respect for the deceased. They announced their presence to Lerato's departed soul, each person introducing themselves and stating how they were related to her.

The healer placed the *kalana* on the bed, then started chanting incantations, pleading with Lerato's ancestors to safely journey with her to her resting place. He did this symbolically by dragging the twig from the bed, then to the floor, where her body had been placed by Lawrence and Kudzayi, according to Lawrence's recounting of events. They would transport the *kalana* from the house and drag it to the vehicle they had travelled in to symbolise that they were moving her spirit from Lawrence's home all the way to its final resting place, where it would be laid along with her body in the casket.

The healer inhaled the snuff to invoke the spirits of her ancestors, then splashed water from the bottle to cleanse the air around the place where Lerato took her last breath.

Moshidi spoke to her sister, asking for her soul to be freed, praying to God to release her from any wrongdoing and imploring her ancestors to travel back home with her.

Lawrence stood uncertainly by the door, careful not to interrupt the family, but mindful of what his father had said. He felt a strange sense of calm as he witnessed the family saying their goodbyes to his lover's spirit. Somehow it felt as if there was a sense of cleansing or reclaiming of that small space where Lerato's body had last lain. The fear and uncertainty he had felt earlier was replaced by a deep sense of connection to the moment and to these people who had come to reclaim their beloved.

He felt oddly sad that her husband could not be part of this ritual.

He said a silent prayer for Lerato to be granted a peaceful rest.

D-Day

Noma was still in her gown and morning slippers. She was in an irritable mood. Phokeng was at least one and a half hours away. Was this man really expecting her to travel all that way on her own to go to a funeral?

Maybe she should call Paul and travel with him and Tom? She looked out the window. Gloomy grey skies stretching endlessly over the horizon.

She took out her third dress that morning, not sure which one of her favourite black garments would be suitable for Lerato's funeral. It was slightly chilly this morning, yet she still wanted to look as stylish as ever.

The Duke was wearing jeans, a light jacket and sneakers.

So he hadn't changed his mind then, even though he'd been up since the crack of dawn.

Why was he so damn edgy?

She could not believe he was going ahead with his fake protest. She had not spoken to him since their last argument about the issue on Sunday evening. Pretended he wasn't even there.

What she really wanted to do was wear something sexy just to piss him off. It didn't look like the weather was going to be on her side, but still . . .

She heard the squeak of his sneakers downstairs near the front door, squeak-squeak, back and forth he paced. What was the matter with him this morning?

'Do you think this dress is too short?' asked Noma, posing provocatively on the staircase.

He barely registered what she was saying.

Since the early hours, long before it had grown light, he had been mentally running over all the details. He did so again for the umpteenth time.

In fact, Quicks Tshabalala had just texted The Duke on his burner phone to let him know that the men were on standby waiting for his cue.

He hoped he hadn't got too rusty. He'd last done a job like this eight years ago. And even then, Noma had been none the wiser. She'd enjoyed the perks that had come with his ill-gotten gains, oh yes, and the step-up he'd given her on to the corporate ladder. But ever since then she'd become doggedly determined to bury this aspect of their lives. Unfortunately, a life of crime had a strange way of trailing a man.

Hopefully, though, this was his last gig.

By the time he looked up from his phone, the staircase was empty and he could hear the shower water running. He could not brook another argument with Noma about the bloody funeral. Or comment on yet another outfit. And anyway, it was time to go.

The Duke went to the storeroom in the garage to collect the instruments he had organised for the job: bottles of chloroform; swabs for the chloroform; stun guns, gloves, industrial rope; pepper spray and spray paint; hammers and chisels. Quicks had organised batons, guns, masks and Royal Guard security uniforms for the crew.

He placed the gear into a heavy-duty duffel bag, loaded it into his beat-up Mercedes-Benz and drove to Quicks' house in Kew.

All eight of the crew were there, ready and waiting. Two were dressed in dark clothing while the other six were dressed in Royal Guard uniforms; the same company used by Rockefeller Diamonds for their armed response security. They'd wear the masks later.

He greeted everyone and went through the plan one more time. Once done, the crew got into their three vehicles and made their way to the Rockefeller building. Quicks, The Duke and a guy called Thabo were in Quicks' Audi A4, with Quicks driving; three of the guys were in a black Golf GTI; and the other three had a Royal Guard bakkie – Quicks had a friend who worked at a branding company. They kept a distance of about two hundred metres between them as they drove, the Audi leading the way.

Quicks drove up to the security entrance at the office park and parked by the gate.

The security guard stepped out of the guardhouse. 'Hi. How can I help you?'

'*Sawubona, mfowethu*,' said Quicks, pressing down the driver's window. 'We're looking for Rethabile Tours? It says it's here in this building?' He took out a piece of paper as if he were reading the address from it. 'This is number 45 Zambezi Drive, right?'

The security guard came closer and took the piece of paper that Quicks handed to him.

'Number 45 Zambezi?' he said. 'No . . . this is number 51. You passed the building—'

Before he could finish what he was saying, the other two vehicles had pulled up behind the Audi and three men were out of the cars in a flash. One placed a swab with chloroform around the guard's mouth and delivered a kick to his shins to overpower him, while the other two bounced into the guardhouse to silence the second guard on duty before he noticed what was happening. The drivers stayed in the cars.

The second guard was on the ground and on his stomach in an instant, wrists tied together behind his back. They used the effective 'highwayman's hitch': forcing the hapless man's arms up his back, passing the cord around his neck, then back and around his wrists again. They bent his legs backwards and tied his legs together. They then rendered him unconscious by administering chloroform. They tied up the first guard in the same way. In the meantime, the fifth robber had coloured the security cameras with spray paint.

So far so good.

The crew put on their masks. Wiese had been adamant that there be no bloodbath, but each man was armed just the same, with either a Glock 19 or a Sig Sauer 9mm handgun. All the guns had silencers. Holding weapons was what worried The Duke the most since there were no guarantees as to how the guards would react and though he'd never admit it to his present company, he hated guns. But Quicks and Thabo were good shooters so if force had to be used, he'd coached them to aim where there would be minimal damage.

Two of the men in Royal Guard uniforms ran up to the Rockefeller Diamonds building on foot to overpower the security guards at reception. They found them standing as if cued for some action, their morning coffees going cold.

'Thank God you guys got here so soon,' said one. 'We think there was an incident at the gate but the cameras are blurred—'

At the sudden appearance of guns and tasers their eyes grew very wide.

'Shit!' said Vusi. 'So you've alerted security, hmm? Bad move.'

Before they could blink the two crewmates shot the guards with steel darts from the stun guns, then expertly tied them up like the others. They dragged them into the staff kitchen on the ground floor and locked them in.

Back at the entrance to the office park, Quicks slipped into the guardhouse to get the remote for the boom gate. Once he pressed it open, The Duke was already in the driver's seat of the Audi. He drove in, followed by the Golf GTI and the fake security vehicle. Themba, dressed in a Royal Guard uniform, stayed behind in the guardhouse to watch over the unconscious guards and man the gate.

They knew the location of all the security cameras courtesy of Wiese's intel, and many paper rehearsals with The Duke. It was Thabo's task to spray paint the outside ones, which he now did, quickly and with gusto.

Inside the building the crew paused and listened. No sound, no movement. Good.

They knew that the manager would be at the vault, which was located on the fourth floor, with three guards, busy with the inventory. Armed and masked, they went up in the lift, and stepped out without making a sound.

'On the floor! Now!' ordered The Duke. 'Or you get a bullet to your head!'

The four staff members dropped to the floor, fear clouding their faces.

Thabo and Quicks stunned them by shooting steel darts from the tasers, then tied them up while the rest of the crew got to work in the vault.

Expensive watches, diamond rings, necklaces and all manner of assorted jewellery and gemstones gleamed and glittered at them but they wasted no time in admiration. They began stuffing everything into the bags they'd brought with them for the haul.

The Duke looked at his watch.

Twenty minutes since they'd started the operation.

They were running five minutes later than scheduled.

The day shift would be arriving any second.

He urged the men to hurry, to get a move on – which they did. Bags bulging, and the crew sweating behind their masks, they scrambled out of the place, adrenalin coursing through their veins.

The Duke's heart was racing. They had made it!

At the gate they were met by response guards from Royal Guards.

The Duke's heart skipped several beats.

Why hadn't Themba alerted them? He'd been at the gate all along.

Then Thabo stepped out of their own branded Royal Guard security vehicle.

'Hi, gents. How can we help you?'

The real guards sat in their vehicle and looked at the fake guards in their uniforms.

'We got an alarm signal here at Rockefellers,' said one.

'Yes. So did we,' said Thabo. 'We got here ten minutes ago. There was a break-in. The cops are on their way.'

'Shit. Are there any casualties?'

Thabo shook his head. 'No. No casualties. We actually have to rush to another call. This is one crazy Wednesday morning!'

As Thabo moved to get back in his vehicle, one of the guards held up a hand. 'Aren't you going to wait for the police?'

'No,' said Quicks from the window of his car. 'You guys can take care of that. Besides, nothing was taken.'

The guard looked at him dubiously, then shook his head. 'I think you need to wait,' he insisted.

In a flash two of the crew jumped out of the Audi behind Quicks' security van and positioned themselves on either side of the Royal Guards' vehicle.

'Out of the car now!' they ordered.

One of the guards got out but made the mistake of tackling Thabo, trying to get hold of his gun. Thabo pulled up the gun and kicked the guy in the groin. Then he punched him in the face. Quicks and The Duke got out of their cars and pointed their guns at the two men.

'Don't try anything stupid,' Quicks advised. 'Unless you want your guts all over the pavement!'

A few swift blows with batons and the guards were on the ground. Pads soaked in chloroform sent them to dreamland and allowed the men to bundle them back into their vehicle without resistance. The Duke pocketed their car keys and, as they drove away, Quicks fired a few shots at their tyres for good measure. There was no time to tie them up. The police really would be on their way by now.

Speeding away with the loot – one hundred million rands' worth of jewellery! – The Duke could scarcely believe it. The smile on his face would stay there until the crew had dumped the cars at Quicks' panel-beater friend's scrapyard. He'd also made sure to dump the burner phone where it belonged . . . into the Jukskei River.

Nothing would be left to connect any of them to the job.

One hundred million rand! Now that was a good twenty-eight minutes' work!

Wie Sien Ons

Noma had not succeeded in landing a lift with Paul and Tom. Paul first had to pick Tom up from Rosebank on his way and another detour would make them late arriving in Phokeng.

So, she'd had to drive solo.

She fumed all the way there and all the way back on the highway, getting even crosser when her husband failed to pick up any of her calls.

When her phone rang and it was Paul, she almost snapped at him.

'Hi, darling,' said Paul, 'how're you feeling?'

'Depressed. That was one of the saddest funerals I've ever attended.'

'Yes . . . all that underlying tension didn't help, did it?'

'Mm-hmm. I'm just so tired.'

'Are you too tired to drop by our place? What's a funeral without *wie sien ons*?'

Noma laughed softly. She hadn't heard that term in a long time. These days they called it 'after tears'. South Africans honestly found any excuse to party. Before tears, during tears, and after tears. It just went on and on and on. And that bloody Duke had dared to avoid most of it as if he were some kind of Mzwandile-*Lite*.

'I guess I could use a glass of wine or two.'

'Perfect. You know where to come, right? Tom and I would love to have you over.'

As Noma drove to Shangri La, her mind kept wandering back to The Duke's strange behaviour. He'd left home without even saying goodbye, never mind that she wasn't actually speaking to him. He had mumbled something about working off-site today, but was that even true? Was he really at work?

She decided to call his workplace, something she hadn't done in years. She spoke to the receptionist and asked her if The Duke had reported for work that day.

The receptionist, who was good friends with The Duke, told her that yes, Mr Manamela was at work but had stepped out of the office.

Noma frowned. Maybe he was telling the truth . . . but why couldn't he pick up any of her calls?

Frustrated, she followed the directions on the GPS system until she got to Paul and Tom's beautiful home. Paul was waiting for her at the front door with a glass of champagne.

'Come in, come in. *Mi casa, su casa,*' he said. He had changed out of his formal clothes and was wearing stonewashed jeans and a Ralph Lauren sweater.

Tom was in the kitchen frying prawns and making a creamy tagliatelle pasta.

She drifted into the house, appreciating the décor again. The last time she and Julius were here was the August social club event the couple had hosted. How long ago that seemed suddenly.

'Wow. I still can't get over how gorgeous your house is!' she said.

'Thank you, darling. Now have a seat, while I go get Tom.'

He returned with his partner, who was wearing an apron that said it all: 'Sexy Chef'.

'Whatever you're cooking smells absolutely divine,' said Noma.

'Thanks, Noma. By the way, I love your dress. Is it Valentino?'

'Of course. What else, darling?'

They laughed. Tom went back to the kitchen, promising to call them to the dining room as soon as he was ready to serve the meal.

'So . . .' said Paul when the three of them were seated at the Italian marble dining room table, 'what a funeral, hey?'

Noma shook her head. 'I still can't believe that Mzwandile didn't at least attend his own wife's funeral. I mean . . . who does that?'

'How long had they been married?' Tom asked, licking sauce off his fingers.

'Almost twenty years, apparently,' said Noma.

'Wow. But I bet this was Lerato's first and only indiscretion. Two decades together – and you throw it all away because you found out your wife was having an affair,' said Paul. 'I hope he was worth it.'

'Well . . .' said Noma, 'I actually know who Lerato was sleeping with . . .'

'Do tell!' said Tom, rubbing his hands at the promise of salacious details.

'He works at the company we outsource for our CSI work. Zimbabwean guy . . . tall, good-looking and . . . wait for it . . . he was there!'

'Where?' said Tom.

'At the funeral!'

'No way!' Paul breathed.

'Why would the family allow him to attend the funeral?' asked Tom. 'Didn't he hide her body or something morbid like that?'

Noma shrugged. 'Who knows why? Maybe it was a way of saying up yours to the husband.'

'Do the kids know about him?'

'I don't know,' said Noma. 'Maybe they know of him but probably don't know what he looks like.'

'Wait. I think I saw a guy in a grey pinstriped suit with this tortured, broken-vows type of look. He was standing all alone by the graveside. Was that him?' asked Tom.

Noma giggled. 'You're so dramatic, but yes! That was him. He wasn't alone though. He came with Frans, the Zebula account director. Frans is the one who dished the juicy details about the whole thing. The affair had been going on for months.'

'Wow,' said Tom, taking a gulp of his champagne.

'I still can't believe that virginal Lerato was even capable of an affair . . . a months-long one, for that matter. I mean, you'd think she was born in Nazareth for all her coyness,' remarked Paul.

'Personally, I don't understand why people even have affairs,' said Noma. 'I mean . . . it's all so messy and unnecessary.'

She gulped down her hypocrisy with a glass of champagne, pushing back memories of her crush on Tafadzwa.

Paul shrugged. 'I still say you straight people like to complicate things unnecessarily. The whole concept of monogamy is seriously flawed. How narcissistic would you have to be to think that someone will only be attracted to you for years on end?'

'It's not narcissism!' exclaimed Noma.

'Well, what is it then?'

'Tom . . . does this mean that if Paul cheated on you he'd expect you to accept it because he's not "narcissistic"?'

Tom laughed uneasily. 'It's not black and white like that,' he said, casting his eyes downwards.

Was it embarrassment he felt?

'Forgive Tom,' said Paul. 'He can be Lerato-like about these things. He was a devout Christian before I came along and corrupted him.'

'Oh please, Paul. Don't flatter yourself,' Tom hissed back.

Noma widened her eyes, wondering if she'd stepped into a prickly zone for the couple. 'Anyway, let's drink to Lerato. She turned out to be quite the dark horse, didn't she?' she said.

The two men laughed.

'Well, at least her church contingent was there to send her off. Imagine if they'd also decided to blacklist her like her hubby,' remarked Paul.

'Yeah, but you should have heard the whispers from the three aunties who were sitting behind me at the funeral reception. In between bites of the slaughtered sacrificial cow, they were gossiping away like *shwashi*,' Tom chipped in.

The other two laughed.

'So what were they saying?'

'"Can you believe it? Mrs Pastor herself! So all the while she was standing at the podium making those announcements in church, turns out she was busy running around with younger men in her spare time,"' said Tom, laying on the theatrics for extra effect.

'Poor Lerato,' said Paul. 'Well, I'm not judging her. We all have our faults. Cheers to the enigmatic spirit that she turned out to be.'

'Cheers,' they all said in unison as they clinked their glasses.

Unravelling

Moshidi woke up in yet another grey fugue.

She'd been having a recurring dream that dated back to her childhood. She'd been a perfectionist even then, but one school subject managed to trip her up. In the dream, she'd been crocheting complicated patterns as part of a crafts project. She'd worked painstakingly on it but each time she submitted it to the crafts teacher, the teacher would regard her with a cross expression on her face.

'This is not good enough, Moshidi! You're going to have to undo it and start again.'

This was the third time she'd had this dream in the past two weeks. She'd wake up, heart rocking hard against her chest, mouth parched, throat filled with panic rising up like bile.

She opened her eyes, and turned to look at the unoccupied space on her bed.

She and Solomzi had been sleeping in separate bedrooms since 'the incident' but had had to put up a show of unity during the *matshidiso* period, when some of her relatives had stayed with them.

Now that everyone was gone, she was all alone, dealing with the double blow of simultaneously losing her sister and her marriage.

Lerato – her darling sister. Her soulmate, the one constant in her life. Gone. Just like that. No serious signs of sickness, no drama, just . . . gone.

She could not stand to look at Solomzi, even though he'd been a model husband during the funeral arrangements. The cynical part of her only noticed how present he was now, such a stark contrast to his famous golf outings.

She had often wondered if there was more to those outings than moronically chasing a white ball around.

She shrugged. Not that it mattered anymore. Even if he had twenty concubines out there on the streets, it was fine with her. They could all have him. Shaking her head helplessly, she wondered how it was possible that she had lost a sister and a marriage in the same week . . . practically the same day. What deranged karmic forces were at play here?

Her helper *ausi* Lizzie knocked on her door.

'*Dumela*, madam. Are you okay this morning?'

Moshidi gazed at her and nodded. She must think I'm out of my mind, she mused.

'Um . . . Mr Solomzi asked if you wouldn't mind coming out for breakfast with him.' She looked at the woman, not sure if she'd registered what she'd just said. 'Madam . . . did you hear what I . . . ?'

Someone hurled out a wild, piercing scream.

Lizzie jumped, looking utterly startled.

Did she just do that? Good God! She needed to be checked into a psych ward.

Lizzie approached her tentatively, as if she were dealing with a wild, chained animal, and sat on the bed next to her.

'Madam . . . please. Try and get up. You need to get out of this bed. The children are going to start noticing that something's not right.'

Moshidi just stared into space.

Solomzi walked in.

He looked thinner than how she normally visualised him in her mind's eye. She'd been seeing him a lot in her head. First date. Wedding day. Her pregnancies. A film reel of their lives. He never looked like this. What was wrong with him?

'Babe . . . can I come in, please?'

She shook her head.

He moved slowly towards her. Why was everyone treating her like a poisonous snake? A crazy voice inside her told her to stick out her tongue. Just to see if there were real fangs behind her lips.

She wasn't sure if she listened to the voice.

Then Solomzi was sitting next to her.

'Baby . . . you have to get out of this room. The kids are starting to worry about you. Please, *sthandwa sam*. I know you loved Lerato. She wouldn't want to see you like this. I'm here for you. So are the kids and everyone who loves you. At least take small steps. Get into the shower. Put on something to make yourself feel good. I'll cook you a nice breakfast . . . or anything you want. Or . . . or we can go out to your favourite restaurant.'

'Huh!'

'What . . . what does that mean, hon? Please. Work with me, here. If not for me, then for the kids.'

She shook her head and ducked back under the covers.

Good Spirits

Unlike Moshidi, The Duke had been in good spirits for weeks. At first Noma was sceptical of his sunny disposition, chalking it down to a new extra-marital affair, but she slowly succumbed to her husband's charms. There was such a sense of contentment about him these days. And also he had been very attentive towards her of late.

This morning she was finally ready to tell him about her big decision.

To become the owner of a gold mine in Zimbabwe . . .

What would he think!

She got up early and made The Duke breakfast in bed. While he ate appreciatively and sipped his hot tea with three sugars, he listened to his wife's ambitious plan.

'Wow!' he said when she'd finished outlining the strategy. 'You're a real warrior, Nomathando Manamela! A gold mine . . .'

She had succeeded in impressing The Duke!

'Yes, my hon, and it will bear the Manamela name. The mine currently produces up to twelve hundred tonnes . . . per day! If we play our cards right, this could be the real legacy we leave for our children, grandchildren and great-grandchildren. Just like we always said we would!'

'So what's the asking price and how are you planning to raise the money?'

'The asking price is huge but I'm confident we'll raise the money. With the money we have in our investments and savings, we can make a good case to the IDC or even the Development Bank of SA to provide us with a business loan.'

The Duke nodded thoughtfully. 'Well. What if I have some other money that I could help you with as an advance to fund the mine? I mean, you and I are married in community of property so what's yours is mine, *mos?*'

She looked at him quizzically. 'Are you talking about your pension money?'

He looked at her sardonically and grinned. 'I'm talking about some *money.*'

She kissed him passionately. 'Stop being silly. First of all, I know where all your money is . . . and I know the value of your pension fund to the last cent.'

'*Hey wena,*' he said, pulling her leg towards him, 'are you planning to kill me? Why are you busy calculating my pension fund?'

'Because . . . I need to make sure at all times that I will never spend a day in discomfort.'

'You're such a gold digger! Why didn't my mom warn me about you?' he said playfully, grabbing both legs and strapping them around his naked body.

'I dig for gold in far, faraway lands. That's why your mother had no choice but to love me!' she said as she kissed him and stroked him passionately.

◆ ◆ ◆

Nthabiseng stared out of the window of the domestic quarters, wondering once more if her life was destined to mirror her mother's – working day in and out, catering to the whims of the rich.

She wondered if her mother found any joy in what she was doing.

But more importantly . . . what was her own destiny? Was she going to follow the same path as Tshidi?

No. She was certain her path would be different.

Suddenly she felt such a strong sense of conviction about her own purpose that she found herself feeling boundlessly hopeful.

Then she went back to staring out the window.

Today was a typical South African day. The sun was shining, the skies were azure blue, as if nature conspired to bring cheer to all and sundry. It was mid-morning and nobody was out in the yard. It looked so empty, peaceful and desolate that she could not resist the urge to go outside and chase the glorious sun.

The people in the big house seemed in good spirits today, which meant her mother would be toiling after them all day.

She put on leggings, an oversized T-shirt and a pair of sneakers, then skipped playfully out of the house to the yard. As she was skipping and enjoying the sunlight on her skin, she saw a car pull into the driveway. She sprinted back into her mother's room where she lifted the corner of the curtain and peeped out, hoping the driver had not seen her. A good-looking man in a designer T-shirt, jeans, sneakers and shades unfolded his legs from a gold sports car and walked straight through the kitchen door.

'Hello, parents. How're you guys doing?'

'Khutso. Look at you! You look like some Hollywood movie star,' said Noma proudly, beaming from ear to ear.

Tshidi came into the lounge carrying laundry up the stairs. She placed the laundry on the floor and stopped to look at Khutso. '*He mme we!* Khutso!? Why do you never come to visit us anymore?'

Khutso looked at her and shrugged. 'Busy, Tshidi. I'm out there trying to make some cash.'

'Goodness, Khutso! Does this cash thing never run out? You can't always chase cash,' Tshidi admonished him.

He looked at her from his seat on the couch and chose not to respond. Tshidi picked up her laundry basket and continued up the stairs, not commenting on his rudeness.

'So what's new?' Khutso said, addressing his parents.

'We're doing well, my boy. Your mom and I are on our second honeymoon these days. You know she always worried that when you *piccanins* left, our lives would change for the worse, but things are actually quite good.'

'Really?' said Khutso, crossing his legs. 'So good that you've adopted another daughter? My sister's not going to be happy about that.'

Noma looked at him enquiringly. 'What are you talking about?' she said. She gave her husband a sharp look but he didn't seem to know what Khutso was talking about either.

Khutso shrugged in his arrogant way. 'I saw some kid jumping up and down in the yard when I drove in. She disappeared when she saw me, but she was definitely there.'

'Hey man. Are you hallucinating? There's no kid here in this house,' said The Duke.

Tshidi came down with the empty laundry basket to fill it with more clean laundry to take back upstairs to the ironing room.

'Tshidi!' Noma called out. 'Please come here a minute?'

Tshidi appeared in the doorway and set the laundry basket down.

'Did you see a young child here in the yard?' Noma asked.

'A what? No.' Tshidi shook her head.

'Okay. There you go. Probably just one of the neighbour's kids,' said The Duke.

The Duke and his son went into the games room to play a game of pool but Noma was unsettled by what Khutso had just told them.

She waited for Tshidi to go back upstairs, then, on a hunch, she went out to the maid's quarters.

She found a teenager sitting on Tshidi's double bed, painting her nails.

'Tshidi!' she screamed, arms folded, glaring at the young girl, who had jumped up in terror at her sudden appearance.

'Oh no . . . madam . . . I'm so sorry. I can explain. Please. I can explain.'

'Tshidi!' Noma screamed again.

The maid's quarters were away from the house, but by some instinct it seemed as if Tshidi had heard her all the way from upstairs. Or maybe panic at what Noma's son had said had brought her rushing to her room.

'Ma'am. *Ausi* Noma. I'm sorry. This is my daughter. She is just passing through. I'm going to take her to the taxi rank just as soon as I'm done with the ironing.'

'What is she doing here?' demanded Noma, ignoring everything Tshidi had just blurted out.

'She is just passing by to get money for some school stationery. As soon as I'm done with the ironing, I'll walk her to the taxi rank, I promise.'

Noma looked at Nthabiseng with distaste, then marched back to the house.

'She'd better be gone by midday,' she said over her shoulder. 'I didn't sign up for a buy-one-get-one-free package here.'

Desperate Times

Lawrence and Kudzayi's lawyer had been working on a plea bargain deal with the prosecutor on their case. The evidence leaned heavily against them, but because they were first-time offenders Munyaradzi hoped to get them a suspended sentence. The hearing had been going well so far.

Kudzayi had been wrongfully arrested in his early twenties when he had just arrived in South Africa. He'd been dating a young local woman whose gangster boyfriend convinced her to lay rape charges against Kudzayi to prove her loyalty to him. The young woman had gone along with the plan and had even managed to get her boyfriend's friends to testify that they had been witnesses to the alleged rape. She later recanted her story when Kudzayi was about to be sentenced to jail.

Munyaradzi had made a strong case that the two foreign young men had acted out of panic based on prior experience with the South African justice system. He had pulled records from the trial to substantiate his argument.

The lawyer had also asked Lawrence to reach out to Moshidi to see if she would be willing to appear as a witness for the defence.

Lawrence was nervous about talking to Moshidi after the funeral, even though she had been pleasant, if a little cool, towards him at the service. He had not known how to interpret her attitude.

Clearly she was grieving. There could have been any number of reasons for her detached demeanour.

He had called her three times and left a message on his third attempt. Two weeks had now passed without hearing anything from her.

Munyaradzi insisted that a good word from a member of Lerato's family would augur well for their case, but Lawrence was already guilt-ridden about the whole debacle. He wondered if it wasn't best to just accept whatever sentence was meted out to them.

But then there was Kudzayi, who had had nothing to do with the affair. And now that he knew the reasons behind Kudzayi's paranoia, he felt even more sorry for dragging the guy into his mess.

He was busy mopping the floor in his kitchen when his phone pinged.

It was a text from Moshidi.

Hi Lawrence. I'm sorry I haven't been able to return your calls. Tough couple of months. Call if you can.

He gazed at his phone, scarcely believing that she had finally reached out to him. He dropped the mop in the cleaning bucket and went to sit down on the couch, contemplating what he was going to say. Just as Moshidi had felt about their first meeting – a lifetime ago, it felt to him – he reckoned his request needed a face-to-face conversation.

He rang her.

'Hi, Lawrence. How are you?' said Moshidi.

'I could be better . . . and I guess I could be worse.'

'Join the club. I saw a couple of calls from you but I haven't been well. My sister's death took a toll on me, if I'm to be honest.'

'I understand, believe me. Moshidi . . . is it possible at all to meet me for coffee? I need to discuss something with you.'

'Hmm. I haven't been able to do much of that. I only went back to work this week. Not sure if I'm up to coffee.'

'Please? If it wasn't important, I wouldn't ask. I know you owe me no favours, but I would really appreciate it if you could give me just an hour of your time . . .' Lawrence said. 'An hour max,' he added.

She paused, then said, 'Sure. I suppose I can make time. When do you want to meet?'

'Anytime when you're free. Maybe tomorrow?'

'Okay. Tashas in Morningside. Around eleven?'

'That's great. Perfect. Thank you,' he said.

Moshidi had been seeing a psychologist after she realised that the trauma of her recent experiences was taking a severe toll on her. She was on anti-depressants and beginning to feel a bit better. She had started being more involved with her children and had even gone for a few runs around the estate. She had also managed to secure a divorce lawyer but hadn't scheduled a meeting with her yet.

The situation at home remained tense. They could no longer say they owned a house in Zimbali and the same might soon be true of the Knysna mansion. And the boat. She'd seen a Final Demand for Solomzi's golf club membership, which was the only thing that had made her smile in a while. What a mess.

To her surprise she discovered that she did not care all that much about losing the material assets that she and Solomzi had acquired over the years. All she wanted was a simple life in which her children's future would be secure. These days, she found herself wondering how she and Solomzi had landed in this race for more and more and more. All it had done was make them both miserable and overworked. And in debt. But she didn't want to think about that part just yet.

When she arrived at Tashas, she found Lawrence tucking into a beef burger.

He smiled when he saw her.

'Sorry,' he said. 'I got here an hour ago. I was starving, so I helped myself to a meal. Please sit down. Have something to eat . . . or drink.'

She sat down and placed her bag on the chair next to her. It felt strange to be meeting up with Lawrence after all that had happened. Stranger still that she had now officially seen more of him than she had of Mzwandile.

Lwazi and Bongani had been visiting regularly at the house. They were part of the reason she found the strength to pull herself off the clasps of depression. They seemed so lost that she felt compelled to take on a more motherly role towards them. Their father stubbornly stuck to his position of cuckold. How do you give the silent treatment to the dead? Such utter fuckery.

Lost in her train of thought, she was roused by Lawrence's voice.

'Moshidi, the waiter asked if you'd like something to drink?'

She shook her head out of the spell and raised her head.

'Hi,' she said to the waiter. 'Can I have a chai tea, please?'

'Sure, ma'am,' he said.

'Thank you for coming,' said Lawrence. 'How've you been coping?'

'Not well . . . but I'm taking things a day at a time.'

He nodded. 'This has been really tough . . . I can't believe it's been two months.'

Moshidi fidgeted with her scarf. 'Yes. So what did you want to talk to me about?'

Lawrence looked at her nervously, scratched his face, then said, 'You and I might be the king and queen of awkward meetings.'

She didn't smile.

'Moshidi . . . I need to ask you something . . . and if you're mad at me for even asking, I'll understand.'

Moshidi folded her arms.

'Look. You know that I'm facing charges for . . . for moving Lerato's body from my place,' he said, pulling pieces off the paper napkin on the table. 'I was wondering . . . I know it's too much to ask for but is it possible to just . . . maybe . . . put in a good word with the prosecutor on the case. I mean, I know your family's not happy with me but . . . I'm looking at possible jail time and I—' He pinched his forehead.

Moshidi shook her head. 'Wow. So you want us to say we're okay with you having moved my sister's body from your apartment?'

Lawrence let out a long sigh. 'Look, I know this is asking too much . . .'

'You think?'

He pursed his lips. 'Shit. I'm s— I'm sorry for having even asked. I guess . . . I guess I should just accept my fate. I shouldn't have asked,' he said, casting his eyes downwards in embarrassment.

Moshidi stood up and took her handbag. 'I'm sorry, Lawrence,' she said. 'I can't help you.'

Then she walked out of the restaurant without looking back.

Switcheroo

Noma had left for Zimbabwe on Thursday and would only be returning home on Tuesday.

The Duke was excited to surprise her with the money that he would be getting for his share of the haul from the jewellery heist.

He'd enjoyed reading up on what the news sites were calling the 'Great Jewellery Heist' at Rockefeller Jewellers. Words like 'daring' and 'dangerous' were used to describe it.

Danie Wiese, as ever, was a chess master who always played two steps ahead of the game. Even though the total value of the jewellery The Duke and his crew had stolen was about 100 million rands, he'd noticed that the press reported it to be worth 210 million. Clearly the old jackal was planning to claim double the amount from his insurance.

Being the mastermind behind the heist, The Duke had taken his time to study the stock and its individual value so that he could ensure that he had his twenty million share. He had also managed to find a buyer – some Greeks – for half of his stock. They were willing to take it for seventeen million; a whole three million less than its value but selling on the black market always came at a price. The Greeks were due to come the next morning, Sunday.

With Noma away, The Duke was alone in the property on Saturday night, except for Tshidi, who was in her living quarters at the back of the house. Early in the evening he made his way to the garage, his plan being to remove half the spoils from their hiding place in the storeroom at the back and decant them from the duffel bags they were in into some other receptacles. He stood contemplating the scene and surveying the crammed storeroom shelves. A couple of those laundry bags he'd seen Tshidi use would do nicely, he suddenly thought, but where did she keep them? He went back into the house. After a half-hearted attempt to find the linen closet and opening and closing a couple of drawers in the kitchen, he gave up and went back out to the garage. The little storeroom was a mess. The old heavy-duty duffel bag was still where he'd left it two months ago, right there on the floor, and still with some of the stuff inside it that he'd procured for the job. Leftover chloroform bottles, rope, tasers . . . Tomorrow. Tomorrow, after the Greeks had been, he would make a trip to the dumping site. In the meantime, he needed those laundry bags. The chloroform fumes were making him slightly dizzy so he went back into the house, feeling tired and suddenly hungry. He realised he hadn't eaten all day.

This had definitely been his last job.

But what a great way to retire.

◆ ◆ ◆

When Tshidi heard her phone buzz, she regarded it with irritation.

'Mama. Your phone is ringing,' said Nthabiseng.

After she had been discovered two months ago, Nthabiseng had stopped spending time at the Manamelas. But once again, xenophobic attacks had resumed in their township and so, with the old lady away somewhere for a few days, Tshidi had snuck her in on Friday evening.

Their particular area was also a hotbed of crime. They were considering moving Nthabiseng to Soweto, but Tshidi was very uncomfortable with this plan as her relative there was a single man who'd once been accused of sexual assault, although he consistently cried innocence. The other option was to send Nthabi to Lesotho, but again, she was not happy with the quality of education in Sekhutlong village and the teachers were constantly going on strike because they often did not receive their salaries. The more she thought about their situation, the bleaker and more desperate it seemed.

She looked at the phone once more and rolled her eyes. '*Bathong*. It's eight o'clock in the evening. Am I ever going to get any rest?' she moaned.

'Mama, just go. You don't want him coming here to check on you, do you?'

She answered the phone. 'Hello?'

'Tshidi. I need your help quickly. Can you bring me three of your drawstring laundry bags?'

'Excuse me?'

'I need your cotton laundry bags.'

'Um . . . really? What for, sir?'

'*He banna*. Just bring me the bags, Tshidi!'

Tshidi stood up irritably and put on her housecoat.

'What does he want so late?' asked Nthabi.

'*Ngwanaka*. That man is just strange, strange, strange. He wants me to bring him laundry bags. Imagine. Sometimes I think that old man is a thug. What's he doing with laundry bags in the middle of the night?'

Nthabi laughed. '*Yho*, Mama. Rich people,' she said.

Tshidi took out the laundry bags from where she kept them in the bottom of her wardrobe and went into the house through the kitchen door. She found her boss waiting in the pajama lounge.

'Ah yes, thanks, Tshidi,' he said, taking the bags from her.

As Tshidi turned to go, he stopped her.

'Listen, can you fix me a glass of Lagavulin, put in three ice cubes, and bring it to me before you go to sleep? *Eish* . . . and can you warm that dinner for me? I didn't have a chance to eat . . .'

Nthabiseng thought her mother was taking quite a long time to drop the laundry bags. She looked out of the window, saw that the light was on in the kitchen, and saw her mother's shape move inside. All was quiet outside, and she went back to her book. Suddenly she heard a strange noise coming from somewhere in the yard. She peered out and then jumped back with fright. A tall, lean figure dressed in black and wearing a dark balaclava had just walked past.

Terrified, after a minute she peeped back out again, lifting the smallest corner of the curtain. To her alarm, she saw a second man, also all in black, but this one was scaling up the wall of the house on a rope! He moved swiftly and was soon by the balcony of one of the rooms on the second floor. What did her mother call it? Oh yes. The pajama lounge.

It looked like he was trying to prise the balcony door open. After a few minutes of struggle, she saw it open, and the man disappeared.

'Oh my God. Oh my God,' she whispered.

What to do? She needed to call someone.

Maybe she could call Mr Manamela?

Did her mom's phone even have airtime?

The Duke felt a cold metal push against the back of his head.

'Hey, Old Timer . . . keep still. Nothing's gonna happen to you as long as you follow my orders, okay?'

Before he knew what was happening, another man was in front of him, pointing a gun at his chest.

Shit. What the fuck?

The man behind him put masking tape on his lips, grabbed hold of his wrists and tied him up with a tight rope. The one in front left the room as silently as he'd entered it.

He had a terrible thought. Tshidi! She was downstairs in the kitchen fixing his dinner.

Then he had a truly terrible thought. His jewellery! His jewellery was sitting in two duffel bags right there on the storeroom floor in the garage, just sitting there for these scumbags to take! The garage was right next to the kitchen. He'd left it open, intending to go back with the laundry bags.

He had another thought. Did these two already know it was there?

Was this some sleight of hand from that bastard Wiese?

How did these thieves know to come here? Tonight of all nights?

Or could it be the Greeks?

Fuck. No. This definitely had Danie Wiese written all over it.

He heard Tshidi scream, then something that sounded like a heavy blow, and silence. He tried yelling but of course only muffled sounds came out of him. He of all people knew how effective masking tape was.

The man in the pajama lounge pulled him to his feet and marched him along the passage to the master bedroom. He sat him down on one of the occasional chairs, then tied him to it. Once he was satisfied that The Duke was powerless, he took off the masking tape.

'Okay, Old Timer. We're not here to play. Show me the safe and give me the combinations. If you cooperate with us, we'll be out of here in no time. Okay?'

The Duke looked at him. He had a tall, lean body, but his face was completely masked. His paranoia was in overdrive. Was this one of the bastards that were part of the Rockefeller robbery with him? One of Quicks' boys? Themba maybe, the one who'd proved unreliable in the guard house? But surely, he'd recognise the voice if that was the case? He'd spent a fair amount of time with the team in the pre-planning phase.

'What's happening downstairs? What have you done to my maid?' he asked, a sudden vision of the gleaming diamonds in the garage, just a few metres from the kitchen, coming into his mind.

The guy hit him hard on the head with the butt of his gun.

'Old Timer, I said I don't have much time here. Give me the combination to the safe. Now!'

The Duke showed him the safe and gave him the combination.

In seconds it was open and the thief wasted no time clearing it out and shoving the contents into his backpack, while The Duke watched helplessly.

There were cash notes of about R150 000.

His and hers Rolexes, Louis Vuittons and Tag Heuers.

Noma's expensive jewellery – rings, bracelets, necklaces.

Keepsakes too, small things of no value, but things he and Noma held sacred from the decades of their lives together.

The thief was so happy, he was whistling.

'Ha! Today's the day! Today *is* the day. My God is good oh! Eh . . . my God is good oh,' he kept saying, whistling the tune to the popular song while smiling from ear to ear. When the safe was empty, he turned back to The Duke.

'Okay, Old Timer. What else, what else? Where's your wallet?'

The Duke felt hopeful. If the man was this excited over their private collection, then maybe he didn't know about the loot in the storeroom.

The thief came over and hit him hard on the mouth with the gun.

He could feel his gums bleeding.

'*Hey wena, sthipha*. Where's the rest? Are you deaf?' the man shouted.

The Duke told him to open the walk-in closet. Inside it there was a display unit with more jewellery, expensive bags, designer shoes. The value of these items was more than a million rand. The thief called down to his friend.

'Hey, Samson! Come up here fast! Bring the maid.'

Tshidi looked like she was in shock. She was gagged with a torn cloth and her hands were tied with rope. Her face was bruised.

The bastards!

'Tie up that bitch and let's get moving! There's enough stuff here to set us up for life.'

The one called Samson did as he was told. He pushed Tshidi down on to another chair and tied her to it. Then he started piling all the luxury items into his own backpack.

They had collected sizeable pickings when they heard the sirens.

First far away, then closer.

Closer.

Then right outside the house. Blue lights flashing.

'Oh fuck. Fuck. Fuck. Who called the cops! Who the fuck called the cops?' demanded the first thief, kicking The Duke on the mouth with his heavy, military-style boot.

'Was it you, bitch?' asked the one called Samson, punching Tshidi in the face.

'Samson, let's get out of here,' said the first guy, heading back towards the pajama lounge, where the balcony door was still open and the rope they'd used to scale up the wall still hanging.

'Come down slowly or we shoot!'

There were six officers in all, each one with a weapon drawn.

'Fuck,' said Samson, as he scaled helplessly down the wall to his impending fate.

Cops and robbers, but this wasn't a game.

Both men were handcuffed, relieved of their bulging backpacks, and shoved unceremoniously into the back of a police van.

The whole job took less than twenty-eight minutes.

Possessions

The three remaining cops went inside the house to check on the victims.

One of them, Prince, was not unfamiliar with this house and its inhabitants.

He remembered responding to a domestic violence call about a year ago, which had turned out to be a false alarm. He hoped the couple was unharmed. He had taken a bit of a liking to the old man, the one who owned those fancy cars. And that brave young girl, the one who had opened the door for them and was now rushing past him like a tornado into the house, was their helper's daughter.

Nthabiseng had been right. Tshidi's phone hadn't had enough airtime for her to make the call to the police so she'd had to be resourceful. She had sent a 'Please Call Me' text to Mrs Manamela, who'd called back right away. Nthabi explained the situation as clearly and as quickly as she could. Luckily, Noma had been too shocked to ask her what she was doing there.

In the end it was Noma who had called the police. All the way from Zimbabwe.

While his two colleagues hurried upstairs after the child, who was worried sick about her mother, Prince looked around the rooms on the ground floor to make sure there was no one else there. Then he followed his colleagues upstairs.

Thankfully, the old man seemed relatively unharmed, save for a nosebleed he was nursing.

The maid also seemed fine though shaken.

'Mr Manamela, are you okay?' Prince asked.

The Duke looked at him, seemingly not registering his face. He nodded absently and continued giving his statement to Detective Khanyi Ndyodya. The other officer was talking to the child's mother and taking down her account of events.

Seeing that his colleagues were in control of the situation, Prince could not resist going downstairs to admire the exotic Lamborghinis. When he got to the garage, he took out his Samsung phone to take a snap of the two Lambos, maybe a quick selfie. He drew in his breath. There were four other cars in the huge garage – a Maserati, a beat-up Merc, and two Porsche Cayennes.

What did these two do for a living to afford such a luxurious lifestyle?

As he walked around the garage, he noticed a duffel bag on the cement floor just inside what looked like some kind of storage room. He walked over and pushed at the bag with his boot. It sagged open and he saw something gleaming inside. He got down on his haunches to take a closer look and was shocked to see a bounty of expensive-looking jewels of different kinds. Earrings, watches, necklaces, diamonds and gold, glittering up at him like something out of an upscale jewellery store. Curious, he went inside the storeroom, which was crammed to the rafters. A second duffel bag, a little way off from the first, contained even more jewellery. But what shocked him the most were the contents in the third duffel bag, an old heavy-duty one that looked like it had almost outlived its lifespan.

What the hell?

He took his phone out again and took pictures of all the items inside the storeroom, the items on the floor, the cars, everything he could think of.

What was going on here? Could these bags have been left by the thieves?

But that didn't make sense. When they were coming down, they were presumably leaving the job they'd just done. And their backpacks were full.

Maybe the plan was that they'd come back again for this bounty.

But that didn't make sense either.

And the ropes and the strong-smelling stuff in those bottles and the stun guns? What would those be doing in there?

Hang on . . . the jewellery . . . there was something about it that looked familiar.

He went to his phone's WhatsApp icon and clicked on the chat group he shared with some of the guys in the Murder and Robbery Unit.

He scrolled back to a conversation they'd had a month and a half ago. Ah . . . there it was! Pictures of the items claimed to have been stolen from 'The Great Jewellery Heist'. The case had boggled the minds of the guys at the precinct, as the brazen robbers seemed to have disappeared without a trace. They'd puzzled over it for weeks on end.

Bingo! He knew there was something about this bounty that looked familiar!

He went upstairs and joined his fellow officers.

'Guys, have you gathered the statements from the witnesses?'

Sergeant Khanyisa Ndyondya nodded.

'Can I have a look, please?' asked Prince.

She handed The Duke's statement to Prince.

He read through it, then said to Tshidi, '*Ausi*, the other robber . . . where did he find you?'

'*Shoo, Ntate. He marra.* I swear I nearly died today! He scared me. I was in the kitchen warming *Ntate* Manamela's food when the man just came out of nowhere and grabbed me by the throat. He strangled me then gagged me with this dirty piece of cloth.'

'And then what happened?'

'He asked me who else was in the house . . . he took out the cloth for me to speak. I told him it was just me and *Ntate* Manamela. He took me around the house . . . to make sure there was no one else.'

'Where in the house did you take him?'

'We went to the guest room, the bar, the lounge and the dining room, then his friend called him to come upstairs.'

'Can you repeat the rooms that you went to?'

The Duke interjected. 'How can you expect her to remember that? She was gagged and was panicking. What does that have to do with anything?'

'Sorry, sir. I know you're both traumatised. It's just important that we establish the sequence of events while everything is still fresh in your minds. Please continue, *ausi*.'

'First, we went to the lounge, past the dining room, then the two guest rooms, then that's when the friend called him to come upstairs.'

Prince nodded. 'Okay. And he didn't go anywhere else . . . maybe to your room or the garage or anything like that?'

'No. There was no time. I think his friend wanted them to get everything here in the bedroom because all the expensive things are here. You can just see. *Yho!* My madam is going to be so mad. I hope you managed to get everything back . . . *yho mme we*! All those Rolexes! Her bags! *Yho!* I just pray you have everything back.'

The Duke's face turned to ice. If the tall police officer had been to his garage . . .

'No, don't worry, *ausi*. We got them on their way down, so we have the bags. We have everything. We just need to log it all into evidence, but everything will be returned safe and sound.' He turned to The Duke. '*Ntate* Manamela, can you please come downstairs with me. Sergeant Ndyondya, please join us,' he said.

The senior policewoman looked at him askance. Prince just nodded and gestured for her to follow his order.

The three went downstairs, leaving Tshidi with the other officer.

Prince walked confidently to the garage, but The Duke stopped and hesitated when he saw where he was leading them.

'Everything okay, sir?' asked Sergeant Ndyondya.

'Eh . . . where are you taking us?' asked The Duke.

'Sergeant Ndyondya, I've made some interesting discoveries here. Come . . . both of you.'

The sergeant followed Prince to the storeroom, and gasped as he showed her the two duffel bags with the jewellery.

The Duke slowly walked into the garage and folded his arms.

'Mr Manamela, do these items belong to you?' Prince asked.

What to say? The tall cop had already established that the thieves hadn't entered his garage.

'Yes. Of course they do. That's why they're there.'

'Are you a jewellery trader?' asked Sergeant Ndyondya.

The Duke scratched his beard. 'Er . . . yes. I am.'

'So you will be able to show us certification for these assets? It's an unusual amount of jewellery to be kept in someone's garage,' said Ndyondya.

'Um . . . I think the thieves . . . they might have run away with the certificates.'

Prince laughed. 'Well. That's very convenient,' he said. 'You do realise we have everything they took in our evidence bags at the station, right? Sir, can you come closer?' He beckoned with his index finger.

Reluctantly, The Duke went to where Prince was standing next to the storeroom.

Prince took out the bag with the chloroform bottles and other incriminating items.

'Can you explain these items?'

The Duke looked at him spitefully. 'I think it's you who owes me an explanation,' he stalled. 'Why are you people questioning me when I'm the one who's just been burgled? It's obvious these thieves planted this stuff to make me look bad.'

'But I thought you said the jewellery belongs to you?' said Sergeant Ndyondya.

'And your helper said the thieves didn't go into the garage. Mr Manamela,' said Prince, 'you need to come with us to the station on suspicion of possession of stolen goods. You have a right to remain silent. Anything you say will and may be held against you in a court of law . . .'

Mercy

Moshidi's father had come to Johannesburg to visit a sick friend. When he called Moshidi, she asked to first meet him at a restaurant before he came to see his grandchildren at her home. She had not yet shared her intentions to dissolve her marriage to Solomzi, but she felt that it was time to discuss the issue with her father. After Lerato, he was her most trusted ally.

Her father had agreed to meet her at noon at a family restaurant not too far from her home.

As Moshidi pulled into the parking lot, she saw her dad stepping out of his old grey Volvo. He was wearing a light-green jacket, baggy jeans and a T-shirt. Summer was here but her winter of despair remained. She was still unhappy, still sad, but she hoped her father would not see through her forced smiles. She did not want to worry him. But at some point, she had to make her intentions known.

As he turned to go into the restaurant, he spotted her and stood waiting, his arms wide open. Moshidi rushed into them and stayed there, warm in her father's embrace.

'Aww! *Ngwaneke!*' he said, as he held her tightly.

Eventually they broke away from each other. He appraised her appearance and frowned. 'You've lost a lot of weight. Have you been eating?'

She smiled. 'No Papa. I'm on a diet.'

'A diet? You look like a twig. Don't you know that African men like some meat on those bones?'

She laughed dismissively. 'Okay then. Let's go eat. I promise to order half a sheep off the menu.'

'I'll hold you to it,' he said.

A waiter walked them to their table and they sat down. Her father asked after her husband and children. They made light banter about family and life until their food arrived.

After tucking into their meals, Moshidi ordered red wine for both of them.

'Papa, there's something important I want to talk to you about.'

Her dad wiped his mouth with a napkin and sipped his wine. 'I gathered as much. What is it, *ngwanake*? Is everything okay? Have you heard from your brother-in-law?'

'Oh no! Mzwandile? *Mxm!* Don't tell me about that one. That man is as cold as ice. I speak to the boys every day. Bongani managed to pass his matric exams, I don't know how, and he wants to get out of that house as soon as possible. Apparently, Mzwandile's whole life now revolves around his church life but he wants nothing to do with our family. The only thing that he's focusing on as far as Lerato is concerned is cashing her life cover. He's despicable that one, Papa.'

Her father shook his head. 'You know, I used to like that boy so much. I never thought he'd turn out to be so mean-spirited. To think that if this had been the other way round, my daughter would probably have even tried to hide this from everyone just to protect his reputation. Can you imagine how much worse things would have been if he had found her in that man's bed from day one?'

Moshidi was taken aback by her father's comment. '*Hawu*, Papa. Do you honestly believe that Lawrence did the right thing by concealing the fact that she died in his house?'

Her father shrugged. 'I've thought a lot about this whole thing and I have to confess that I think I would have probably tried to do the same if I were in his position. As much as I hate Mzwandile for the way he has treated my daughter, it's a big thing for a man. Imagine having to go and identify your wife's body at another man's house? I may not like what Lawrence did but I understand where he was coming from.'

'Speaking of Lawrence . . . he reached out to me last week.'

'What did he want?' asked her father.

Moshidi downed her wine. 'He asked if I would testify in his favour regarding his case.'

Her father looked at her with concern. 'What did you say?'

She shrugged. 'I told him the law must take its course.'

He frowned. '*Bathong*, Moshidi. Is that what you said to him?'

She nodded. 'More or less. What else was I going to say to him, Papa? I can't get involved in that. I have my own pain to deal with.'

'But . . . how is that different from your brother-in-law's attitude?'

'Papa! It's two completely different things!'

'Have you ever thought what it took for that man to honour our request to come to his house to perform our rituals? Can you imagine his fears . . . doubts? We could have been a family seeking vengeance. We could have had all sorts of intentions, but he chose to honour our request in spite of everything that hung in the balance. Come on, Moshidi, I think the least we can do is inform the state that we bear no ill will towards the man. So much has been lost. Do you really want an innocent man to spend years in jail because he chose to love your sister?'

Moshidi looked at her father incredulously. 'He wouldn't be going to jail for loving my sister! He'd be serving time for . . . for moving her body.'

'But do you think Lerato would be happy with that outcome? After the man has proven to be more of a loving companion to her than her own husband? Mzwandile did not even show up at her funeral, but that young man was there, even though he knew he could be going to jail over this whole thing. *Nana*, I'm not asking you to say he didn't do what he's accused of, but my life won't be happier if Lawrence serves time in jail. I doubt this would do anything to better your life either. The only person who will be happy about that outcome is Mzwandile, who's busy cashing in on your sister's death.'

'So what do you want me to do?'

'Just give an official statement regarding our wishes as a family. Let it be known that we bear no ill will towards the man and that we have forgiven him. That is all. Why destroy his future over this matter, hmm? Is it worth it?'

Moshidi sat quietly, digesting her father's words.

How did this meeting end up being about Lawrence?

Hmph.

'*Eish*, Papa. You're asking too much of me, *waitsi*. I've got my own problems. Now you want me to focus on Lawrence Moyo's problems too? Do you know what actually irritated me when I saw him?'

'What?' asked her father.

'He was eating a beef burger there at Tashas. Imagine. A whole beef burger!'

Her father laughed. '*Bathong*. Now we're putting people in jail for eating beef burgers?'

She kept shaking her head. 'You know, when I realised I had lost Lerato for good . . . I could hardly do anything, Papa. I couldn't sleep, couldn't work, couldn't eat . . . nothing. I realised that my life was always cushioned by the knowledge that my sister would always be there for me. She was just someone who made all the sweet moments sweeter, and all the awful ones more bearable. We laughed about almost everything. When I saw Lawrence that day, I couldn't believe he could just carry on with his life like that. Just order a whole beef burger, Papa. Imagine.'

He took her by the hands, and held them. 'I loved your sister more than life itself. I understand your pain . . . you know that parents should never bury their children. Your poor mother! I can barely afford to spend a night away from her. She is completely gutted. We're all suffering, my darling daughter, but you know I never raised you to be vindictive. Sorry, my little one, but you know I've always said, "First do no harm". What joy are we going to gain by having that boy locked away? Hmm?'

She shrugged. 'I know. I know, but . . .' She sighed.

'But what? Think about Mzwandile. Do you think he's had a moment's peace since making his decision to denounce my daughter for what she did? Almost twenty years of marriage, then he deserts her for faltering just that one time? We're better than that, Moshidi. Mercy and forgiveness say more about your character than anything else in the world. That Mzwandile can go to church every day if he wants to, but I can assure you he has no peace.'

Moshidi sighed. 'I'll see what I can do, Papa.'

He smiled, his eyes twinkling. 'That's my girl!'

She smiled back.

'Okay, so tell me, what is it that you wanted to talk to me about, hmm?' her father asked.

Moshidi looked at him. He was so kind-hearted. So forgiving. She knew he'd ask her to give Solomzi a second chance.

'Arg . . . it's nothing serious,' she said. 'Tell me that joke again . . . the one about Mama and those ladies at her *stokvel*.'

A Year Later

Noma did not want to be late for her appointment with her investors at Kuenda Mberi gold mine. Today was their official signing off on a deal to invest more than 400 million rand in her new company. She had been working on this deal for more than eight months and was excited to finally see it come to fruition.

'Aunty Noma, sit still while I finish styling your hair,' said Nthabiseng as she skilfully wove the styling tong around Noma's extensions.

Noma looked at her reflection in the mirror. 'Hmm. You young people are good at everything. Where did you say you learned how to style like this?'

'On YouTube. It's super easy! I can even do your make-up now. Just like a professional,' said Nthabi.

Noma appraised her. 'You're only fourteen years old. Don't focus too much on hair and beauty. You need to make sure you get good grades. Remember, Crawford College has high standards. The kids you go to school with have had more exposure to private schooling than you have.'

Nthabi smiled confidently. 'Don't worry about my schoolwork, Mama Noma. I won't disappoint you. My tutor is very good, and she says I'm strong at maths. She says I'll go very far if I keep working hard.'

Noma gazed at her and said, 'You'd better. Failure is not an option with me.'

'I know, I know,' said Nthabi, as her mother came in to bring tea for Noma.

'Oh no, Tshidi. It's too late for that. I have to rush to my meeting. Wish me luck, you girls,' said Noma.

'Good luck!' chorused Nthabiseng and her mother as Noma rushed out the door in her vertiginous Louboutin heels.

As she got into her chauffeur-driven Mercedes-Benz, Noma reflected on the meeting ahead. She had worked so hard to get to this point, she thought, taking in a deep breath. Sometimes she wondered how she'd been able to hold it all together, given the events of the past year. As always, she thanked God for the presence of Tshidi and her daughter in her life.

When Nthabiseng had texted her on that fateful night, so many emotions ran over her on hearing the teenager's voice on the line.

She'd been in Zimbabwe, having back-to-back meetings to finalise the purchase of the mine when she got the 'Please Call Me' from Tshidi's phone. That call had changed the entire trajectory of her life. When she returned to South Africa to discover that her husband had been arrested, she was full of righteous indignation. She hired the best lawyers, certain that a grave miscarriage of justice had been committed. It was only when The Duke confessed everything that she knew they were in trouble.

Now, a year later, her husband was in jail. As for Khutso . . . he just pretended that his father was not a prisoner of the state and continued putting on the appearance of a privileged golden boy who remained untouchable. At least he still came by to check on her, even if he refused to discuss his father's fate.

At first, Noma had been resentful towards Tshidi and her daughter for being privy to her family's not-so-perfect life; for being the first to shatter the façade that she had worked so hard to keep up . . . decades of trying to reinvent her past.

But, as always, the past always caught up with you. Had the police not been called, what would have happened that night? Were the thieves going to simply leave without harming Tshidi and her husband? Would they have stayed longer? Killed them? Who knew?

In the end, all she could do was count her blessings that their ill-gotten wealth had been kept a secret for as long as it had.

It was The Duke's foolishness that had exposed them, but she refused to go down with him. She was Nomathando Manamela. A self-made titan of business.

Of course she knew nothing of her husband's nefarious business dealings!

This was the narrative she stubbornly told, and she had sworn to herself that she would not deviate from it.

When she realised that she was now all alone in her beautiful home with her beautiful cars, she decided to allow Tshidi and her daughter to move out of the servants' quarters and into the main house. After all, she couldn't exactly carry on without company in the huge mansion. She hadn't been sure about this decision, but her life had been falling apart all around her. If those two had not been there to keep her company, she often wondered what would have become of her.

As for The Duke, she had committed to visiting him once a month. It was the least she could do. If not for him, she wouldn't have continued to live this life of luxury in the first place.

Basics

Moshidi waited for her man to pick her up from work. She was dressed in a simple chiffon and cotton dress and sandals, and was enjoying the warm September breeze.

As soon as she saw the black Jaguar pull up to the parking lot, she ran to meet it.

He stepped out the door and went up to kiss her.

'Where to, today?' she asked him, giggling like a schoolgirl.

'We agreed that date night will always be a surprise,' he said.

'Okay. Dazzle me, then, you darling man!'

As they drove to their destination, Solomzi filled her in on the kids' antics during the drive back home from school.

'The twins are really enjoying the soccer team, hey? I'm thinking maybe one day, they'll go professional.'

She looked at him fondly. 'I never thought the day would come when Solomzi Jiya would entertain thoughts of having professional soccer players under his roof.'

He shrugged. '*Andithi uthe*, we should simplify our lives. So here I am. I'm going back to basics . . . for you, my darling.'

She laughed. 'You're such a quick study,' she remarked.

He pulled up to a large brick building with two unmistakable golden arcs flashing at the top of the building.

'We're here,' he said.

'Erm . . . this is a McDonald's.'

'Yes, baby. What's wrong?'

'But . . . but . . .'

He turned to face her and looked her in the eyes. 'Babe, remember we said we're ditching the mad chase for the most expensive thing – the latest bag, five-star restaurants . . . etcetera, etcetera?'

'But, baby . . . it's McDonald's!' she moaned like a petulant child.

'Yes, but you're at McDonald's with your loving husband who will do anything to keep you in his life. Even if it means downscaling his tastes.'

'*Yho mme we!* Okay. I know we said we're done with Keeping Up with the Joneses. But my love . . . maybe we could try Spur or Mimmos . . . for starters.'

He laughed. 'What's wrong with McDonald's?'

'Ah . . . babe. It reminds me of that accountant – the one I dated before you,' she said bleakly. 'I think it's taking things too far.'

Solomzi looked at her then burst into laughter. 'Okay, fine, my uptown girl. Let's go to Mimmos then.'

'Phew. At least.'

On The Other Side Of Town . . .

Lawrence was on his morning jog, breathing in the air and enjoying the freedom of the neighbourhood park. He looked at his pedometer, counting each step and feeling a sense of accomplishment for keeping to his commitment to this new daily ritual.

He still could not believe how close he had come to losing his freedom. During the plea-bargaining process, he had often felt like his life was hanging by a thread. One false move and he'd be in jail for . . . who knew how long? Five years, ten years? What would become of him? What would life as an ex-convict look like for someone like him?

He shook his head, trying to block out the negative thoughts.

He and Kudzayi had been fortunate to get a smart lawyer like Munyaradzi, but their guardian angel was surely Moshidi. The testimony that she gave on behalf of her family was the pardon they had needed to sway their case in a different direction. In the end, the judge had decided to hand him and Kudzayi a five-year suspended sentence.

Did his life change because of the sentence?

Of course, it did.

For starters, he lost his job at Red Marketing.

For six months, it seemed as if his life had come to a cruel cul-de-sac with no silver lining in sight. His fate changed when Frans convinced him to partner up with him in a new venture, Frans's own CSI marketing company.

Fortune smiled on them when Frans landed a major client within weeks of starting his own enterprise – Kuenda Mberi Mining – a company owned by one of the ex-directors on the Zebula Mining account.

With Kuenda Mberi's Zimbabwean links, Lawrence was a natural contact to bring on board, and together, they had already managed to host the company's first fundraiser. Through the golf event, the owner of Kuenda Mberi, Nomathando Manamela, managed to attract a funding deal worth almost half a billion. Not a bad start at all for their small company.

As Lawrence lengthened his stride, he passed the gorgeous tall woman whom he often encountered on his runs.

She smiled at him, and he smiled back.

When he came back for the second track around the park, he found her stretching by one of the park benches. He went to stretch next to her.

'Hi again,' she said, smiling up at him.

'Hi. Beautiful day for a run.'

She stood up to her full height. 'My name is Kefilwe,' she said, stretching out her hand to greet him.

The sun reflected a shiny glint on her left ring finger.

Oh boy.

A wedding ring . . . the equivalent of a flashing red sign for him.

'Hi, Kefilwe. My name is Lawrence,' he said. 'I'm pleased to meet you.' She really was gorgeous. 'So, anyway . . . gotta run!'

GLOSSARY

Urban South Africans mix different languages in their daily speech because of the cosmopolitan nature of Gauteng, the province where Johannesburg is located. South Africa has eleven official languages, and the speech of urbanites blends most of these languages, as you will discover when you read the book.

So, to help those readers unfamiliar with South African dialect, I have put together a list of words and phrases that my characters use in the book.

amadodana (isiZulu) – young men. In the context of the book, amadodana specifically refers to the Young Men's Guild of South African Methodist churches

amarhada (Tsotsi Taal, slang) – police

amapiano – new genre of South Africa music. Mixture of house and kwaito music

andithi uthe (Xhosa) – remember you said

ausi (Setswana) – sister

ayeye (slang) – expression meaning something is about to go down. Could be good or bad

ba re (Setswana) – they say/they said

Baba (isiZulu/Xhosa) – father

bafo (isiZulu, colloquial) – brother/bro

bathong, ngwana ke (Setswana) – oh dear my child

bethuna (oh bethuna) (isiZulu/Xhosa) – goodness me!

bo-ausi (slang) – domestic workers (a respectful term)

braai (Afrikaans) – a barbecue

CIPC – register of companies in South Africa

doek (Afrikaans) – headscarf

dololo (slang) – nothing

dumela (Setswana) – hello

eish (South African, colloquial) – used to express a range of emotions, such as surprise, annoyance, or resignation

ema (Setswana) – wait

hawu (isiZulu/Xhosa) – an expression to express surprise or shock

hayi (Xhosa expression) – no

hayi mani wena (isiZulu expression) – no man!

hayibo (isiZulu) – exclamation of shock or surprise

hayisuka (isiZulu/Xhosa expression) – damn it

he banna (Setswana) – hey man or oh man!

he marra (slang) – my goodness though . . .

he mme we! (slang) – oh my goodness!

hey wena (isiZulu/Xhosa) – hey you

i job yi job (slang) – a job's a job

indaba (isiZulu) – conference. Also means news

ja-ne (slang) – expression of surprise or resignation

jislaaik (Afrikaans) – expression of shock or surprise

to jol (slang) – to celebrate

kalana (Setswana) – twig

kana (Setswana expression) – remember

kasi (slang) – black residential area/township

ko (Setswana) – at

kotiza (isiZulu/Xhosa) – a period where the bride spends time at the groom's home mostly conducting domestic chores

Kuse kasi wena la (isiZulu) – this is the hood

kwerekwere (slang) – foreigner (derogatory)

leya tagwa (Setswana) – you drink heavily

lobola (isiZulu/Xhosa) – the traditional bride price or dowry

maar wena (slang) – but you . . .

makoti (isiZulu) – bride

matshidiso (Setswana) – condolences

mfana (isiZulu) – small boy

mntwanam (isiZulu) – my boy

mos (expression) – affirmation

moXhosa (Setswana) – Xhosa person

Mxm – expression of anger, irritation or annoyance

nana (Setswana) – baby/my baby

ndoda ndini (Xhosa/Zulu) – silly man!

neh? (expression, slang) – right?

nkosi (isiZulu) – Lord!

nogal (Afrikaans) – moreover

ntate (Setswana) – a respectful form of address to a man, or Mr, e.g. Ntate Manamela: Mr Manamela

nywe nywe nywe (slang) – blah blah blah

o le wa skielbog – the one with squinted eyes

Papa-we (Setswana) – Hey, mister

piccanin (slang) – small person/small child

rakgadi (Sesotho/Setswana) – aunt (paternal)

ratu, short for *moratuwa* (Sesotho/Setswana) – love or my love

sangoma (Xhosa/Zulu) – traditional healer/shaman

sbali (isiZulu/Xhosa) – brother-in-law

sha/shamwari (Shona-Zimbwabwean) – friend

shandwa (isiZulu/Xhosa) – my love

shoo (slang) – a sigh

shwashi (slang) – a gossip, or gossips (singular and plural)

sies (slang) – expression of disgust

sisi (isiZulu) – sister

sisonke (isiZulu)– We're all together

Sawubona, mfowethu (isiZulu) – Good day my brother

Spaza (slang) – a tuck shop mostly in a township

sthandwa sam (isiZulu) – my love

sthipha (slang) – idiot, moron, dummy

stokvel (slang) – informal savings society or investment society

taba e (Setswana) – this issue

tata (Xhosa) – father

thatha (isiZulu/Xhosa) – take this

thyini (Xhosa) – an expression of surprise

tshidisa (Sesotho/Setswana) – funeral condolences

tshini (Xhosa) – an exclamation of surprise

tsotsi (slang) – thug

tsotsi-taal (slang) – township street language

ufunani? (isiZulu) – what do you want?

unjani (isiZulu) – how are you?

uphi u (isiZulu) – where is

ubaba wase khaya (isiZulu) – the man of the house

ukubekezela (isiZulu) – patience, tolerance, endurance

ukukotiza (isiZulu) – a period of performing bridal duties at the groom's parents' home

uMthakathi womlungu (isiZulu) – White Sorcerer

unjani (Xhosa/Zulu) – how are you?

uyabazi abazalwane kodwa (isiZulu) – do you know 'born-again' Christians, though?

voetsek (Afrikaans) – fuck you

wa (Setswana) – you're

waitsi (Setswana) – do you know

wie sien ons (Afrikaans/slang) – literal meaning is 'who sees us?', a phrase used to refer to a party held after someone's funeral to celebrate their legacy

ya (Setswana) – belongs to

yho mme we (Setswana) – Oh Mother! expression of shock or helplessness

yintoni ke ngoku (Xhosa) – what now? What is this now?

A NOTE ON SOUTH AFRICAN SEASONS

South African seasons differ from European and US seasonal ranges. For reference, below is the South African seasonal split:

Spring: September, October, November

Summer: December, January, February

Autumn: March, April, May

Winter: June, July, August

ABOUT THE AUTHOR

Photo © 2018 Nicolise Harding

Angela Makholwa was born in Johannesburg, South Africa. A qualified journalist, she cut her teeth reporting on crime stories in the 1990s. The case of a real-life serial killer went on to inform her debut novel, *Red Ink* – the first South African crime novel with an African female protagonist. Her writing has gained her critical acclaim and several literary award nominations, including the 2020 UK Comedy Women in Print Prize, for which her novel *The Blessed Girl* was shortlisted. She is a keen yogi, reader, occasional dancer and a juggler of businesses – as well as writing novels, she currently runs a public relations agency. *Critical But Stable* is her fifth novel.